MW01093776

Flying
Dismount

The Grabbing Mane Series: Book 2

Natalie Keller Reinert

This is a work of fiction. Names, characters, businesses, places, events, locales, and incidents are either the products of the author's imagination or used in a fictitious manner. Any resemblance to actual persons, living or dead, or actual events is purely coincidental.

Copyright © 2021 Natalie Keller Reinert

Cover Photo: Jakub Gojda/DepositPhotos

All rights reserved.

Paperback Edition

ISBN-13: 978-1-956575-01-9

Also by Natalie Keller Reinert

The Hidden Horses of New York: A Novel

The Grabbing Mane Series
Grabbing Mane
Flying Dismount

The Eventing Series
Bold (A Prequel)
Ambition
Pride
Courage
Luck
Forward
Prospect
Home

The Show Barn Blues Series
Show Barn Blues
Horses in Wonderland

The Alex & Alexander Series
Runaway Alex
The Head and Not The Heart
Other People's Horses
Claiming Christmas
Turning for Home

The Catoctin Creek Series
Sunset at Catoctin Creek
Snowfall at Catoctin Creek
Springtime at Catoctin Creek

Chapter One

HANNAH WAS GALLOPING around the arena with that wild look in her eyes again.

Casey sighed to herself and gently tugged back on the reins, tucking James into a corner of the arena. She wanted her horse somewhere out of trouble. Just in case Hannah's teenage enthusiasm and her own horse's wild-eyed exuberance blended into something neither of them could control.

"Outside line!" Hannah shrieked, leaning into her turn as she pointed Caruso at the jumps set up along the long side of the roping arena.

"You've got it!" Casey called, trying to be encouraging. Sure, Hannah's riding gave her the willies at times, but the sixteen-year-old was Casey's only riding buddy. Their eighteen-year age difference rarely meant much—horses were a great equalizer with maturity—but when Hannah got keyed up about jumping, it reminded Casey that her friend was still riding with that famous teenage sense of immortality.

Casey had lost that feeling a long time ago.

Across the arena, Caruso went rocketing towards the jumps, his hooves scrambling in the deep gray sand, his head high and his eyes wide. James seemed to like Caruso's style. He sidestepped and mouthed at the bit, throwing his head up and down, and generally acted like a big impatient baby. Casey pushed against his side with her outside leg, reminding him to stay against the high wooden fence where she'd told him to stand. He obeyed her, but moved too fast— James moved too fast an awful lot these days—and she felt her half-chap brushing against the rough wooden planks. Another step over, and he'd be squashing her leg against the fence. She hissed a warning.

"James! Stand up and be a good boy!"

James dipped his head against the bit again, but at least he stood still. His feelings had been hurt, though. He tipped his ears back to her, and Casey thought she could read his thoughts.

I'm always a good boy.

"Yes, I know you are." She ran a hand under his short ruffle of dark mane, scratching his withers with her fingernails. "But Caruso over there? He isn't. He's a goblin. And he's a terrible example for you. Close your eyes."

The goblin in question, a slim and wide-eyed chestnut gelding with a dished face and an appetite for trouble, was currently hauling Hannah over the first jump with an undignified scramble. Hannah, as lanky as her horse, had no problems sitting chilly in the saddle through her horse's most uncoordinated attempts at jumping. Casey couldn't help but feel jealous of the younger girl's serene confidence. She was pretty sure she'd be on the ground by now. But Hannah stayed in Caruso's center as her horse's long legs ate up the ground, clearing the five stride distance between the fences in four and a half, then chipping the last six feet and bounding over the small fence with his eyes bugging out. Casey was able to restrain herself from gasping dramatically, but it took an effort.

Hannah let Caruso bolt past them, and James flung out his nose, eager to follow. Reluctantly, Casey let him move into a walk, trusting Hannah would slow her horse to a more sedate pace.

She did, eventually. It just took two laps of the arena.

"Too fast," Hannah panted, finally bringing a jigging Caruso alongside James. "Right? That was good, but it was way too fast. I think. I'd have to get that distance better at a show."

Casey shrugged noncommittally. She wasn't Hannah's trainer; she wasn't in the market to be Hannah's trainer. They rode together, they swapped notes. That was that. Should both of them be riding with trainers? Yes, absolutely. But life was expensive here on the outskirts of West Palm Beach, and neither of them were able to afford the coaching they needed. So, they made do with what they had. "I mean, it was a five-stride, and you left half of the last stride out. So yeah, it was fast."

"Are we sure it's a five-stride? Maybe we measured wrong."

They pulled up their horses and looked at the jumps for a moment. The fences certainly looked like they were five strides apart. They'd walked the distance on foot earlier, using the long strides their coaches had used—back when they'd both had coaches. That luxury felt like a very long time ago.

For Casey, her last time with a coach had been about six months ago, at St. Johns Equestrian Center, two hours north and a world away from here. For Hannah, it had been two years ago, at the Rusty Stirrup School of Horsemanship in her old town of Palm Lakes. Privately, Casey thought Hannah's old trainer had left out some important basics. But who was she to judge? Before spending most of last year regaining her balance in the saddle, she hadn't even ridden a horse in fifteen years. Casey had no illusions about her riding ability, and she was definitely not a professional. She was in the same boat as Hannah, trying to keep up her skills in an expensive sport.

So when the girl asked her for advice, or suggestions, Casey was always very hesitant to offer. What if she steered her wrong? Hannah might wind up injured. Or dead. And it would be her fault.

But what if, Casey wondered, staying silent was just as dangerous?

"Well, they seem right to me," Hannah volunteered at last. She walked Caruso in a figure-eight around the fences. "We could get a measuring tape?"

"Or maybe we shouldn't be jumping at all today," Casey said, knowing this idea would be met with jeers.

"Casey, come on! We can do this. Why are you always so down on yourself? James is a great horse! And you're a great rider!"

One of those things was true, Casey thought. "I only mean jumping without a trainer can be really dangerous."

"Look at these fences, Casey. They're like two feet tall. Nothing is going to happen. People jump without trainers all the time. You just got spoiled at your old place." Hannah laughed, kicking her feet out of the stirrups. She swung her legs at Caruso's sides while her horse danced sideways. It was the kind of thing that made Casey squirm. She was certain Hannah was going to get hurt.

That was about the only thing she was sure of these days. Jumping, trail riding, anything that wasn't walking and trotting around the high board fences of the roping arena got her insides all wrapped up with nerves. It hadn't been too bad at first; she'd arrived at Twin Palms Ranch with determined optimism. The farm was tiny and isolated, with a small barn, an arena, and a five-acre pasture that backed up to the mix of wetlands and range north of the Everglades.

Besides herself and Hannah, the other five boarders were very casual horsepeople. They mostly came to the barn after work, where they alternated between slow horseback ambles around the arena and long conversations in the collection of lawn chairs sitting under the barn's front overhang.

After the first week at Twin Palms, Casey had wondered if she'd made a terrible mistake in moving to West Palm Beach. Yes, she loved Brandon. Yes, he deserved his chance to work his dream job, saving the ocean. But how was she supposed to keep training and showing James? She watched a pair of riders walk their horses around the arena at a slow walk, gossiping away about their days, and her heart sank. That wasn't the life she wanted for herself.

Then Hannah found her. With her Anglo-Arab gelding Caruso and a heart full of passion for riding and jumping, she thought Casey was her long-lost best friend. She had more enthusiasm than skill, and more talent than knowledge. But she was sweet, and willing to go faster than a slow, western pleasure jog on her horse. Casey fell in with her without even meaning to. Who else would she ride with? They started timing their arrivals to ride together. Casey even started leaving work early when possible, sneaking out of her home office whenever she knew her bosses up in the Space Coast wouldn't try to catch her on a video call. If they beat the Olds—Hannah's name for the other boarders, not hers—to the arena, they had all the room they need to jump.

And there were jumps. Hannah dragged them out of the hiding place behind the arena with an air of triumph. Casey and Hannah had some work to do to revive the rotted standards, hammering back the crossbars on the feet and encouraging the wasps living in the jump holes to relocate. Before Casey quite realized what was happening, they had set up four fences in the arena and Hannah was petitioning weekly to raise the heights above the bottom three holes.

In that argument, at least, Casey prevailed. If the fences were low, they were less likely to get into trouble.

But on days like this, when the distances weren't working out, she thought even two-foot fences were a bad idea.

"I feel like if that were five strides, it would have ridden better," Casey said finally. "You weren't going that fast. I could try it, I guess?" Her voice ran up at the end. She didn't really want to try it. James had a lot of kick to him today. If she didn't get him where she wanted him and he put a foot wrong...

Hannah was egging her on. "Casey! Do it. James has a way different stride than Caruso. I bet you can get five strides."

"Oh, I don't know." Casey looked up at the sun, which was shining cheerfully down on them from a cloudless blue sky. She squinted back at Hannah. "It's boiling today. Could be time to just wrap it up."

"It's April! Of course it's hot! It's going to be hot until November. And we have our horse show in a few weeks. You have to jump him now, or neither of you will be ready."

Casey was pretty sure they wouldn't be ready either way. When Hannah had picked out the schooling show at the end of April, it had seemed ages away. In the months since, Casey had experienced more than a moment's doubt about her entry, sitting in someone's inbox. She hadn't shown since she'd left St. Johns. Since she'd left her friend and trainer Sky. Without Sky's tutelage, wouldn't she completely screw up?

But Hannah insisted they'd be fine. And in a moment of weakness, Casey had believed the teenager.

Which was probably her first mistake, but it wasn't like she had anyone else to give her advice, either. Brandon didn't know a thing about horses. The Olds didn't know a thing about horse shows. Or if they did, they weren't talking.

"Okay," she said, agreeing to her second mistake. "Give me some space."

She picked up the reins and James immediately went on high alert, huffing and puffing with his head held high and his ears pricked sharply at the jumps. "Settle down, goofball," she told him, as she asked for a trot and receiving something between a pogo stick and a frog hop. "Why can't you just be nice and quiet like you used to be? Easy, easy, easy!"

Casey finally let James drag her towards the first jump, her jaw tense and set. She tried to keep her weight back, tried to keep his attention on her. But James was sure of what he wanted, and he wasn't much bothered by what she had to say about it. She didn't like the horse he'd become at Twin Palms. He'd been like a jumping bean ever since they'd moved here. Always ready to go, and go, and go. She just couldn't seem to wear him out. To say nothing of keeping his focus on her.

Hannah insisted it was his personality coming out. "This is what he's like when he's having fun. Horses having fun always act all loopy. Look at them in the pasture. They go nuts out there!"

But Casey had her doubts about Hannah's explanation. James had been a happy horse at St. Johns, but he'd still displayed a laid-back personality. Even when he'd gotten fit and perked up naturally as a result, he hadn't been this up, this in her face, all the time. And he wasn't even all that fit now—lately, she'd only had time to ride a few days a week, and he'd lost some of his condition since last fall. By rights, James ought to be cooler and calmer now, with less energy to burn.

They popped over the first fence, and Casey perceived she was giving too much release—she landed hard on his neck as he landed and James snatched his head downward, nearly unseating her. She'd gotten herself back in the saddle and was trying to focus on the fence ahead when a sudden beating of wings thumped against the air, and white flashed in front of them: a large flock of cattle egrets appeared in front of them. The long-legged birds landed in the sand beyond the second jump, looking around placidly as if they had no idea a horse was plunging towards them.

Casey was so startled she forgot to sit down and take control, and so when James threw up his head at the sudden flock of birds and turned abruptly, galloping hard across the arena, Casey neatly toppled over his shoulder and somersaulted into the deep sand.

The fall didn't actually hurt; she sat upright immediately, to let Hannah know she wasn't dead, but she didn't bother standing up right away. She just sat in the dirt and contemplated her life's choices up to this point.

None of them seemed good.

"You okay?" Hannah was circling Caruso around her. The horse was snorting at her, pretty sure she shouldn't be on the ground. "You need help?"

"I'm fine. Annoyed, I guess."

"There goes James," Hannah observed, as Casey's horse thundered past. Caruso ducked his head and jigged, anxious to join the Thoroughbred. His hooves spun close to Casey. "You gonna catch him?"

"I'm going to catch him," Casey said wearily, rising to her feet and regarding the state of her breeches and chaps. She was absolutely coated with damp sand. "And then I'm going in."

"Always get back on." Hannah parroted the old saying in a sing-song voice which made Casey grit her teeth.

"I have to go home anyway," Casey said. "My boyfriend has people coming over today." Work friends—engineer types, not big on playing outside. They already thought she was kind of crazy for riding. She wasn't about to let them see her trudging into the house covered with dirt and horsehair.

Hannah made a face. "Some IT crowd get-together?"

"Yeah, but they're nice. Computer people get a bad rap but they're really normal people."

"Normal people are gross."

Casey rolled her eyes. Teenage exceptionalism. She'd had it once, too. "Anyway, I gotta go." She held out a hand, hoping James would suspect she had a cookie and come towards her. "Keep riding if you want to, but I'm done."

"No, it's hot, like you said." Hannah let Caruso jog after James, who turned and looked at his friend with interest. "I just want to be sure you're not backing out of the horse show. I can't go without an adult, my mom said. And you know this is my first horse show ever. I can't miss this."

"Don't worry. I'm not backing out of the horse show." They had too much at stake for Casey to wuss out now. She'd already begged to borrow the truck and trailer from Liz, their reclusive barn owner, and sent in their entries. Sure, it was only a schooling show. She'd be out a hundred and fifty bucks if they didn't go, nothing too crazy. Money wasn't the issue here—for once. Casey hadn't taken James to a horse show since last year. Mentally, she knew she had a lot riding on this little schooling show—like her ability to train James without a full-time coach overseeing her every move.

She hated to put too much emphasis on one silly horse show, but it meant something. If they couldn't make this work, what kind of future did she have with James, or any horses she might have after him? Casey had been a serious show rider in her teenage years.

Competitiveness was all she knew. Without it, what on earth was riding for?

She knew that was an over-the-top sentiment. She didn't really believe it, not really really. But she also didn't want to end up like the Olds. Showing up every night to putz around the arena, talking about her day at the office.

Fine, she'd probably never be a professional rider. But she didn't want to be the opposite of that, either.

Once she had his attention, James gave in fairly easily and allowed himself to be caught—he was hot, and probably embarrassed about spooking so hard at a flock of pasture birds. Casey walked him into the barn to strip his tack and give him a quick shower.

She had to admit, she liked the barn itself, which was open to the breeze—when they had one—and had the very basics she needed to keep a horse: a paved aisle she enjoyed sweeping clean, a wash-rack with a hose that spat out both hot and cold water, a fridge for cold drinks and carrots, and a window air conditioner in the tack room, which labored night and day to keep the humidity from eating away at the saddles stored inside. The barn met the basic needs of civilized equestrian life.

And, most importantly, the horses liked it. When they were in their stalls, they were free to lean over the half-walls and groom each other, or nip and tease each other, depending on their moods. If they wanted to nap, there were ceiling fans to keep the bugs off, bent with age but still capable of tossing a breeze. A cluster of oaks helped shade the metal roof, along with the ranch's namesake twin palm trees.

For a pleasure rider, a place like Twin Palms Ranch was a godsend. Inexpensive, unpretentious, and surrounded by miles of trails into the wilderness of interior Florida. The kind of barn where a boarder could keep a six-pack of Bud Lite in the feed room fridge and no one would have a problem with it. The kind of barn where a group of boarders were just as likely to sit around in cheap patio chairs as get on their horses and ride. It was a casual place, built for easy friendships, not for competitiveness or rivalries. It would have been great if that had been what Casey was looking for in a barn.

She clipped James to the old trailer tie hanging from the wooden rails of the wash-rack and started spraying him down as Hannah walked Caruso into the barn.

"I jumped him one more time," Hannah said. "To get the five strides."

"Did you get it?"

"No. Still four and a half. He's not good at distances, though."

"Well, he's got to learn him someday. How long have you had him, anyway?" She realized she'd never really gotten the horse's backstory. Hannah lived in the future; she rarely talked about her past.

"I've had him two years," Hannah said cheerfully. "Got him from my old trainer. He was a very bad lesson horse." Hannah tapped Caruso's white-tipped nose to underscore her words. The horse snorted at her. "I used to let her use him in lessons to work off board, but you know...a horse can only dump kids so many times." She laughed. "He stopped earning his keep pretty quick. We had to go. And then my parents were moving, so..."

"And that's how you ended up here," Casey finished. It was the equestrian tale as old as time. Girl buys horse, girl can't afford board, girl lets trainer use horse, trainer realizes horse is unsuited for job and ends arrangement, girl finds new barn. And so here Hannah was, in the same boat as her: ambitious, keen to prove herself, and unable to afford the astronomic costs of show barns in south Florida.

Hannah slipped off Caruso's bridle, leaving a dark ring of sweat behind his ears. "Well, this place isn't so bad. And, when you have to pay your own board out of a part-time job, you take what you can get. My parents don't help much."

"Honestly, it's not much better when you have to pay your own board out of a full-time job, either."

"You're not giving me a lot to look forward to," Hannah laughed. "Adulthood sounds like a real bummer."

"It really can be," Casey admitted. She angled the hose down James's neck, and the horse lipped at her shoulder. "But try doing it without horses. It's absolutely the worst."

"Hah! I'll never quit horses. Only a crazy person would do something like that."

Casey put her hand on James's warm neck. She felt his muscles quivering beneath her, his life-force that was so much bigger than hers. "Literally," she told Hannah, closing her eyes for one moment of indulgence. "Only a crazy person."

Chapter Two

THE LONG, TORTUROUSLY straight road back to civilization always made Casey want to doze off, even with the sun beaming at its usual ten million watts. Empty grassland, chewed-down pastures, sugarcane fields, scraggly citrus groves, desolate lots piled high with pieces of tractor trailer and abandoned boats and one puzzling half of a large passenger aircraft: the scenery could be simultaneously alien, depressing, and reassuring. One thing was certain: when you looked out the window and saw a chunk of a Boeing sitting next to a sign for gator jerky and orange-blossom honey, you knew you were in Florida. With all its disorienting glory.

After about seven miles of sameness, the rural highway came to an abrupt change, intersecting with Interstate 95. North: Daytona Beach. South: Miami. In the middle: this place, the sprawl of the Gold Coast, from the Palm Beaches to Fort Lauderdale. A concrete jungle with everything from roadside motels to country clubs in its thorny vines. Even horse farms, if you had enough money.

Casey's route kept her going east, past the interstate, past the highway hotels and fast-food joints, digging deep into the heart of suburbia. The traffic thickened and snarled; the stoplights glared red above the heat rising from the cars and the blacktop. Strip malls offered simple solutions to all life's wants: chiropractors, florists, quick divorces, vape juice, smoothies. On every corner, a succession of nearly identical chain restaurants offered nearly identical menus. Behind shopping centers anchored by super-sized pet stores and big-box electronics outlets, subdivisions announced their names on stucco signs. The newer ones boasted their nature-based titles like a casualty list of the things they'd crushed: Osprey Hammock, Eagle's Roost, Sawgrass Estates, Everglades Trace.

Casey lived where everything was a little older and a little cheaper —not by much, but still—so her development was close to the main road, its parking lot shadowed by live oaks which predated the Spanish-style condominiums. The sign welcomed her with a slightly damaged facade—car crashes were not uncommon here—and rusting metal letters: *Vista Lago.*

Of course, the lagoon view in the name was referring to a retention pond out front, dug to drain the site and hold all the water that ran off the parking lots, but there were a pair of Muscovy ducks living there, and several herons and egrets who had staked it out as prime fishing real estate, and was the alligator there today? Casey craned her neck as she drove past the pond. Yes, there he was, sunning himself on the grassy embankment running down the pond.

"Good morning, gator," she said, and pulled around to the back building. She tucked her car under an ancient green carport and looked for a moment at the arches on her building, then beyond that, to the covered picnic court where Brandon had already laid claim to the tables with the property office's *Reserved* signs.

They missed their backyard at the townhouse back in Cocoa, that was for sure. Before moving here, Casey hadn't realized how much having one's own space had mattered. But things were more expensive down here, and buying even *this* condo hadn't been easy. Sometimes Casey looked at the rising costs of real estate around Florida and suffered a brief pulse of despair, like she'd never get more space than what they had in this dark little box they'd bought.

Oh, the fun of adult life, good times like fussing endlessly about where to live and how to finance it. Even Casey's parents hadn't had to settle for starter apartments while they were in their thirties. The beautiful house she'd grown up in had cost pennies compared to what it was worth now. Casey shrugged it off and let herself inside.

Inside, delicious cooking smells filled the condo. Casey paused on the patch of linoleum that passed for their foyer and inhaled deeply. "Smells amazing," she called. "You're the pulled pork champion!"

Brandon's voice issued from the kitchen. "Totally got my hands full, babe, or I'd come and give you a kiss. Everything go okay at the barn?"

"It was fine, thanks." Casey shed her boots and walked into the kitchen. She knew she was leaving things out, not admitting she'd gotten dumped in a stupid spook. But it was just that—a stupid spook—so why tell him about it? "I got caught up in some things with Hannah. We reset the jumps in the arena and tried to smooth out some of the really dug-up spots. And we rode for a full hour after that."

"Wow!" Brandon rinsed his hands in the sink and turned around. His tan face was a little sweaty from the heat rising off the full stovetop. "An hour, in this weather! You guys are dedicated."

"It wasn't too bad. It was only—what—" Casey checked the temperature on her watch. "Okay, it's eighty-seven *now,* but it wasn't that hot earlier." A lie. She'd been right to tell Hannah it was too hot to ride. The humidity had to have the heat index close to ninety-five or more. But no point in bringing that up. She always tried to keep barn things smooth and light with Brandon.

Not just barn things. Work things, too. And things like persistent loneliness, missing her friends back home, or the overwhelming claustrophobia she sometimes experienced living in this tiny condo. Casey smothered them all. She didn't want to worry Brandon; didn't want him to think it was his fault.

She'd *chosen* to move here. She'd picked him over staying home, alone.

"Dedicated," Brandon repeated. "Also, it's like a hundred and one in here, so I'm probably projecting my overheating body onto yours. Why did I decide to prepare anything that needed the oven set at four-fifty? We should eat a bunch of cold watermelon soaked in vodka and call it a day."

"I'm sorry. I should have come home sooner to help." Casey looked around at his mess. Brandon had gotten seriously into cooking. She suspected his interest was partially to save money now that their living expenses were higher, and partially because Casey was often at the barn on weeknight evenings, giving him more time to fill on his own.

"No, you're fine. These fried zucchini fingers were my idea and they're my problem." Brandon laughed a little breathlessly as a kitchen timer dinged. "Go shower. In twenty minutes this stuff will all be ready to take out to the pavilion and you'll never know what a mess you walked in on."

"Okay. Thanks, babe." She gave him a quick kiss before heading to their bedroom at the front of the condo, pulling off her belt and unbuttoning her breeches along the way. Saving time, she figured.

She'd get showered in ten minutes and go help Brandon.

He was so nice about everything, all the time, but she still felt guilty when she was off riding while he was sweating in the kitchen.

Casey turned on the shower and began to step in, but something on the counter caught her eye. It was her phone—the screen lighting up with a new message. She sighed and picked it up. Sharon, her boss at Atlantic Horse Show Productions. On a Saturday? That couldn't be good.

"What now, Sharon?" she muttered, flicking up on the notification.

She read the message. She sighed again. Harder. Heavier. With real exasperation, this time.

Atlantic Horse Show Productions had been a dream job seven short months ago. Remote work, marketing horse shows, the occasional meeting back in Merritt Island, which could coincide with a quick lunch or dinner with her friends or her parents? She'd hit the jackpot. After slogging through years of boring email marketing and unsuccessfully attempting to relive her teenage years by grooming for Sky, Casey thought that putting her marketing skills to good use for a horse show company had been the answer to all her prayers.

Now, it seemed like her good-natured bosses were trying to squeeze every last drop out of her.

Casey put down the phone and stepped into the shower, her brain now wrapped up with the potential consequences of Sharon's message. She and her business partner, Phillip, were meeting with a west coast-based show production company on Monday, and they wanted a marketing deck from Casey. Not the one she'd already provided them: the ready-made, polished, perfect deck which Casey used when approaching new sponsors for their horse shows. No, Sharon was requesting something purposely made for their meeting.

Something to make Atlantic look like a much bigger company than it currently was. And, naturally, it would have to be done in the next two days.

"Weekend work," Casey told her bar of soap, "should be against the law."

The really annoying thing was that she was already thinking of ways to make the deck perfect. Already figuring out what stats to showcase, and the best ways to present them. She stood under the shower until the hot water faltered, designing the perfect deck in her mind.

Brandon tapped on the door.

She started, splashing water out of the shower.

"Hey, Case." Brandon peeked in at her, mildly concerned. "You were in here a while, and I was starting to worry. Thought maybe you fell down, and I didn't hear you."

"Oh my gosh." Casey turned off the shower and groped for a towel. "I'm so sorry. I had a message from work and I started thinking about it and—listen, do you mind if I jot down these ideas? I know we need to get things down the pavilion but I just need to—I'll be quick—" She was already pushing past him, dripping water on the bathmat, reaching for her phone to take notes. If she didn't get this stuff down now, she'd lose it. Shower thoughts were like rainbows—you had to take a picture quick, before they faded forever.

"Of course I don't mind," Brandon said, backing out of the bathroom. "You do what you need to do. I'm going to get started."

"I'll be right there," Casey promised, but she was tapping already, getting the words down, making checklists. By the time she finished, the bathroom was cold again, and Brandon had emptied the kitchen of all its treats—right down to the heavy cooler of iced drinks.

Casey tugged one of her sundresses over her head, so hastily she nearly popped a seam when she forgot to unzip it all the way. She raced to the front door, smoothing the skirt with one hand, and peered around the corner. She saw Brandon at the pavilion, greeting the first few arrivals. Here he was, throwing a party for ten all by himself. She hadn't done a thing to help.

Brandon wouldn't blame her for putting work and James ahead of his party—he never did. But she still felt bad about it.

Well, what choice did she have? Her work, her horse, her life: it all took a lot of time. Sure, someday, things would calm down. They had to, right?

Until then, she'd keep balancing as best she could.

And hope Brandon stayed this patient and understanding for as long as it took.

"I really didn't mind," Brandon said, for the third time that evening. "It was my party. It was my idea. You didn't have to worry about it."

"Can you just be mad at me, like, a little?" Casey forced herself to laugh. "I said I'd be there. I expected I'd a bit of extra work to do later. I didn't realize Sharon was going to call and want to talk for two hours about strategy. I left you alone with all your friends." She didn't add what Sharon had said when Casey had suggested she just use the marketing deck already provided. *You knew this was a start-up with extra work to get us off the ground when you started, Casey. Are you not up to this? Tell me now, because we're only expanding and if you're not on board, we need to know.*

She'd stood absolutely still for a long moment after Sharon finished her threat, trying to comprehend what was happening. Her kind, funny boss couldn't possibly have said such a thing to her, could she?

But it had happened, and Casey had to stammer an assurance that of course she was on board, of course she'd get the new deck completed by Sunday evening, of course she wanted to be part of whatever bright future Atlantic Horse Show Productions was heading towards. It's not like she had the wherewithal to quit, after all.

She didn't want to tell Brandon about it, either. He'd never speak to an employee like that, never threaten them, and he wouldn't understand how she'd put up with it, even if she put her bank balance in front of him and pointed to how much James, gas, and car insurance were costing her down here in the snarled concrete jungle.

"Alone with my friends, a fate worse than death," Brandon said dryly.

"No, I know that's silly. But it's just—" Casey sighed, searching for the words. "I can't imagine what they assume about me, for one thing. Not showing up to her own boyfriend's party."

"They think you're very busy," Brandon told her, pulling her close. "And they think you're very successful." He planted a loud, theatrical kiss on her forehead. "And they think you're very athletic." Another smacking kiss, on her cheek. "And, even though, I tell them not to think of you that way, they think you're very sexy." A lingering, teasing kiss on the lips.

"Brandon, you didn't tell me your friends were pervs," Casey murmured, getting into the spirit of things despite the worry eating away at her.

"Oh, the worst," he assured her around kisses. "I shouldn't even associate with them."

She laughed and snuggled against him, tucking her head against his shoulder. "They *are* nice, though. I'm impressed with how you made friends as soon as you moved down here. I obviously haven't done that."

"Well, it's different for you and me. You don't have any coworkers here. Making friends can be pretty easy when you're all working on the same project. We get together for lunches, we shoot the breeze, we grab drinks after a successful day, and before you know it, we're pals. Plus, they like that I can cook," Brandon added seriously. "Never underestimate the power of cooking."

"It's a damn fine hobby." Casey straightened again, easing her neck from side to side. Funny how casual intimacy in your thirties could cause a crick in your neck. "Feel free to expand into baking."

"Oh, yeah? Want to make a cake with me tomorrow?" Brandon gave her a teasing smile. "I'll let you lick the beaters. I'll even turn off the mixer first."

"I can't. I made plans to ride with Hannah in the morning, and then I have a pile of work to do for Sharon in the afternoon." To say the least. "I can *eat* the cake, though. And shout encouragement from the office while it's being made."

"Ah. Well, we'll see if I'm up to it tomorrow. I have to admit, I'd hoped I had you to myself for at least a few hours this weekend."

She saw him fight to keep his expression from showing his disappointment, and her heart tugged within her chest. They spent so little time together these days, other than bumping around one another as Casey made her way between her home office and the kitchen or bathroom. She wished she had some leeway with James, but this wasn't the time to let up on riding. Not when James was being such a space cadet. Not when she'd promised to go to a horse show with Hannah in two weeks. Maybe work would calm down after this merger. Maybe James would quiet down as the weather grew more oppressive. Maybe she'd figure out a magical spell which would set her life in order.

But until then, all she could do was make sure he knew that her schedule wasn't her choice. "I'm really sorry. I didn't expect the extra work. It came out of nowhere this afternoon. Sharon claims to need all this stuff for her meeting on Monday morning and it's really ridiculous, she already has everything she needs if she'd just *use* it—"

"It happens." Brandon transferred his gaze to the television, which had been playing softly across the room all this time. "I understand."

"But, Brandon, listen. I'm *really* sorry." She wanted him to look at her, to tell her he wasn't angry with the familiar, gentle expression he seemed to reserve just for her. "Things are so crazy right now with this acquisition they're trying to make. But hopefully when they buy this other company, things will calm down. We'll have more people to shoulder all this work."

Brandon shrugged. "It might."

"Brandon, seriously—"

"Casey, I'm just saying you've said that before. But they keep piling more on you while they go off and run horse shows, whatever that means. They leave you at home with all the work." Tension flattened his voice. "It just keeps happening, that's what I'm saying."

"Okay, that happens, but they do a lot at the horse shows," Casey said. "I wouldn't want that assignment. It's all kinds of face-to-face nonsense. At least if they throw all the office work at me, I can do that from here."

"For now. Make sure they don't start sending you out on the road, too. Because I wouldn't put it past them."

Casey stared at him, wondering when he'd decided to dislike her job. How long had he been simmering silently over her workload? "I had no idea you were so against Sharon and Phillip," she said, making it about the people instead of the work. She *liked* the work. She enjoyed marketing. She loved writing emails encouraging people to come to their horse shows. The work itself was a dream come true— which was why she was putting up with the other stuff, the assignments they kept piling on her which had nothing to do with her job title. Or her paycheck, if she was being totally honest with herself.

"Hey." He looked at her now, blue from the television dancing in his dark brown eyes. "I'm not against *them*. But I am against the way they make you feel, which is like you never work hard enough and you always have more to do. I don't blame you for having to do your job. No one can help it when their bosses are unreasonable. Let's just ride this out, okay? It's your work. You're doing what you have to do. I promise to be patient. But I'm also going to speak up when I can see they're pushing too hard."

"Thanks," Casey murmured, sliding close to him on the sofa. She rested her head on his chest, listening to his heart slowly beating, and said yet another silent prayer that after this month, things would calm down.

I can find balance, she told herself. *I did it before. Back home, things got rough, but we figured it out.*

But back home, she'd had a different sort of life. Friends. Family. Sky. The girls at the barn. Support mattered, no matter how much she tried to tell herself she was strong enough to do everything on her own.

Casey loved Brandon, and she knew he loved her. Still, sometimes she wondered if their love was enough to sustain her. Shouldn't he be enough? Why did she need a horse, why did she need to ride every day, why did she need to find passion in her work? Why couldn't she live with good enough? She hated to think she was a person who needed more than her share. But sometimes it seemed as if she was asking for the moon every morning when the sun rose, not content with just one celestial body to light her way. Like she needed to have it all, and then some.

Chapter Three

SUNDAY, EIGHT O'CLOCK in the morning. A flock of turkey vultures floating over the condo parking lot as Casey walked to her car. The juvenile alligator snoozing on the lake bank as she drove past. Blinking blue and red lights at the entrances to local churches, escorting the faithful through clogged intersections. Spirituality gurus on the radio stations, as the corporations did their weekly penance. Casey put on the nineties satellite channel and listened to Nirvana, quietly amazed that she still remembered all the words to the songs she'd listened to in middle school. The palm trees and wizened orange groves west of the interstate flashed by in a blur of brown and green.

Hannah was already in the arena pacing out strides when Casey arrived. The spring sun was steaming hot, quickly burning off the fog that had been trailing through the pastures, twining around the palms and shielding the cattle egrets from sight. Hannah's face was pink and damp with dewy sweat. She looked up as Casey walked out to meet her, gesturing towards the four jumps she'd set up.

"How is this grid? I tried to put them on the best footing I could find, but it's getting deep out here. We need to drag the arena."

"Yeah, I can see that." Casey kicked at the gray sand. It was local sand, hauled in years ago from some worksite and never properly set up with drainage or a base. Hooves churned it up quickly and the ring really needed dragged after every few rides, but Liz only hitched up the drag once a month or so. With this kind of ground, trying to find safe places for jumping got more complicated by the day. What she wouldn't give for the balanced clay footing back at St. Johns Equestrian Center! "I guess there's a lesson here for us: never put a fence around a flat piece of ground and call it a riding ring. There's more to it than that."

"That's the way most people do things around here, though." Hannah shrugged. "I've never been able to afford a barn with a nice ring."

Casey shook her head. Chances were, she'd never be able to afford nice rings again.

They trudged back to the barn and found Maria inside, grooming her Appaloosa gelding, Chico. A Florida native in her late sixties, Maria was stringy and deeply tanned; she looked a bit like an old-growth tree. She was wearing her usual riding clothes: a pair of cut-offs, decrepit and grayed sneakers, and a loose tank top which displayed her boney, freckled chest.

She eyeballed Casey and Hannah with no small amount of amusement. Casey knew it was because of their clothes: riding breeches, boot socks, paddock boots, long-sleeved sun shirts. They looked like models from a Dover Saddlery catalog. If models were allowed to get very, very sweaty and red in the face, before they'd so much as groomed their horses.

In contrast, Maria's skin looked cool and dry, as if the oppressive heat couldn't touch her.

"Hey Maria," Hannah said casually, ducking under Chico's cross-ties and heading for Caruso's stall.

"Morning, Hannah." Maria went on rubbing Chico with an old rubber curry comb. "That horse of yours has been pawing at the wall the whole time you been in the ring. Give him some hay the next time you're gonna leave him standing while everyone else is outside. I finally threw him a little flake."

"Oops," Hannah said lightly, unrepentant. "Thanks." She gave Caruso a light slap on the neck and the horse shifted back from the door, giving her room to slip inside and halter him.

Casey paused by Chico's head, giving the Appy a light caress beneath his thin forelock. Chico was tall and broad-chested, with the breed's signature rat-tail and a mane that was more theoretical than actual, but his coat pattern was a fantastic blend of strawberry roan and small dark spots, and his demeanor was best described as Old Man Sitting in Park With Hard Candies. "Hello, Chico," she told him. "Your mama taking you on a trail ride?"

"Wouldn't be Sunday without a trip to church," Maria drawled. "Gotta go out and pay respects to the Big Guy." She picked up a bottle of Deep Woods Off and sprayed her bare legs. "Yellow flies are back already, though."

"Yikes." Casey shivered. She hated the very idea of yellow flies, long-bodied bloodsuckers that lived in the swamps and were so hard to kill, you practically had to crush them with your fist to end their evil lives. She couldn't imagine riding bare-legged with those monsters swarming. "Don't get sucked dry out there."

"Well, the Off helps a lot. And I have a fly whisk. You all ought to come. It's a real pretty, clear morning, even if it's hot." Maria winked, faded blue eyes twinkling. "I mean, it's always hot, so that ain't no detractor."

"Can't. We have to practice for our show in two weeks," Hannah declared, snapping Caruso into the aisle cross-ties behind Chico. "We have the trailer borrowed and everything. Gotta work hard every day now."

Maria gave Hannah an indulgent look. "You'll show 'em, honey," she told the girl. She glanced back at Casey, lowering her voice as she said, "Teenagers live for competition. I suppose it's because they haven't yet learned it doesn't matter." She cocked an eyebrow and grinned. "But, what's *your* excuse?"

Casey was used to the other boarders at Twin Palms watching her work hard in the arena with a certain skepticism, but she wasn't quite prepared for this full-on attack. Certainly not so early on a Sunday morning, when she was a little dizzy with heat and humidity. Still, she tried to put up a defense. "Horse showing is fun. And...rewarding. It lets us measure how much progress we've made."

Well, it was an attempt. But even Casey could hear the lack of conviction in her voice. Progress? Hardly. This show was going to be a demonstration of how far she and James had fallen.

Maria snickered, though not unkindly—just enough to let Casey understand she didn't buy the argument. As she placed a faded saddle pad on Chico's back, she asked, "What happens if you don't make progress? Chico and I ain't made any *progress* in ten years. We're still pretty happy. No one's come and taken him away from me. Ain't no horse police, checking up on our show record."

"Progress is...progress. It's getting more skilled. I don't, um, it's like —" Casey hated the way her words were fumbling. This argument should be simple. She loved riding, and being an excellent rider meant hard work and training. That was a given.

Right?

Maria was saddling Chico with brisk, practiced motions. "Now, I'm not being mean. You just seem tireder than you did when you first got here. And I see you and Hannah hustling all the time. If you ever want a break, now, we'd love to have you go out on a trail ride and relax a little. You don't even have to ask permission. You see us out here, well, tack up and come with."

"Thank you," Casey replied. "So nice of you. But we're fine."

"You ever even been on a trail ride since you got here? You don't know what you're missing. Beautiful out there."

"No, we stick to hacking around the barn." A wide green swath of grass surrounded the barn and arena, and Casey often let James walk the perimeter on a loose rein after their workouts. She liked to watch his neck stretch, to discover the moment his ears loosened and flopped with every stride. But he also looked hard at scurrying lizards and mumbling flocks of ibis, reminding her that their few trail rides back at St. Johns had always been fraught with spooks and drama. Gwen had helped her work through his silliness, but Gwen wasn't here, and Casey felt the absence of her youth and confidence. She shook her head. "We're fine, really. It's only...there are some big goals we've set for ourselves, and to reach those goals we have to work really hard. That's all."

"You must crave hard work," Maria remarked. "Ah well, it's a game for the young. Hard work and climbing the ladder and winning ribbons and all that. And of course, I mean well when I say y'all are crazy." She smiled at Casey from beneath Chico's neck.

"I'm sure you do." Casey smiled. "I promise we're not crazy, though. Big goals, like I said. And I gotta be honest, here. I don't know who I'd be without my goals. They're what get me up in the morning." And kept her up at night, if she was being honest with herself, but that wasn't the point.

"You'd be yourself," Marie reminded her. "Ah, I think I see your trouble. Don't you know if you spend all your time chasing success, you don't spend anytime getting to know yourself?" She tugged the bridle over Chico's brick of a head. "Take my advice. You need a trail ride. Some quiet time. A big old break from *goals*." She said the word like it was filthy in her mouth. "And that man of yours probably would like to see you more, too. Although I'm just guessin' now."

"I appreciate your insight, thanks," Casey told her with a gulp, a strange sound which came from nearly laughing at Maria's disdain for her horse show plans, while nearly choking at Maria's accurate assessment of her relationship. "But I think I have the balance right."

It was a bold lie to tell to such a knowing woman. But Casey really, seriously, didn't want to talk about it.

"Okay, did not expect the threatening weather," Casey called as she rode James out to the arena. Hannah had beaten her out there and was already trotting Caruso. He carried his head high, and his eyes were bugging out. As usual. Hannah never seemed to notice her horse's hollow-backed movement or general air of unease. Sometimes Casey wondered if she'd ever ridden a horse who was moving with calm, comfortable engagement.

Hannah glanced up at the dark clouds blowing in from the east and shrugged her shoulders. "I mean, it's Florida. When isn't it storming? We've still got so much work to do. Can't stop for a little rain."

Casey gave a little shrug of her own and leaned down from her saddle, tugging the gate closed as James fought to sidestep away. The wind ruffled his black mane and tossed his long, luxurious forelock over his eyes. Casey questioned whether they should be in the arena at all. There was a definite smell of rain in the air, and that was probably a low rumble of thunder in the distance, too. But Hannah was right. Even in the dry winter and spring months, south Florida attracted rain like a magnet attracted horseshoe nails, and if they were going to get anywhere with their horses, they'd be putting up with some rough weather along the way.

"Watch for when Maria comes back," Hannah shouted, trotting past. "She knows the weather best. If she comes in early, we go in early. Deal?"

"Sounds good," Casey called back. "But if there's any lightning close by, we have to go in. Maria or no Maria."

One nice thing about the foul weather: the sudden onset of clouds created some welcome shade, along with a gusting breeze that rattled the palm tree fronds and kicked up the thin layer of dust resting atop the damp sand beneath. The breeze blew cool against her sweaty face, and Casey felt her spirits lifting as they warmed up, trotting and cantering in big circles around the arena. Everything was better when the air moved a little.

Of course, the cooler temperatures and the whipping wind raised James's spirits as well. A particularly powerful blast of wind whistled through the railings of the arena. Keyed up and looking for trouble, James threw a small, experimental buck.

Casey felt her teeth clenching as she leaned back in the saddle, pushing against his movement. *"No,"* she snapped, as if she was disciplining a naughty dog. *"Do not!"*

"Give him a kick!" Hannah cried, galloping past. Caruso still had his head straight up in the air, his nose poking out. But that was how he liked to travel, and Hannah didn't know how to teach him to soften and round his spine. Casey had been trying to help her with it for a while, even breaking her rule about no teaching. Unfortunately,

Hannah was impatient, and Caruso was uncooperative. She'd complained they didn't need to be round and "dressage-y" to compete in the jumper divisions, and Casey had looked at the current crop of top riders gracing the equestrian blogs and knew Hannah was right. Round and measured was out, flat and fast was in. Also, right now she was in no position to lecture Hannah, who hollered, "Go on! A big kick! Remind him who's boss!"

Casey should've known better than to follow Hannah's instructions, but James had her frazzled, and the word *kick* penetrated her fuzzy brain. The next time James napped and tried to buck, she kicked him hard with both heels.

Surprised by the assault, James flung himself up and forward, head high enough to rival Caruso's. One gigantic leap ought to be enough for him to express his feelings, Casey thought resignedly. She could accept that she'd made a mistake. But when his forelegs hit the ground, he did it again, launching with even more power.

Casey was already hanging on by reins and toes and sheer grit, but the second big hop was enough to sling her loose from the saddle. With little fanfare, she tumbled into the gray sand, a mouthful of the stuff sifting between her lips, and then the rain began. The fat drops were cold on the back of her neck.

Two falls in two days, she thought, letting the drizzle sink into her skin. With that kind of stat, getting up seemed pointless.

Maria had somehow beaten them back to the barn. The rain pounded down on the roof with a sound like a train roaring overhead, but Maria still gave them smiles and nods as she groomed Chico from the comfort of his stall. It must have been that sense of weather Hannah had alluded to; either way, they'd gotten soaked, and Maria had not.

Casey snapped a snorting James into the cross-ties and then, with a grimace, reached into her shirt to shake more dirt out of her bra. She must look like she'd rolled around in the sandy patch in the pasture, where the horses liked to grind the dirt into their coats.

Hannah set Caruso up in the cross-ties facing her, but Casey tried to ignore her. She didn't want to look at Hannah, or Maria, or anyone. She was too embarrassed. The plan was to curry-comb the sweat out of James's coat, put him away, and hope the storm let up by the time she finished so she could leave without driving through a blinding rainstorm.

Luckily, the rain and the rolling thunder put the kibosh on any idea of conversation. By the time they'd untacked their horses and put them back in their stalls to munch hay, Casey was sitting alone in the tack room, assessing the damage from her fall. It wasn't too bad. She was sore on the shoulder where she'd landed. Her corresponding hip had a throbbing ache, and she'd be stiff as a two-by-four tomorrow morning, but nothing had been broken. At her age, that was the important thing.

And, she hoped, Hannah was thinking about other things now. The girl had a fairly short attention span. Casey glanced out at the rain—still coming down in buckets. She resigned herself to a longer stay at the barn than she'd intended, took out her tack cleaning kit, and oiled her rain-soaked bridle. As the rain continued hammering down on the metal roof, Hannah entered the tack room and did the same. A quarter of an hour ticked by in silence, as Casey indulged in more and more elaborate ways to clean her tack. She even got out the metal polish.

Then, when the last raindrops were falling from the eaves outside, Hannah brought up the fall.

"That was a pretty dirty move James pulled on you."

Casey worked a toothbrush between the brass clinchers on her bridle's brow-band. "The weather played a big role. All that wind. I should have known he'd get freaked out."

"Caruso didn't, though."

"Caruso wasn't exactly relaxed, either," Casey pointed out.

"Well, he's Caruso. He doesn't relax."

Casey bit back a sharp reply. She wanted to tell Hannah that it was *her* responsibility, as the rider, to relax her horse. But she knew that kind of training wasn't something Hannah would figure out on her own. Hannah needed a trainer to help her. Casey thought she could probably help—but she held back. What was she going to do, stand in the middle of the ring and holler instructions to Hannah? She wasn't a riding instructor.

In fact, these days she felt like the opposite of a riding instructor— whatever that might mean. Someone with no idea what they were doing in the saddle. She'd be qualified to help Hannah in a professional capacity right after she stopped tumbling off of James every time the wind blew a little.

Hannah needed someone like Sky, a real trainer. Maybe even a real barn, like St. Johns Equestrian Center. A place filled with supportive and experienced riders, a place overseen by a kind trainer with experience coaching young riders.

And older riders, Casey reminded herself. Everything Casey had now, she was sure she owed to Sky. All those riding lessons, and riding with younger, more experienced, more intuitive riders like Gwen, had set her up for success with James. Things had started so well.

And now she was riding down one long backslide.

And this became a problem which was *really* growing fast if she was falling off twice in two days. She never used to fall off! Now it was becoming a habit. And for what? For stupid spooks and silly antics. For a flock of cattle egrets. For a gust of wind and her own over-reaction.

Casey put her bridle back on its hook. *Time to stop beating yourself up,* she reminded herself. *Time to go home and do work on Sunday, instead, so you don't get fired.*

Maria poked her head into the tack room. "Knock-knock," she rasped, laughing. "Just wanted to tell y'all that rain's letting up and I'm leaving."

"I didn't even know you were still here!" Hannah exclaimed. "You shoulda come in and cleaned tack with us!"

"I was just sitting with Chico, watching the storm," Maria told her. "My tack can last another day or two. It's lasted this long." She glanced at Casey. "You okay, mama?"

Casey watched that glance take in the dirt streaking her pretty riding clothes. "I'm fine. Thanks for asking."

"He needs loosening up," Maria told her. "But that's all I'm gonna say. Ta-ta, you two."

A moment later, they heard Maria's old truck roaring to life.

Hannah mulled over Maria's parting words. "He needs loosening up?" she asked eventually. "How's she mean?"

"She wants me to give James a break." *And myself,* Casey thought, all too aware that when Maria looked at her, she saw a person and a horse in need of some serious chill.

But they didn't have time to slow down now. They'd already lost so much ground. And she didn't feel like she could bear to fall behind with James now, not with the way her life was going. All she *had* was work, and James, and sometimes, Brandon. Work was a mess. Brandon seemed to be trying to wait her out. That left her James.

Casey was well aware that if she didn't succeed with James, she wasn't succeeding with anything.

Chapter Four

THE STORM THAT sent Casey out of the saddle had left deep water ponding on the roads, and a resulting car accident had shut down her road's intersection with I-95. When the car ahead of hers moved into park, Casey followed suit. She tipped her head back against the seat with a long sigh. Perfect. A traffic jam when she had hours of work ahead of her.

The timing was off in more than one way. Trapped with her thoughts, Casey thought if there was one thing she didn't want to hear right now, it was her own annoying inner voice. The one which spoke up when things were going badly, to assure her that everything was wrong and getting worse. Today it had several choice comments for her.

You're not a good enough rider.
You're going to get yourself and Hannah hurt.
James is going nuts and you can't stop it.

"None of that is true," Casey said aloud. And then, because she'd been putting it off for a couple of weeks and there was no time like the present when you were stuck in traffic, Casey told her phone to call Sky. She figured Sky would be in the arena teaching, and she'd only get voicemail, but Sky picked up on the second ring.

"Casey!" Sky's exuberant voice shrilled from the car speakers. "How did you know to catch me right now, between lessons? Amazing timing!"

"Got really lucky, I guess."

"I'll say. How are things? How is James?"

"Oh boy. Honestly? Things are rough."

Sky didn't even hesitate. Didn't tell Casey to call her back later. She was too generous. Too kind. One of the most generous, kind people Casey had ever met. And Casey had just left her, given it all up. She wanted to scream.

"Tell me everything," Sky said.

Casey needed no more prompting than that. She spilled her guts. *Everything.* Well, everything horse-related, anyway. Her fear their rides weren't as productive as they used to be. Her concerns that James was getting more reactive and tougher, and she wasn't fielding his issues correctly. Her plans to get back into showing, after their long winter hiatus, in exactly two weeks. "Which, honestly, scares me," she finished. "I figured we were doing okay, like things were good enough, for the longest time, but the past few weeks...yikes. Like I said, two falls in two days must mean, like...something. Unless you think it's only nerves?"

"I suppose it's possible," Sky mused, but she didn't sound convinced, which made Casey nervous. "Or else you need to get into a lesson program. Some riders just need that kind of support. There's nothing to be ashamed of, if that's the case. Isn't there *anyone* you can ride with regularly? Try for a few months and test your results?"

"Not where we are. I've checked and checked. We'd have to trailer somewhere, and I have to borrow a truck and trailer for a show."

"And you can't get a truck and trailer of your own..."

Casey snorted. "Not in the financial cards right now. Hannah is positive she's going to save up and buy both as soon as she gets out of high school and can work full-time at the diner, but that's two years away and I don't think she quite understands how much these things cost."

Sky sighed. "Well. I don't really know what to say. But you could draw back on showing plans until you can get regular coaching. I feel kind of bad...I recommended Twin Palms to you, and now things aren't going well..."

"It's not the barn," Casey lied. "The barn is nice. The horses are taken care of. James is happy." *That* much was true. "And it's in my price range, which I can't say about most places."

"Well, that's good. That makes me feel a little better. Hey, listen—if he gives you too much trouble, you can always send him up here for a month or two. I could give him a quick tune-up and he'd be good to go for another six months or so. It's possible that would buy you the time you need to find a trainer in your area, or a better transportation option."

Casey hesitated. This wasn't the advice she'd hoped for. Sky was actually suggesting she send James up to her for training? To buy six months of good behavior? And then what? In six month's time, nothing would change. She wouldn't magically have the money to move to a barn with a trainer, or buy a rig so they could drive to lessons. That wasn't how working for a horse show company worked. Her job was more about passion than paychecks.

"Your silence tells me you're not into this idea."

"Oh, I'm sorry, I—"

"I get it, Casey. You're in a tough spot. But don't forget that you bought James with the plan to stay in my barn, with regular coaching and training. You guys just might need more help now that you're on your own."

Ahead, Casey saw taillights flashing as drivers put their cars back into gear. It was the perfect excuse; the best timing she'd experienced all day. "I'll think about it, Sky, thanks. But for now I have to go. Heavy traffic."

"No problem," Sky trilled, as if they hadn't just been in the midst of a very depressing conversation. "Talk soon!"

Casey had plenty of time to digest Sky's words as traffic slowly crept forward. And by the time she'd passed the scene of the accident and sped back up to a normal pace, she'd also had time to get her feelings hurt. She'd gone to Twin Palms Ranch at Sky's suggestion. If it wasn't a good fit for her, if she needed to be at a barn with a coach this whole time, then hadn't Sky steered her wrong?

"She could have done it on purpose," Casey muttered. "She might have been trying to make me screw up with James so I'd have to send him back to her."

A crazy thought? Maybe. But who could tell anymore? She'd been making the best of her bad situations for so long, Casey was losing track of what the good ones even looked like.

"Casey!"

Brandon was calling for her the second she put her key in the door.

She pushed open the door and tossed her purse onto the hall table. "What?" she shouted back, hoping the exhaustion in her voice didn't sound too shrill. Traffic jams took it out of her like nothing else. All that wasted time! She was close to furious over it.

"In the kitchen! Come look!"

Casey sighed and kicked off her paddock boots. She stalked into the kitchen in damp socks, then stopped short. She put a hand to her hair almost involuntarily, thinking of the mountains of sand still clinging to her wet ponytail. Brandon wasn't alone. He was sitting on the tile floor, cross-legged, with a fluffy, panting puppy in his lap. His friend Stevie sat at the kitchen table, a huge smile on her face.

"Look at the puppy!" Brandon crowed, and Stevie laughed.

He sounded like a five-year-old, Casey thought impatiently. "I *see* the puppy. Hey, Stevie. Did you get a dog?"

"More like five dogs." Stevie shrugged, an unrepentant smile on her face. "I'm fostering a litter for the Little Harbor for Dogs. They're mystery dogs."

"Mystery dogs?" Casey surveyed the wriggling fur ball in Brandon's lap. It was a rag-bag of black and tan and white patches, with a pink tongue that escaped its toothy little mouth as it smiled up at her, desperate to meet the new body in the room. "Oh, I get it. Because you guys have no idea what breeds are in there?"

"Exactly. In some ways, this puppy looks suspiciously like a Bernese Mountain Dog. But one of her litter mates at home has long ears like a Basset Hound. So it's hard to say just what kind of paternity we're dealing with here."

"He's super cute," Casey admitted, giving the puppy a careless pat on the head. He caught her pinkie with his sharp teeth, then gave her a swipe with that long tongue when she yelped. "Puppy teeth." Casey grimaced and straightened, heading for the fridge. "I'm absolutely parched. It's like a million degrees plus thunderstorms out there. The whole 95 interchange was blocked for half an hour. And now I have to shower and get to work. It was nice to see you, Stevie." She poured a glass of water and left the kitchen.

Casey was halfway down the hall when Brandon called after her.

"Casey? I was thinking of keeping this puppy."

Casey dropped her water glass. It shattered on the tile, making a spectacular crash.

The puppy yelped in terror and made a break for it, slipping out of Brandon's fingers like a buttered piglet and running for the living room. Brandon toppled forward, trying to snag the dog, but he missed.

"I got it," Stevie assured him, giving chase. "I'll keep her away from the glass."

Casey snatched the little pan and broom they kept by the fridge, and knelt to sweep the mess. She glanced up and noticed Brandon was watching her with a critical expression. She didn't care for it. "I didn't drop the glass on *purpose,*" she snapped. "What's with the glare?"

From the living room: "Got ya! Whoops! No, I don't. C'mere, you slippery devil!"

Brandon ignored the mayhem. "You didn't seem very happy to see Stevie. Or the puppy."

"I'm sorry, but I didn't expect either of them. I'm a mess, so no, I wasn't happy to see company in the kitchen. And I have a lot to do, so I can't visit. Also, I don't think the puppy minded that I didn't jump over the moon when I saw him. He is just fine without me."

"Her," Brandon corrected. "It's a girl puppy."

"Okay. Same answer. The puppy didn't mind. The real question—" Casey stood up and pointed her broom at Brandon. "The real question is why you decided to blindside me with a puppy for adoption. I know we wanted to get a dog back before Christmas, but we also agreed we'd wait until things calm down. I'm too busy—"

"Casey, you're not the only person who lives here. I can work from home a little extra to housebreak a puppy. Plus, it's the perfect way for us to break up the day and get up from our desks. I don't think it's blindsiding when we literally agreed that when we moved here, we'd get a dog. You were so excited about it. What happened?" Brandon's voice was almost pleading, but Casey hardened her heart to him. After all, he had a lot of nerve asking that question.

What happened?

What *happened?* Was he serious? The pile of work on her desk happened! "I didn't ask for work to get crazy and I didn't want to go to a barn where everything is ten times as hard and I'm still not getting anywhere! Maybe if we'd gotten a house with a yard back in Cocoa, things would be a little different, but getting a puppy now? In a condo? When we have to walk it and play with it and I still have people breathing down my neck for work that isn't even my job and my horse is dumping me just because it's a little windy? How can you seriously think you can add a puppy to my life right now?"

She tossed the glass in the trash can and dropped the pan and broom back into the crevice between the fridge and the wall. In the living room, the overly cheerful playing sounds had ceased. Casey was aware that everyone in the condo—Brandon, Stevie, the puppy— probably wondered what the hell had gotten up that mean lady's butt.

After all, who got angry about a puppy?

Casey poured herself a fresh glass of water and tried to calm herself down.

"Wow." Brandon surveyed her with quiet concern. "That's a lot of different issues rolled together."

"You better believe it is." Casey threw back her water and refilled her glass again, wishing it was with something stronger. She missed Sunday brunches with their bottomless mimosas, weekend visits to craft breweries, long afternoons by the pool with her mom and a pitcher of margaritas. Now her Sunday beverage was just coffee at best, growing cold while she hammered away at her laptop. And the change affected Brandon, too. He was stuck home because she was. Bored, because she was busy.

Trying to adopt a puppy, because she didn't have time for him.

"I'm so sorry," she muttered, ashamed to even look at him. "I'm just stressed, more than I can even believe."

"Hey, I get it." Brandon's arms were around her, squeezing her tight, giving her consolation she probably didn't deserve. "I understand. Things are bad right now. But, hey? They'll slow down. Right?"

He was echoing her words, the ones he'd thrown back at her last night.

He was trying, so hard. And she wasn't trying at all. She was at capacity.

"Right," she choked, her throat tight with unshed tears. "Things will slow down. As soon as this acquisition is over. There will be more people, for one thing." She tried to lighten her tone. "We'll have the employees from the west coast."

"There you go. More people. It won't just be you. That will be a big help."

"Yeah." Casey sniffed. She tipped her head against Brandon's neck, not ready to let go.

"No puppy right now," Brandon offered. "We'll wait for things to slow down."

"I'm sorry. You wanted a dog and I've been putting it off—"

"No, it's okay. This one's a little too hairy for us, anyway. She needs a big yard to shake off all that fur."

Casey laughed despite herself. "Honestly, she *is* so wooly, like a little sheep. This place would be all hair."

"She can hear you," Stevie said.

Casey's eyes flew open. Stevie was standing in the doorway, her arms full of squirming, licking puppy. Casey's face must have betrayed her embarrassment—*making fun of an orphan puppy, Casey? Really?*—because Stevie just laughed. "Don't worry about it. I have a list of people a mile long. This puppy's gonna be adopted before the end of the day."

"Where was I on the list?" Brandon asked, sounding wounded.

"Third." Stevie picked up her backpack.

"Third!"

"Well, sorry," Stevie said. "But they give us a rubric, and we score potential adopters. It's not personal. It's math."

"I want to see it," Brandon announced.

"Sorry. Confidential."

"What knocked me down to third?"

Stevie eyed Brandon. "You're taking this really personally."

"Yeah, well, I'd be a wonderful dog dad."

Casey had never heard Brandon utter the words *dog dad.* She studied him, wondering if she was witnessing some hidden side of him being freed for the first time. Suddenly, she felt her left eyelid twitching. It was her biggest stress tell, and she knew just what word had triggered it.

Not dog.

Stevie was shaking her head at Brandon. "Okay, I'll tell you one thing. They prefer married couples. It's unfair, I know, but it's on the rubric."

Casey watched Brandon react to that. "Totally unfair," he exclaimed. "And possibly illegal?"

"They're a non-profit; it's a gray area. Fine, I'll tell you one more thing. Working hours. They specifically ask if the household works over five days a week."

"I almost never—"

Stevie's gaze flicked to Casey. "Gotta go," she said. "I'll call you in a few months. And when we find something with less hair."

She was at her desk five minutes after she stepped out of the shower, her hair knotted up in a bun, her stretchiest leggings and softest t-shirt called in for comfort duty. Brandon brought her a mug of coffee she hadn't had to ask for and then lingered, a hand on her shoulder. She wanted to shrug his touch away; not because she didn't want his consolation, but because she didn't deserve it.

"It's not a big deal," he said eventually. "We *had* agreed this was the wrong time for a puppy, with your work schedule and—everything else. I didn't bring it up again. This is on me."

"It really sucked hearing Stevie say we weren't good enough, that's all." She drew a shaky breath. "To hear, out loud, *you're* the reason your boyfriend can't have a dog."

"Well, she didn't decline because of you. Just your job," Brandon reminded her. "And that's going to get better." He squeezed her shoulder. "I'll leave you to it."

"Brandon—wait." Casey stood up and drew him back to her. It was all hanging on her shoulders now: the missed party the day before, the bad ride and the stupid fall, Sky's lack of faith in her, the weekend work she hadn't planned for, and now the lost opportunity to adopt a puppy. She was almost too exhausted to say her piece. But it had to be said. Before he left the room, left her to sit in this second bedroom-turned-office, to work until evening drew in and the promise of a pleasant Sunday afternoon had been utterly lost. "I'm—this is really hard right now. I thought everything would come together when we moved and I had this job and—it just *hasn't*, you know? And—I'm sorry. I want you to understand I'm really sorry about the way things are going."

Brandon tugged her close. "We'll figure it out, Casey," he said, his lips pressed softly against her damp hair. "And if the only downtime you have right now is at the barn, that's okay. Maybe I can spend some time with you there, too. Horses like me."

She smiled against his shoulder. "It's hardly downtime, what I'm doing at the barn."

"Well." Brandon paused for a moment. "Do you ever think it should be? A little bit, anyway."

She didn't have an answer to that.

"Now, you get to work." Brandon squeezed her shoulder and started to leave.

"What are you going to do?" Casey always felt bad when the office door shut on a weekend.

"Go to the store. Buy some wine. Cook myself a fancy dinner. Might even let you have some of it. Think you can be finished with all of this by, I don't know, seven?"

Casey looked back at her laptop. The fan was already whirring with the effort of all the files she had opened. "It's done by seven no matter what," she decided. "What are they going to do, fire me?"

"There's my girl." Brandon planted a kiss on top of her head. "Fight the power."

And he left her to get to work.

Chapter Five

"IT'S A PRETTY farm," Sharon observed, nodding her head at their surroundings.

"Well-kept," Phillip agreed.

Casey, standing beside her bosses, somehow fought back an incredulous stare. *A pretty farm?* Try horse heaven. This place was exquisite, and *any* equine would trample their current owner for a chance to live in an ostentatiously beautiful property like this.

Well, they would if horses had the same design taste as a typical South Florida wealthy human, anyway. Sometimes over the top, always Spanish revival, and most definitely luxurious: the style palette down here worked overtime to let a visitor know there was money in buckets behind these barns. And for anyone, human or horse, who desired palm-lined driveways, white fences, and gleaming stall fronts, it would be hard to top this farm. When Casey had agreed to go on a site visit to see an equestrian center proposing a "small" series of horse shows, she hadn't expected this level of grandeur.

Places like this were so far out of her reach, she couldn't even imagine attending a show here.

"It's, um, a *really* nice farm," she replied to Sharon, who seemed to be waiting for her contribution. Then she looked around again, aware she was probably moving her head back and forth like an owl who had just woken up.

But it was worth looking a little foolish, just to take the place in. They were standing on a cobbled roundabout which wrapped in front of the colossal main barn, serenaded by tinkling water dancing from the white marble fountain in the center of the circle. Marble seashells framed marble horses, prancing on their hind legs; a coy hippocampos below twined his sinuous tail around a laughing mermaid.

The fountain itself was worth the price of admission, Casey thought. The huge white stables behind it were just icing on the cake. Lined with Mexican fan palms—the same skinny trees that gave Beverly Hills its distinctive feel—the twin-winged barn had windows every twelve feet and a handsome horse head for everyone of them. Casey wondered at first what all those horses could be looking at; then she noticed the wind had blown a few palm fronds down, and gardeners were in the hedges alongside the barns, cleaning up.

"Hello, friends!" A petite, senior woman came out of the barn's entrance rotunda. She was wearing purple Bermuda shorts and a light button-down blouse, tan sandals and a wide-brimmed straw hat over close-cropped gray hair. The woman's obvious age startled Casey; she seemed far too spritely and athletic for the lines on her face and the papery skin on her arms.

"Good morning, Tildy," Sharon called. "Everything's looking beautiful today, yourself included."

"Oh, go on." Tildy waved a thin hand as she approached. "I look my age, which is terrible."

The sea breeze, which had been gusting off and on all morning, chose that moment to roar through the palms. Casey thought Sharon ought to be thankful for the audible interruption—it was pretty awkward to be put in your place about pointless compliments by a woman who was obviously pushing ninety—but she jumped as hard as the others when another palm frond came crashing down, hitting the cobbles a few feet away.

"Oh, these trees!" Tildy exclaimed. "I couldn't get them trimmed this winter and now we're paying the price. You have to baby these fan palms," she told Casey conspiratorially, as if she looked like a person planning her own palm tree oasis. "You can't just let them grow like a nice Florida cabbage palm."

"I'm sure," Casey agreed, with a sidelong glance at Sharon. But Sharon was just smiling and nodding away.

"Into the barn, then?" Tildy clapped her hands. "Let's look around!"

They were walking past the palm frond, which was laying limp on the ground like a carcass, when a dark-haired, middle-aged man came racing out of the barn and snatched it up. He glared at the frond as if it was a misbehaving dog.

"Thanks, Mario," Tildy called as he dashed away, waving the frond at the gardeners. "Mario loves this place like it's his own," she told us confidingly. "He's been my barn manager for fifteen years. I couldn't do any of this without him." She looked around happily. "My dream farm."

"Tildy, it's a wonder," Sharon declared, giving in her to real thoughts on the matter. "I was trying to play it cool, but you deserve better. I'm so impressed with what you've done with the place."

"I'm just jealous," Phillip interjected. "Can you find me an oil-baron husband? I'm an excellent cook and I'm never late for social functions."

Tildy's laugh was a dry rattle. "Phillip, you know how these Texan men are."

Wait, Casey thought, looking at the people laughing around her. *I don't know.* But the others seemed deeply amused and Casey had to chalk her confusion up to some generation-gap situation. Sharon and Phillip were at least twenty years older than she was, and it showed—often. Casey had been secretly hoping the west coast deal would provide her with some more contemporary colleagues. She imagined working with a fellow thirty-something who loved horses, too. Even if they were working remotely, some work friends would be amazing.

She followed the little group as they went into the rotunda and stood still for a moment, taking in the wide barn aisles stretching away from them on either side. Horses leaned over gracefully curved stall fronts and whinnied like extras on a film set. Casey spotted hay carts at either end, and grooms hoisting flakes of hay to throw into stalls. Lunchtime for the ponies.

"Casey, can you grab some photos of the arenas and stabling areas? Quick, before the grooms get down here and there's hay all over the place. And then go to the next barn." Sharon gestured down the left aisle. Through the open doors, Casey could see another long stable glistening in the sunlight. "Just grab anything you can use for marketing. Think luxury. Sound good, Tildy?"

"You have the run of the place," Tildy told her graciously. "Make us look good!"

As if this place could look bad, Casey thought, stalking down the rubber-paved aisle. Her paddock boots, polished to a sheen for this site visit at Sharon's insistence, pounded on the horse-friendly paving bricks. There wasn't a single wisp of hay marring this end of the barn, so she set up a few shots with her bulky digital camera, watching as the horses swiveled their ears towards its beeps and clicks. They were tall, imposing, and groomed to a gleaming shine, but when they saw Casey, all they wanted was their lunch hay.

"Sorry, guys," she called as their rumbling nickers and neighs grew louder. "I'm just the photographer."

Weird, how she'd become the photographer. Weird, that they had called her along on this visit at all. Sharon and Phillip usually handled details like farm inspections on their own. When they'd insisted she visit Ivy Place with them, camera in hand, she'd understood they were trying to sell the property as well as the show to potential exhibitors. She could see why; she just hoped it would not become common practice. Casey had enough to do without traipsing all over South Florida, taking pictures of fancy barns.

She passed the grooms, silently throwing hay without a glance in her direction, and crossed the grass alley between the two barns. This stable block was empty; she assumed they would use it for renting stalls to competitors. When Casey flicked on the aisle lights, the barn's ready, waiting state impressed her. Grooms had stripped the stalls of shavings, then swept them clean, and there wasn't a speck of dust or corner full of cobwebs to be seen. She remembered the barn manager swooping past them, his gaze laser-focused on the single errant palm frond, and figured she was dealing with a real obsessive type here. Someone who couldn't handle the truth about horses: they were messy, dirty animals who lived outdoors.

Casey shrugged and set up some shots of the plain but roomy barn. A wide-angle featuring the aisle with the show-jumping arena just visible at the far end, white sand gleaming in the sunlight. Some thoughtfully composed close-ups of stall fronts with their individual water spigots and double-latched doors. She checked each one on the camera's screen and smiled to herself. They'd be great shots when she cleaned them up.

Casey had taught herself the basics of photography over the past few months, along with a full suite of photo editing tools which had once seemed too mysterious for her to even contemplate. All on weekends, of course. She'd mulled over a foolish idea of making some kind of hobby out of it. Kind of funny to think about now.

She had made her way out to the jumping arena, where perfectly groomed footing and a colorful jumping course awaited, when a cool voice from behind her called, "All you're missing is a horse!"

Casey jumped, fingers fumbling at the camera. Well, that's why she kept the strap around her neck, even if she looked like a middle-aged dad visiting the Grand Canyon. The camera must be kept safe from incidents just like this one. She turned and saw a woman of about her age crossing the arena. This newcomer was all horsewoman from the waist up: pink sun shirt, a ball cap embroidered with a jumping horse tugged tight over her smooth dark hair, Ray-Bans to keep out the glare from the arena's white footing. But everything below her bellybutton was Floridian summer: pale blue cut-offs, a pair of leather flip flops, toenails painted a cheerful sunshine yellow.

"Hey," the woman said as she drew near. "I'm Raina." She held out a hand and Casey took it admiringly: Raina's hand was tan and smooth, with a few hard spots on the palm and the skin inside her fingers. A rider's hand. "I work for Tildy."

"I'm Casey. From Atlantic Horse Show Productions. My bosses are meeting Tildy inside—"

"Oh, I know. I helped my dad get this place into perfect order this morning." Raina laughed musically. "Although he would have wanted this place to be perfect on a random Tuesday, even if you guys *weren't* coming. My dad's kind of obsessive about perfect barns. If you can't tell."

"Your dad?" Did she mean the guy with the palm frond?

"Mario," Raina replied. "The barn manager. You—met him, didn't you?" A shadow of suspicion crossed her face. "Tildy said she would introduce him to the horse show team. Sometimes she forgets how much he does around here."

"I *saw* him. But he was busy. He walked away before we could say anything. There was a...a palm frond."

Raina's sigh gave her away, even as she planted her smile back on her face. "That man. A palm frond? Sounds like him. He worships Tildy, and this farm, to the point of obsession."

"Well, Tildy did say she couldn't do it without him."

"You better believe her." Raina's laugh was flinty this time. "Because he does it all. Anyway, what do you think? You guys are going to take on the show series? Tildy's been wanting to show this place off for a long time. She's just been waiting for the right partnership."

"I can't imagine them turning it down. I mean, just get a load of this place." Casey flung her arms wide. "I've been taking photos for ten minutes and I've probably got enough for a coffee-table book."

"Tildy would *love* that. Don't say it near her, or she'll hire you to do it."

"Oh, I wouldn't have time." Casey chuckled regretfully. "They keep me pretty busy. You know they're going to buy Perfecto Events, right? The show production company based in San Diego? They agreed to a deal yesterday. Actually, I'm not even sure they published my press release yet." She was pretty proud of that press release; she'd taught herself to write them with the help of an online course. And since press releases were pretty close to fitting her job description as the marketing manager, the weekend effort was a lot less onerous than it might have been.

Raina shrugged. "Cool. I hadn't heard that. But listen, it's hot out. Did you get enough arena shots? Want to go back to the barn? I have a secret stash of Diet Coke in the staff fridge, and you look like you could use a cold drink."

"Amazing." Casey lowered the camera she'd been holding like a weapon, still planning her next shot. "I must have enough pictures for this project, anyway."

"I'll bet there are some press photos on my dad's computer, anyway. I'll send them to you," Raina promised.

Casey walked alongside Raina back to the barn, their footprints leaving a trail on the perfectly furrowed arena sand. Once they were sitting in the cool, quiet staff room with sodas in their hands, she enjoyed a calm she hadn't experienced at work in a long, long time. Sitting with Raina felt easy, like a friend she'd known all her life. She could tell they were similar: close in age, lifelong Floridians, lifelong horsewomen. Raina had just chosen the all-horse route in life, the road Casey hadn't taken. It would have been more cut and dry for her, though, with her father running a farm like this.

Casey let her eyes rove over the photos on the wall and Raina ran her through them, explaining who the horses were and where the shows had been. Casey was pretty impressed when she realized the photos with the biggest jumps and most ornate ribbons all featured Raina in the saddle. "So are you like, the barn's show rider?"

"Basically." Raina shrugged. "I've been on the staff as an assistant trainer since I was twenty-five. It's been ten years and Tildy's in no hurry to give me a promotion, even though I do all the work."

"So, who is the head trainer?"

Raina nodded at a man standing in some of the award photos, clutching the reins while Raina sat in the saddle. "Chip. Tildy's son."

Casey got up and looked at a picture more closely. Chip was more oval-shaped than angular, and his skin was pale. He held the reins clumsily, as if they were foreign to his hands. Casey raised her eyebrows. Head trainer? There was no way this guy was training horses to do anything—well, not anything a rider would *want* a horse to do, anyway. "This guy? Seriously?" she blurted, then put her hand over her mouth. "I mean—"

Raina's laugh was appreciative. "I know. Luckily, he doesn't actually try to be head trainer. He just likes the title. It makes him feel powerful, I guess. He's hardly ever here, so I try not to let it bother me. But when we get to the big shows and he swaggers in...I admit that it sucks. For me, more than anyone else. But I think my dad notices, too."

They were quiet for a minute. Casey remembered the way Tildy had called Mario her barn manager, and yet hadn't actually introduced them. Casey wondered if this beautiful farm had some issues simmering just beneath the surface. She sat back down next to Raina. "Do you think you might leave someday, if they won't promote you?"

"It could happen. But probably not. My dad needs me. And anyway, who has the money to keep horses like this?" Raina's outstretched arms encompassed the entire beautiful property. "I'd never find a job at another operation on this level." She shrugged and changed the subject. "So, do you have a horse?"

"I do! I have an off-track Thoroughbred, named James."

"And do you show him?"

"I try. But it's not easy, when I don't have nice amenities like this place has. We barely have an arena to ride in. I get what you're saying about not wanting to give all this up."

"Sometimes I don't know *what* I'm supposed to give up," Raina mused. "Like, I want to be a rider. Does that mean when I put up with nonsense in order to ride, I am not a good feminist, a good Latina?" She grimaced hilariously at Casey, who gave her a sympathetic smile in return. "Am I supposed to give up the nice arena and perks so that I can get some respect? Or am I supposed to appreciate what I've got and just deal with the awful stuff? It's hard to know what's right."

Casey wished she had an answer, but she was sort of out of her depth on this one. She started when she heard her name being called from the barn aisle, feeling a little pulse of guilty relief. "That's Sharon," she announced, standing up so quickly she nearly dropped the camera bag. "I guess we're going."

Raina smiled wearily and pushed hair back from her dark eyes. "It was nice to meet you, Casey. Maybe I'll see you around?"

"That would be really nice." Casey liked Raina—liked her instantly, in a way she hadn't felt in years. Maybe she finally had a friend of her own down here in Palm Beach. Maybe she could stop mooching off Brandon's crowd.

Although she had no idea how she'd find the time to hang out with a friend.

They could be texting friends, anyway. "Let me text you real quick," she suggested. "So you have my number."

Raina's face lit up. "That would be great!" She recited her number, then shook her phone when Casey's initial *hello* reached her. "Got it! Let's grab coffee sometime." She laughed at Casey's hunted expression. "So soon, right? But trust me. I know a cafe next to a tack shop. We can make it a work trip."

"Perfect," Casey sighed, giving Raina a sheepish smile. "Because that's the only kind of trip I can take right now."

"A work trip!" Casey stared at Sharon.

Phillip went on eating his sandwich, but at least Sharon had the grace to put down her fork and give Casey her full attention. They were sitting in the window at a strip mall cafe near I-95; Phillip and Sharon would have to get on the road back to the Merritt Island office after lunch. Ivy Lane had been their only errand in Palm Beach.

Casey usually enjoyed a lunch with her bosses, especially one near home so that she could race home after, get changed, and hustle out to Twin Palms to ride James. But Sharon had really soured things with this new pronouncement.

Sharon, who was looking at her with such surprised eyes. "It's to San Diego, not Anchorage. You're going to love it. We'll book your flight out on Monday. That gives you Tuesday through Thursday to handle the Perfecto office, then you can come back. You won't even know you were gone."

"I'll write down some of my favorite restaurants," Phillip said. "Good food in San Diego."

Casey looked between her bosses in shock. "But I *can't* go to San Diego. Not next week, anyway. I have a show next weekend."

Sharon picked up her fork again. "You can still show next weekend. Just have someone else get James ready. You'll be back by Friday night."

Yes, she'd be back by Friday night...jet-lagged and probably nursing a cold from two transcontinental flights in five days. She kicked her boot against the ground and winced as it brushed against the steel foot of the table. Probably scuffing her good boots on top of everything. *Way to go, Casey.*

"So you're giving me three days in the Perfecto offices," she said eventually. "This really can't be a video session?"

Sharon took a bite of potato salad and looked out the window.

Phillip put down his sandwich reluctantly, recognizing it was his turn to reason with Casey. "There won't be anyone to video with," he told her, wincing a little with the admission. "It's just you."

"Wait—what about the Perfecto teams?" Casey had been counting on them like a fleet of guardian angels waiting to swoop in and save her the moment the papers were signed. "Their marketing people, their planners, what about *them?*"

"They quit," Sharon said, still looking out the window.

Casey stared at her. "They *quit?*"

"They wanted out of the business," Phillip said hastily. "That's why they sold."

"But they never—I never heard that—"

"Well, whatever they said beforehand, when we finalized the deal, they all said they were leaving when we took ownership," Sharon announced, her tone flat. "And we take ownership on Monday. So that leaves us to pack up the office starting Tuesday."

"And Wednesday, and Thursday," Phillip added. "You have three full days. It won't be too bad."

Casey gaped at him. "Packing up the office?"

"Emptying it," Sharon clarified. "We don't need paper copies of everything. Just digitize what's on the list and shred the rest."

"There's a list," Phillip said. "Or, there will be. Of the things we'll need."

"I don't understand." Casey was floundering. "Why didn't you tell me the San Diego team quit? I expected we were all going to work together."

"Well, it didn't work out." Sharon waved to the server, holding up her empty glass.

Phillip leaned over the table, his face organized in sympathetic lines. "I know it's a big ask, but we're at a turning point here. And Sharon and I can't do it—way too much on our plates in the office right now. You've been so helpful, Casey, don't think we haven't noticed that you've been going above and beyond for a while now. This is how start-ups are sometimes."

Sharon nodded in agreement. "Of course, you're wearing a lot of hats, and you're thinking some of them don't fit. But think how great it's going to be when we're expanding and you were with us on the ground floor the whole time."

Casey didn't say that she'd thought that's what this moment would be: that when they bought Perfecto, that *was* the expansion, that now was the time to congratulate herself on sticking out the hard times. But no. Apparently, she was still on the ground floor. And the next floor was nowhere in sight.

The disappointment added an edge to her voice when she asked, "So, just to clarify, I'm doing the work of four people now? Myself, plus three people who quit? Do I have that right?"

"That's one way of looking at it," Sharon said, fussing with pink sweetener packets—Casey didn't know anyone else who still used saccharine in her iced tea. "But don't get mired down in those kinds of details. This is just a minor bump on the road to expansion."

"We're all just doing what needs to be done," Phillip agreed. "It's not a competition."

"Even though we're putting on competitions!" Sharon giggled.

Casey picked up the bread that had come with her salad and bit into it. With carbs in your mouth, no one could hear you scream.

"So I told Hannah I had to go to San Diego and couldn't make the horse show, and she almost broke down crying right in front of me. And that's my day! Oh, and of course I got home late, but you noticed that."

Brandon shrugged. "I figured you'd be home after eight. It's no big deal."

Casey looked around the kitchen table, where she had been eating a fantastic chicken casserole. Hers was the only place setting on the table. If Brandon hadn't chosen to sit with her and have a glass of wine, she'd have been eating alone. He'd eaten at least an hour ago, while she'd still been at the barn. He'd cleaned the kitchen and wrapped up leftovers before she'd gotten home. And he'd abandoned his TV show to sit in the kitchen and watch her eat while she moaned about her day.

"I'm getting really boring," Casey realized.

"No, it's just work kicking your ass." Brandon poured a little more wine. "But going to San Diego—that's huge. Aren't you a little excited?"

"No. Not even a little." It was the answer a boring person would give, of course.

"Casey, have you ever *been* to San Diego? It's beautiful."

"And if we were going on vacation, that would be great. But this is a work trip. I probably won't even see the Pacific."

"It's hard to miss," Brandon mused. "It's right there."

"Watch. I'm going to be wedged into some tiny office like the one in Merritt Island, with no one around—it'll be me and a bunch of files to digitize and upload for the entire trip." Casey dug into her supper with a sudden vengeance.

"I'm sure it will be better than that," Brandon chided. "It almost always is. Was I aware you were a pessimist? Or is this new?"

Casey flicked her gaze from her plate to his face. His air of gentle concern was getting through her wall, leaving her guilty and defenseless. She came home late, and she piled on her sob stories? Not what Brandon deserved at all. "I think it's temporary?" she said, attempting a smile. "But I'll try to get over it."

"It's fine either way." Brandon leaned back and taking a long sip of his wine. "I'm with you for your looks, anyway."

Casey laughed. "Big mistake, buddy. Don't you see these worry lines on my forehead? I'm fading fast. This job is aging me."

Brandon leaned forward. "Hey, let's be serious for a minute. *Is* this job a poor fit for you? I mean, I've been cheering you on for a while, trying to keep things positive, but—well, now I wonder if I was overlooking the way it's really making you feel. Is it getting worse when it's supposed to be getting better?"

Casey fiddled with her food. "I don't know."

"The working on weekends, the office visits back up in Merritt Island..." Brandon prompted. "Seriously. Do you think things truly are going to calm down? Because if not, I don't want to just keep encouraging you to do something you hate. We can find you a new job."

"I don't *hate* this job. I enjoy working in horse shows. I had a really fun site visit this morning, actually. Met a nice girl there and everything." Casey sighed and pushed her long bangs behind her ears. "Honestly, I just want *less* of this job. I keep hoping once we expand, we'll get more staff and I can go back to just marketing. I really thought this acquisition was going to bring more people on board. Not give me the work of three more people."

"Well, maybe this trip will give you some time to really think about where the company's going. And if that direction is going to work for you."

"I don't know what choice I have, honestly. This job is ruining all my plans, but it also gave me the opportunity to move here. With you. Remember?" Casey shook her head. "I have to stick with it. Things will iron themselves out, eventually."

Brandon topped off her wine glass. "Do what you can," he suggested. "And in the meantime, finish your chicken. I made a cheesecake for dessert."

"Oh my goodness." Casey started shoveling food into her mouth. Brandon's cheesecakes were a reason to live on the worst of days.

Chapter Six

ON THE FRIDAY before the San Diego trip, Casey blew off her last few hours of work and met Hannah at the barn. She stopped along the way to grab chocolate milkshakes, hoping to make some small amends for her sudden abandonment of their horse show plans, as well as pick up peanut butter sandwich cookies from Publix for the horses. Peanut butter was James's favorite, to the point where he'd started turning down other, lesser flavors. She'd had to donate an entire package of lemon creams to Hannah—Caruso didn't care what he ate, as long as it progressed into his mouth as quickly as possible. Casey was pretty sure she'd seen him eat a chicken nugget out of a McDonald's bag one day, although Hannah swore she'd gotten the bag away from his marauding mouth in time.

"Hey, Hannah," she called as she walked into the barn, goodies in hand. "It's quiet here right now!"

"Yeah, it's nice this time of day." Hannah had been pulling their tack out, setting it alongside the cross-ties in the aisle. She ran a hand through her dark hair, then tugged it into a knot. "A million degrees, but nice."

"That part, for sure. But it's nice without the other boarders, you know?"

"No one peering at us like we're crazy for jumping, you mean?" Hannah laughed. "Yeah. I used to ride at this time a lot before you came. But it got boring riding alone, anyway."

"Not to mention really dangerous?" Casey suggested.

Hannah shrugged and continued working on her milkshake. Sixteen-year-olds were not concerned with danger.

Casey got to the heart of the matter. The real reason for the milkshakes. She'd been agonizing over the idea all weekend, but finally decided she didn't really have a choice. It was Hannah or no one, and no one was marginally more worrisome than Hannah. "I have a favor to ask of you. Well, it pays. So I have a job to ask of you. Do me a favor and take the job, is what I'm saying."

Hannah lifted her eyebrows. Her cheeks were sucked in with the effort of extracting milkshake from the straw.

"Will you ride James for me while I'm gone?"

Hannah stopped slurping the milkshake. Her face had brightened considerably. "Ride James? Like, train him?"

"I was thinking more, just keep him exercised..."

"I would love to! Yes!"

"Well, great." Casey hadn't exactly expected Hannah to say no, but her extremely enthusiastic agreement made her a little sad, too. Hannah would rather have Casey gone and a second horse to ride—for money—than have Casey around. She swallowed her disappointment, telling herself that teenagers were fickle creatures at best, anyway. And at least James wouldn't be out of work all week. "Well, you know how he goes and where his tack is, obviously. Just don't ask too much of him. He's going to be confused with someone else riding him."

"When are you going, again?"

"Monday. And I'll be back Friday, but I won't want to ride until Sunday. So you get him for five days. Is fifty bucks okay?"

Hannah had been furiously typing something into her phone, probably sharing her good news with some old chum from her old barn, but now she looked back at Casey. She lifted her chin. "Sixty-five. I charge fifteen dollars per ride."

Casey nearly burst into laughter, but Hannah was dead serious. And she needed Hannah—it was almost embarrassing, how much she needed Hannah. So she forced herself to nod and held out her hand. "Sixty-five bucks."

Hannah shook her hand with great solemnity. Then she went back to typing.

Casey sighed and looked around. With that task taken care of, she supposed they'd better get down to business and go for a ride. She walked down to the paddock and banged the chain against the gate. The flat expanse of pasture glowed green under the tropical sun, dotted with palm trees and the occasional cattle egret. A short distance away, the horses grazed contentedly; one by one they looked up and considered her, then looked at one another, as if trying to decide whether or not they should go in. Finally, James turned towards her, followed slowly by Chico and Caruso. The other horses put their heads back to the grass.

Casey watched her dark horse amble towards her, his thick black tail swishing over his back, and felt a ridiculous surge of sadness, as if she was leaving home for good and this was the first swelling of homesickness.

Five days, she reminded herself. Hardly a lifetime. She'd gone on last-minute vacations which lasted longer and created more chaos in her life than this one brief business trip. A hop to San Diego and back, no meetings or anything stressful, just cleaning out an office. In fact, it would be restful. A change of scenery. She'd go to lunch by herself and read her phone. She'd listen to some podcasts. She'd take hot baths and go to bed early.

But even as she listed the positives of her trip, the timing remained terrible. One thing on her calendar for the past two months—one thing!—and this trip had to be at the same time. She'd been working so hard to get James ready for this show, sometimes she felt like schooling her horse had occupied more space in her brain than her job.

James shoved his nose against her closed hand, and she released the cookies she'd been gripping there. He snatched at them greedily, his lips pressing against her palm. His muzzle was a teasing combination of velvet and prickles, his unshaven whiskers poking at her skin. She listened to him crunch the cookies with his molars. His chocolate-brown eyes stayed glued on her face, waiting for her next move.

Here it came: she picked up the battered leather halter hanging on the fence post and slipped it over his head. James snorted and came with her through the open gate, while the other horses jostled along the fence-line, looking for their own cookies. Caruso whinnied shrilly, his gaze going right past her; Casey spotted Hannah emerging from the barn, her phone finally pocketed.

One last ride, Casey thought, knowing she was being melodramatic but leaning into it. This wasn't just her last weekday afternoon ride before a quick trip; it was the *end* of something. This was the conclusion for goals she'd set months ago, goals which hadn't worked out. She knew perfectly well that the horse show would have ended in failure. They weren't ready. James had been getting tougher for months. She had been getting worse for months.

They were failing at this, and so this work trip was really a blessing. She was flying away from her problems for a few days, choosing a voluntary dismount over an involuntary one. What had Sky called it, when they'd practiced kicking their feet from the stirrups and leaping clear of a cantering horse? Ah, right—a *flying dismount*. Pretty apt, Casey thought, grinning to herself. She'd hop right off this runaway horse and right onto an airplane out of town.

"You didn't want to show anyway," Casey told James, patting him on the neck. "And when I get back, it'll be May, which is practically summer, and showing in summer is for suckers."

Even if they'd been progressing reasonably well on their own, Casey wasn't about to show under the sizzling Florida sun until at least September. Even September was pretty questionable. She knew people did it, but was it really worthwhile, baking out there for some ribbons?

So that was that, for showing. San Diego could be a blessing, not a curse. Casey just had to remember to look at it that way. She led James into the barn, noticing a battered old pickup was coming up the driveway. Maria's truck.

"So much for our quiet time," she muttered to James. Why was Maria here so early in the afternoon?

Maria parked and got out of her truck, slamming the door so hard that Casey flinched. "Sorry," she called in her usual drawl. "Door don't latch otherwise. What are y'all up to, here so early? I don't usually see you around here before five or six o'clock."

"I have to go away for a few days, and we have stuff to do this weekend, so I took off work early today." Casey snapped James into the cross-ties. "It's hot, so I'm just going to take a little ride around the arena, nothing serious."

"It's always hot, but that don't usually stop you from working hard." Maria laughed, drawing her arm across her forehead. "Phew! You're right, though, it's a scorcher. Must be almost ninety degrees. You ought to come out on a trail ride with me. I know a nice, quiet, shady trail."

"We can't go on a trail ride," Hannah said, walking Caruso into the barn. "We're getting ready for a show."

Casey raised her eyebrows. "What? We are?"

"Yeah, of course we are." Hannah clipped the cross-ties to her horse's halter. Caruso turned his head as far as he could and whinnied to the horses in the pasture, an ear-piercing sound. Hannah laughed and swatted at him. "Honestly, Casey, if we can't go this month, we'll just go next month."

Casey shook her head. "Hannah, I don't see the May show in our future. It's going to be super hot."

"It's hot *now*," Hannah reminded her. "We're all hot all the time. It's Florida."

The girl had a point. But Casey knew kids didn't feel the heat the way thirty-something adults did. And as fun as Hannah could be to ride with, she still sometimes made decisions that didn't take her horse's best interests into account. An entire day at a horse show when the temperatures were in the nineties and the humidity was high enough to match definitely fell into the Not Great for Horses category.

Plus, Casey could feel her momentary reprieve, her brief relief at being let off the horse show hook, slipping away.

"I don't want to show in May," she said, but Hannah was shaking her head.

"We have to," she insisted. "Or what is any of this for?"

The words made Casey's hand still halfway into her grooming tote.

What is any of this for?

"None of it's for anything," Maria said, sounding amused. "You young folk get so fussed about things. Just live a little!"

Casey wished she could be as cool and unfussed as Maria. It must be incredibly liberating, having no goals, living without the constant howling demon of perfectionism on her shoulders. She couldn't relate. "We don't have to get a ribbon to know we're improving," she pointed out.

"I've never won a ribbon," Maria said cheerfully. She started out to the pasture.

Hannah glared at Casey. "You're just like her now."

"Like who? Like Maria? I don't think so."

"Admit it! You don't want to show. You want to just poke around the arena after work like everyone else. I thought you were different," Hannah snarled, "but you're just like the rest of them."

"Hannah, that's not true!" Casey knew she was over-reacting—she shouldn't be so dependent on a kid's opinion of her. But she couldn't help it. Ever since she'd started riding again, she'd been trying to prove she still had that spark, that passion and drive for the sport which seemed to blossom to its fullest in teens. She'd been the oldest person at St. Johns and she'd worked hard to get the aggressively passionate teenage girls there to accept her. Even though in the end, she'd realized that their backbiting and constant one-up-man-ship was a lifestyle best left in her adolescence.

So even as a little voice she'd tuned out before asked, *Why do you care so much what these kids think of you?* Casey was already pledging her devotion to the cause again. "We'll go to the show in May. I promise. I'll talk to Liz and get the trailer lined up, and we'll go. Okay?"

Hannah's face lit up and her anger was forgotten, burnt out as quickly as it had flared. "Seriously? Yes! Thank you, Casey! Awesome. Listen, can you keep an eye on Caruso for just a minute? Maybe brush him off? I'm just going to run out to the arena and move a couple jumps around."

They didn't need to jump this afternoon. They could have just walked their horses around on a loose rein, and that would have been the perfect ride for the weather and for Casey's rumpled state of mind. But she couldn't turn down Hannah's enthusiasm. Sometimes, she thought Hannah was all that stood between her and turning into one of those after-work pleasure riders. And while she couldn't quite understand why such a fate was so bad, she still shuddered at the thought. She was a *competitor*. She had *goals*. She was still like Hannah, and the girls back at St. Johns: Gwen and Arden and the rest. Serious riders.

"I'll knock the dust off him as soon as I groom James," Casey promised, and gave both horses a few more cookies while Hannah bounded off to set fences.

Behind her, she heard Maria's knowing chuckle, and she knew the older woman thought she'd just been bullied by a teenager.

Well, Maria was probably right. What about it? Casey picked up her curry comb and got back to work on James's dark coat.

They had work to do.

Chapter Seven

A GOLD AND pink sunset, made exotic with the dark silhouettes of distant palms, was just getting underway in the west. Casey admired the view as she mopped the sweat from her face with the fresh towel she kept in her barn bag. Another hot ride tonight, but Hannah's enthusiasm knew no bounds.

Hannah's mother had called while they were cleaning up the horses, and Hannah happily filled her in on their long evening ride and their new plans to show in May. Casey cringed as she heard the story pouring out; she knew Missy Talbot considered Casey too old to spend so much time with her daughter. And now she was probably thinking Casey could just be a *little* more of an adult in this situation and shut down Hannah's incessant horse show planning.

But wanting to go to a horse show wasn't a juvenile endeavor, Casey told herself. If that was the case, the A-circuit shows wouldn't be packed with adult amateur classes. The entire equestrian industry was built on the exuberant spending of middle-aged women outfitting their show horses. No one was saying they were a bunch of overgrown children for wanting to win some ribbons for their riding.

Well, no one who was doing the actual showing, anyway.

Casey gave a lengthy farewell to James, and waved goodbye to the other boarders, who were sitting around drinking beer and talking about all the riding they were too tired to bother with, and got into her car.

Almost instantly, her phone rang. She groaned when she saw the caller and didn't even bother to answer with a smile. All her boss got was a morose, "Hi, Sharon. Everything okay?"

"It's fine. Sorry to call you so late. But can you do me the biggest favor? I mean, I'll owe you for life."

"That doesn't sound promising." Casey looked through the windshield at the darkening sky ahead of her. How could it be so late? She never got out of the barn *at a decent time.*

"Well, here's the thing. Tildy wants to sign off on the show series by Monday morning, but she lost the contracts we left with her."

"I can email her the PDFs," Casey said, grateful for an easy fix. "Not a problem."

"It's a little more complicated than that."

"Let me guess. Tildy can't open a PDF."

"I don't even think she can open an email. Now her assistant is away and her son isn't home, and she doesn't have anyone else who can help this weekend. And of course we're two hours away," Sharon added, as if distance was suddenly a huge problem in this business when they thought it was fine to ship Casey across the country with just a few days' notice.

"So, I have to go home, print out the contracts, and drive them back up to Tildy's place. Tonight."

"That would be great," Sharon said. "Thank you."

* * *

Brandon hovered in the office doorway as Casey printed out the contracts. "This is too much," he said for the fourth time. "They're abusing you now."

Casey opened a file folder and shoved the papers inside. "What difference does it make? This is my job. I can't just quit it. In fact, since this was the job I took after literally going on sabbatical and trying to find out what I wanted to do with my life, quitting is probably the wrong thing to do, even if I had the money saved. Apparently, this is how I want my life to be."

"Casey. Come on."

"I can't come on, Brandon, I have to get going and I still smell like barn!" Casey gestured at her dirty breeches, her sweaty top. "I'll be home by ten. I'll eat something in the car, so don't wait for me to eat supper."

She was out the door again before he could say anything else.

Ivy Place was nearly an hour away, but Casey made the trip in under forty-five minutes, a stat she wasn't proud of. She sat at the elaborate front gate for a mind-numbing five minutes before Tildy figured out how to open it, and she had to restrain herself from driving like a demon up the palm-lined driveway. At last, she pulled up in front of Tildy's white mansion, left the car idling under the Grecian-style portico, and ran up to the imposing double doors, file folder in hand.

To her surprise, the person who opened the door wasn't the tiny Tildy, but Raina, looking tidy in a pair of clean jeans and a cream blouse. Casey looked down at her own horse-stained attire and immediately wanted to hide behind one of the colossal columns lining the porch.

But Raina smiled as if there was nothing unusual about receiving a late-evening visitor wearing sweaty riding clothes and smelling of stable. "Casey! How nice to see you!"

She waved the file folder weakly. "I brought over the contracts for Tildy to send to my office. Which, I just realized, she won't be able to fax. Can she get a courier to FedEx them?"

"I can use the fax. Sorry that you had to come rushing over here. I wasn't up at the house yet."

"That's great." Casey faltered. "I'm sorry, I'm confused. Do you—live here?"

Raina's smile turned into a grin. "I live above the main barn. I have an apartment. But Chip is in Tampa, and Tildy's assistant is visiting her mother, and Tildy gets lonesome when she's home alone, so I come up and stay with her. It was my dad's idea at first—she always listens to him. So now I just come up when I know her assistant isn't here. If I wait for her to call and ask me, she's already been alone too long and she's irritable." She gave a little shrug that seemed to say, *What can you do?*

Casey had thought she understood all-encompassing jobs, but now she realized there were work-life boundaries that even Sharon and Phillip hadn't yet breached. "Well, I'll just leave these with you, then...?"

"They're safe with me," Raina assured her, taking the folder. "Listen, I'm sure you probably want to get home, or I'd ask you in for coffee. You want to meet up later this week? I'd really love to hear more about putting on horse shows. Your job sounds fascinating."

Casey looked at Raina for a minute. A rider from one of South Florida's most fabulous equestrian centers thought *her* job sounded fascinating? She couldn't quite think what to say.

"I'm sorry," Raina said quickly. "That was pushy."

"No—no—it's just, I have to go to California on Monday. I won't be here all week. Maybe we grab that coffee next week?"

"That would be really nice."

"Thank goodness. I'd like to have *something* to look forward to when I come back." There was a pause as Casey realized she'd said something terribly bleak. She hastened to explain herself. "I mean, I had to cancel my horse show plans next weekend and I've been kind of down about that open space on my calendar, you know?"

Raina's smile returned. "I totally get that. I'm the same way. If I don't have plans, I don't know who I am."

"Yes! It's like that!" Someone who got it! Casey felt her face light up. "How is the Monday after next? Can you do lunch?"

"On Mondays? Usually. I'll text you the place I was talking about."

"Awesome!" Casey lingered on the doorstep for a moment until she realized they were just staring at each other, waiting for the other to end the conversation. In the sudden silence, Casey could hear a television inside, blaring at an uncomfortable level. It must be for Tildy—who would probably look for Raina if she was gone much longer. "Well, I guess I should go. It's crazy late, right?"

Raina laughed. "Go have fun in California. I'll see you next week."

Casey slipped back behind the wheel as Raina closed the doors of the mansion, returning to whatever her life was inside those walls. Casey could feel herself slipping into the delicious clutches of a girl-crush. She couldn't wait to get back from her trip and find out more about Raina.

And get her own life back on track after this untimely interruption.

Chapter Eight

SHE WAS STARTING to think she'd gotten lost.

This trip had begun so simply. Casey had picked up her rental car at the San Diego airport and dutifully gone straight to the office, putting in a full afternoon sifting through the remains of the office. The small space in a dingy strip mall wasn't much different from the office back in Merritt Island, but the departing horse show promoters had taken their posters and calendars down, leaving blank, staring beige walls pockmarked with tiny thumbtack holes.

The bleak surroundings hadn't been much of a greeting after five hours in the air. But Casey soldiered on, organizing the paperwork left behind in stacks, until her eyes were crossing with tiredness. She'd driven the city streets back to her hotel in a daze, astonished by the sheer power of jet lag.

Then her phone rang.

The sound surprised her so much that she swerved and nearly drove right off the road. Casey swore and straightened the car before she ended up crashing. Possibly, she should have expected Sharon to call her at that late hour; perhaps, she should have known ahead of time that her bosses would come up with some crazy extra task she hadn't signed on for. Well, she hadn't. Foolish as that was.

And now here she was, heading out on a site visit to Sungold Ranch.

If she ever found the place.

Then: magic. The road curved gracefully around a round, bald hill. On the far side, a sign with the farm name appeared, its hanging board waving gently in the breeze.

"Finally!" Casey pulled into the driveway and looked at the gate, then at its surroundings. "I seriously thought I was going to end up in Mexico or something."

The welcome email from Goldie Harper had said she'd have to climb out and open the gate the old-fashioned way; the automatic opener was broken. What she hadn't mentioned was that the gate straddled a notch in the hills, and that when Casey got out to open it, she would be able to see for miles across a fawn-colored landscape of rolling hills and grazing livestock.

"So this is why people live out here," she muttered, as if the Pacific Ocean and the perfect weather weren't reason enough to move to the southernmost tip of SoCal. "I've never seen anything like this."

This was definitely no Florida: the rolling landscape, the rocky slopes, the short green trees clinging to beige, grassy hills. White clouds, fat and fluffy as cartoon sheep, floated through a candy-blue sky and cast drifting shadows across the hills. Beyond the closed gate, the driveway curved sinuously, fitting itself to the hillside. She saw where it ended in the distance, at a collection of wide, steel-framed buildings. Horses stood near a pasture gate, either waiting to be brought inside or just looking for some attention. Nearby, a dark blue pond glimmered beneath the protective branches of a cluster of pine trees.

So this was Sungold Ranch, her surprise new client. Sharon's voice had been full of urgency when she'd called, informing her that Perfecto had left the balls in the air with this trainer's potential summer show series. "Goldie Harper could be huge for us," Sharon told her. "Do a site visit, get the contracts signed, and start the process."

"That's not what I do." Casey scarcely believed she was daring to argue. "I can't do this, Sharon. This is your job."

"You're there. We're not. We need you to close this deal." Sharon's voice turned stern. "I'm forwarding you the directions."

And that was that.

Casey looked through the windshield at the farm, wondering how on earth she was supposed to close a deal. She probably could have managed this through a series of emails. The written word was her thing. In person? Conversation? She'd forget something important; she was sure of it. This was going to be a disaster.

"One more disaster," Casey said softly, "in a series of disasters."

But this would definitely be the worst one.

Her phone's calendar app chimed gently, reminding her she was supposed to be introducing herself to Goldie Harper, owner of Sungold Ranch, right now.

"Here I come," she muttered, hopping out of the car to open the gate. "Ding-dong! Avon calling!"

"It's a beautiful property," Casey said for the umpteenth time. She couldn't help herself. Goldie had been showing her around the place for fifteen minutes, and Casey still hardly believed this ranch was real. Everything about it amazed her: she loved the open-sided barns, allowing a breeze to play through the aisles and stalls, the big arenas with their reddish sand footing which was both giving and supportive beneath her feet, the massive pastures which stretched over the hills, dotted with grazing horses. Sungold Ranch was a true beauty.

Goldie Harper smiled and nodded at every compliment to her farm, taking the praise as her due. Casey thought she ought to pay this woman a few compliments, too. Middle-aged spread hadn't touched the angular Goldie, and while her dark red curls weren't natural, they weren't sparse, either. Goldie clearly spent all day, every day, in the saddle, and the lifestyle had left her taut with muscle and bursting with life.

"Really," Casey said as they finished the tour. "This place is a wonder. The white perimeter fence is a pleasant touch, too."

"Thank you! I thought the white might be a little much, but the boarders love it and it brings in traffic from the road." Goldie pointed to the farm's long road frontage. Then she turned and gestured at the arenas behind them, flanking a long and tidy barn. "And of course, that's all new fencing and footing in the rings. Just redone in the fall. It was time. I like to keep sprucing old things up."

"Nothing seems old. I'd say, established. How long have you been here?"

"Thirty-four years this summer," Goldie replied, pride in her voice. "When I started, it was five acres and a run-down shanty for the horses. I built it up from there. Always improving. The main barn is only six years old."

"Well, it's magnificent. Amazing that you've been able to work on the place for so long. Most people seem to come to their properties late in life." She was thinking of Tildy, tottering around her beautiful farm, watching younger women ride her horses.

"I wouldn't have a shot now. Land down here costs a fortune."

"Right place at the right time?"

"I guess. The only place for me, so thank God I was here to put down roots before the prices went up." Goldie looked around. "Yep. This is all I ever wanted."

Casey couldn't help a brief pang of jealousy. Imagine knowing what you wanted! "You sound so sure."

"Well, I figure, that's what you have to do in life, get to know what you want and go after it with everything you've got. I try to teach my students that, too."

"What's your student population like?" Casey tried to stick to the script, even though Goldie's words sent another wash of emotion over her. She made it sound so simple! Just know what you want! Meanwhile, Casey couldn't even figure out how to enjoy her horse, or work normal hours at her job. *It must be easier said than done,* she supposed.

"They're mostly juniors, and about a third of them are showing rated." Goldie droned some stats clearly pulled from her prospective student spiel. "And then we have some very accomplished ammys in the barn. I'd like to build up my adult amateur business even more, but it's hard to get everyone to rated shows—they're so expensive. That's one reason I was trying to put on a show series, a nice one, not just slapping together some classes and calling it a schooling show. I figure that giving them a nice show at home this summer will help convince some of them to step up, and maybe it will scratch the itch for the ones who just won't ever afford the big shows."

"Sure, that makes sense. A lot of our clients are doing something similar." It relieved Casey to find her own spiel returning, the words shaking off her tongue with little input from her brain. She had never seen herself as a sales rep, but apparently if you worked in marketing long enough, the ad copy part of your brain just translated itself into verbal pitches.

By the end of the site visit, Goldie was ready to proceed with the contract she'd originally been considering with Perfecto. Which was great, of course, but Casey was privately concerned as she carried the signed paperwork to her rental car. There was no one on the ground here. Who was going to work with local businesses to pull together sponsorships? Who was going to set up vendor accounts and get the show organized?

She had an awful feeling it was going to be her.

And there was nothing she could do about it.

Sure, it wasn't her job. But when had that stopped Sharon and Phillip before?

"And hey, what's one more thing?" she muttered, driving back over the winding roads towards San Diego. "My days are already completely full, so why *not* add more?"

She couldn't help being rather bitter. Putting on all these horse shows, while she shelved her own showing plans yet again. Was it so much to ask that she have a riding life in addition to a fulfilling job? Or was life really one thing or the other, to the exclusion of everything else, every single time?

It was beginning to feel that way.

The thing to do, Casey decided later, sipping a calming beer at the hotel bar, was to find a role model who had her shit together, and emulate *her*. And since no one came to mind as strongly as Goldie Harper, that was who it would be. She had to go back to Sungold tomorrow, so she'd use that time to get to know Goldie, and in doing so, figure out how the other woman had gotten her life together. A day wasn't much, but she was a quick study.

A perfect plan. Casey congratulated herself with a little toast to her reflection in the mirror behind the bar and ordered another beer.

* * *

Sharon had deemed the office clean-up a three-day job, but adding the Sungold show series to her workload was seriously eating into that time. The next morning, Casey woke up with a start at three a.m., jet lagged, disoriented, and too anxious to get back to sleep. She ended up driving out to Sungold at eight o'clock, two coffees deep and in a serious mood.

So, Goldie put her on a horse.

"You need a ride to clear your head," Goldie declared. "And I ain't taking no for an answer."

Casey looked down at her toes. She hadn't packed for site visits, and while her jeans wouldn't give her any trouble, she couldn't imagine climbing into the saddle wearing strappy gold sandals. "I'm not dressed for riding."

"Oh, this is a riding school. We got boots in every size."

"Plus, this isn't what I'm supposed to be doing." Casey gave a little chuckle, trying to hide her nerves. She wasn't great at standing up to authority figures. "We're supposed to be going over class lists and taking an equipment inventory. I have the whole checklist from Sharon here—"

"Oh, email can do all that. I meant to tell you that last night. Didn't want you to be driving out here on my account when you're jet-lagged out the wazoo, when I'm just gonna give your lists to my crew to handle, anyway. But, since you're already here," Goldie continued, patting the neck of the palomino mare that a slim girl in breeches had walked out to them, "I figured we might as well get to know each other. No better way than in the saddle."

"Well, that's really kind." Casey smoothed the mane of the palomino mare Goldie's working student had saddled for her. "If you think there's time."

"There's always time for riding," Goldie assured her. "This is Daisy. A real nice girl."

Casey looked from the horse to the woman adjusting the saddle, confused by which one was the nice girl. The young woman saw her wide eyes and laughed. "The mare is Daisy," she explained. "I'm Sharmayne."

"Of course," Casey said, relieved. "She's lovely. Um—I'm Casey. Nice to meet you."

"Nice to meet you." Sharmayne had soft vowels, kind brown eyes, and a broad smile. Her long black hair was braided and tucked beneath a kerchief. "I'm a little jealous of you. Always wanted to go to Florida."

"It's really humid." Casey dismissed her homeland with a wave of the hand. "You're probably better off here."

"The competition, though!" Sharmayne slipped a latigo bridle over Daisy's head, tucking one ear through the headstall. "I'd like to show big-time. Big, big, big-time."

Goldie laughed outright. "Sharmayne wants to be a Grand Prix rider."

"Then she should," Casey said, already loyal to the working student. "Can't you go to Indio or one of the California circuits?"

"She will when she's ready," Goldie interjected. The look she gave Sharmayne wasn't unkind, but Casey sensed there was some old trouble there. Best not to get into it. She subsided, taking Daisy's reins from Sharmayne with a nod of thanks. Another groom brought up a second horse, a strapping bay warmblood gelding, and handed him off to Goldie.

"Here we go!"

At the mounting block outside, Casey poked her borrowed boot into the stirrup and swung easily into the saddle. Daisy was wider than James, and she marveled for a moment at the difference in feel—she hadn't been on a strange horse in months. Then Goldie was hooting for her to move up, giving her room to climb up on her lop-eared gelding. He tugged at her and tried to trot away as she settled into the saddle, but Goldie clearly wasn't bothered.

"Oh, hush," she laughed, handing the horse all the rein he asked for. She looked over her shoulder at Casey, who had moved Daisy out of the way. "Don't mind him. This is Sunny Jim. He always wants to feel like he can run away at a moment's notice. It's like a security blanket for him, having loose reins."

"That must be...interesting." Casey was thankful Daisy was more like a veteran school horse. "I like his name," she offered. "It's kind of close to my horse's name. James."

"Now, that's a good name for a horse," Goldie proclaimed. She made an almost imperceptible movement with her body, and Sunny Jim began walking forward at a quick clip. Daisy followed, her golden ears pricked.

Casey expected to go into one of the beautifully groomed arenas, but Goldie let Sunny Jim stride right past the rings, making for an open gate at the end of the barn area. Ahead, Casey saw a narrow path of red, rocky dirt dug into the fawn-colored grass. It meandered in a long, curving line right up a tall hillside. Unused to changes in elevation, she deepened her heels a little to prepare for the hill.

Goldie glanced back at her and smiled. "I know you Florida girls never get a good view from the saddle. So let's ride up to the ridge line and take a look at the farm from here."

"I did see it when I drove in," Casey offered. "It's pretty impressive."

"It's even better from over here," Goldie assured her. "Come on, ride up next to Jim and me."

Casey would much prefer not to ride alongside someone else on that narrow path. But she remembered her goal today: learning how Goldie had gotten such spectacular control of her life. So she set her nerves aside and nudged Daisy with her heels until the quiet mare responded, jogging up alongside the long-striding Jim.

"That's it," Goldie said approvingly. "Easier to have a conversation when you're not always turning around in the saddle. Jim likes it better with a friend, too. Horses know best: everything is better with friends."

Casey felt her heart sinking just a little. If having friends were the ticket to happiness, she was out of luck. She'd left her best friends behind when she'd moved to Palm Beach, and there was no replacing them. She'd known them both since high school, for heaven's sake. They had the goods on each other in ways that even significant others couldn't quite match. If she'd worked out of an office, she might have met some agreeable people, but would it go anywhere? Office friendships were nice and all, but mumbling about the weather to someone by the water cooler wasn't exactly the stuff of lifelong companionship. And while Hannah was fun to ride with, she was also nearly twenty years younger than Casey. They weren't exactly heading to brunch together.

Goldie seemed to notice Casey's brooding silence. "You have any riding buddies, Casey?"

"I have one," Casey replied. "A teenager who has big dreams and not a lot of money. So, kind of like me, only younger."

Goldie glanced at her and nodded. "I know the type. My head working student down there, Sharmayne, she was like that. She started riding here when she was fifteen. Now she's twenty-five. That's ten years of working with me. She's a good rider, a good worker. Sometimes she struggles to fit in around here, but I make sure no one talks down to her."

"That's good of you." Casey hadn't seen many of Goldie's boarders, since she'd only been here while most professionals were sitting at their desks, but she could picture them pretty easily. "It's a tough sport if you're not born rich."

"That it is, and everyone deserves a chance to ride. If it's in their blood, like it is ours, then denying that is just cruel. I don't care what someone's background is or what they look like or whether they fit someone else's view of what a rider ought to be. And neither do horses. I'm just looking for people who want to learn and are willing to do whatever it takes."

Total dedication, Casey thought. Not a tall order at all, right? She smiled to herself, shaking her head. Last year, she'd pretty much proven to herself that she *didn't* have what it took to be a professional horsewoman. Well, certainly not a groom, anyway. Goldie wasn't aware of that little tidbit, or perhaps she wouldn't be so open and welcoming to Casey. Maybe she'd think Casey was just another empty promise, another woman who could sit pretty on a horse but didn't take advantage of that talent. And possibly, she was right.

They reached a high point atop the ridge, and Goldie drew back on Sunny Jim's reins, then let go almost immediately. The horse flung his head but stood still. Daisy stopped alongside him without prompting, and beside her, Goldie flung one arm wide. "Now *that's* the best view."

Casey looked around and gaped at the land stretching out around them. Under the blue dome of sky, the low grasslands and the rocky hills seemed to glow with a warmth she'd never seen in photos or movies. This was a landscape unlike anything she'd ever experienced, and she suspected it was made even better by her seat on the back of a horse. It felt like land meant for horses. You couldn't easily walk on two legs through these scrubby, boulder-strewn highlands, but a good horse could pick out a path, and take you anywhere you needed to go.

Suddenly, Casey thought she understood how Goldie had become so certain. It wasn't any particular inner quality. It was this beautiful land. "I feel like if you were out here every day, you'd know exactly where you belonged," Casey said slowly. "There wouldn't be constant questions about who you are or what your purpose is."

"It's easy to know yourself when the country is like this," Goldie agreed. "Built for horses, made for horses. I imagine it's tougher in a place like Florida. Buggy and wet and hot all the time." She grinned at Casey. "But it's home, right?"

"I think so. I mean, I always thought so before." She looked round again, still trying to take in the sheer scope of the wild country around her, and the tidy contrast of the horse farm below. "You...uh...you hiring?"

Goldie eyed her knowingly. "You don't want to work for me. You want to build something for yourself."

Casey resisted the urge to cry out, *"But what? What do I want?"* She didn't know if it would do any good to out herself as just another confused millennial to Goldie. So instead, she smiled and shrugged, and pretended to listen as Goldie started talking about the farm again.

"It's a lot to ask of you, I agree. But you're still coming home Friday, aren't you?" Brandon sounded a little concerned. "I mean, they wouldn't make you stay any longer?"

Casey flicked her bangs out of her eyes. She had been studying her reflection in the hotel room mirror, that big rectangular one which always seemed to hang over the desks in these mid-range places, as if they'd done extensive market research and found that tired women on business trips loved to look up from their work and study their smile lines and crow's feet. Since Casey had been doing just that all afternoon, perhaps they were right.

"I'm still coming back Friday," she assured Brandon. "But Sharon wants me to come back in two weeks. And stay for two weeks, doing show prep."

It had been a low blow, getting that email—Sharon hadn't even had the courage to call her up and tell her. No, it would be safer to break the news over email, where Casey could stare at the words in utter disbelief before slamming her fist against the laminate hotel room desk, howling in pain, then letting loose a list of swear words—half about her bruised hand, half about her job. She counted herself lucky no one had called the front desk about her; she'd steeled herself for a knock on the door, checking up on her.

On the other end of the call, Brandon was apparently still processing the news. "I'm a little shocked, honestly. And...wait...this means you'll be gone for your birthday. Oh, Casey. I planned a party for you!"

"Come on, Brandon, we don't have to make a big deal of my birthday. It's not a big round number or anything." Thirty-four hardly seemed like something to be celebrated, anyway. Casey wasn't so sure she felt up to recognizing *any* more birthdays, honestly. What year could possibly be worth celebrating at this point? Thirty-five? Forty? Would she have any idea what she was doing with her life by the time she hit any of those so-called milestones? It seemed increasingly unlikely, and for that reason, she was considering opting out of all future birthdays.

At least being in San Diego would make ignoring *this birthday* easier. Note to self: plan all future business travel over birthdays to avoid potential celebrations.

"I might as well tell you right now, I had some pretty fun plans for this birthday." Brandon sounded grumbly now. "But I guess I can push them back."

Don't bother, she thought, but knew better than to say it out loud. If Brandon wanted to plan a party for her, she had to let him. Even if she'd rather stay in bed with her pillow over her head. "Really, Brandon, the date doesn't matter to me. Any time we're just having fun with our friends is good for me."

"Well...good." His tone was still mulish, but she knew he'd come around. If she could handle this—and she could, bruised hand and blue language notwithstanding—then so could he. Just a couple of weeks away. A drop in the bucket for two people who had lived together for years.

Really, the only reaction to this new business trip which worried her was the one from James. But she wasn't about to tell her boyfriend that her horse was her primary concern.

"What about James?" Brandon asked, surprising her. Was he turning telepathic? Was this one of those long-term relationship things?

"I guess Hannah will keep riding him. Hopefully that's still going well. She hasn't texted me, but her Instagram is full of videos of her feeding him cookies, so I know they're both still alive."

"Maybe she's just using him for a model and not riding him at all," Brandon suggested. "For internet clout. I mean, he's a lot better looking than Caruso."

This was undeniable, but Casey still appreciated hearing it from a non-horseman. Caruso was not an attractive horse, in her opinion. "I guess that might be happening. I've found that posting solid James content guarantees at least three new followers per post, with the right hashtags. Sometimes I get as many as ten or eleven on one cute video."

Brandon was chuckling now. "You social media people and your metrics."

Well, she had him cheering up now. That was something. Casey let Brandon catch her up on the other doings around the condo and his office before she made an excuse to get off the call. It wasn't that she didn't want to talk to him. It was that she felt weird about needing Brandon to be okay with her traveling, when she wasn't okay with it at all.

Perhaps this was because the thing she missed most about Florida was riding James, and the thing she was most upset about was losing her chance to show him yet again. Not losing time with Brandon. And shouldn't that have been the bigger issue?

And no, she reminded herself, it *wasn't* because she didn't miss Brandon while she was away. She did, a lot. But Casey knew her boyfriend would manage without her for a few weeks. He was a grown-up and he would be just fine.

James, on the other hand...he was barely holding it together when she was around to ride him every day.

She and Brandon would be fine. Casey was worried about how this sudden travel might hurt her relationship with James.

Chapter Nine

"HE WAS SO good," Hannah gushed. "You should go away more often!"

Casey gave the teenager a wan smile before returning her gaze to her horse's freshly trimmed mane, clipped fetlocks, and banged tail. Clearly, Hannah had taken her assignment to ride James a few times while she was away and run with her own interpretation of the job. Had no one ever told her that giving another person's horse a haircut was a serious transgression?

Granted, she'd done nice a job with his mane, but Casey would not have cut his tail quite so short; it was halfway to his hocks. "You, uh, gave him a real spa day, huh?"

"I just wanted him to look good for his mama." Hannah wrapped her tan arms around James's neck and gave the horse a hug that was a tad too proprietorial for Casey's taste. She twitched the lead-rope slightly, and James took a step towards her, dislodging the teenager.

Hannah backed off, giving James a confused look. "Usually he's fine with my hugs."

"Oh, you know horses," Casey said breezily. "So unpredictable."

Hannah shrugged it off. "Anyway, I loved riding him. And playing with him. Caruso isn't as chill as he is for baths and stuff. I even practiced braiding him so we'd be ready for the show."

"Well, he looks great," Casey assured her. "Thanks for working so hard on him." The words cost her. All those minor jobs Hannah had done were *her* responsibility. Casey was sure that being jealous of a teenager for pulling a horse's mane wasn't rational, but she'd been a horse owner for less than a year. She wasn't ready to cede control just yet.

And his tail really was too short.

Hannah had already pocketed the small stack of twenties Casey handed her and waltzed off down the barn aisle, her slim hips barely holding up her coral riding tights. Casey turned back to James with a grimace. "Well, it was probably for the best, moving to a barn that wasn't all teens," she told him with a sigh. "Seems like these days, I can barely handle only one of them."

James rubbed his head against her, his tiny star leaving short white hairs all over the front of her sun-shirt. Casey looked down at the mess and grimaced. "Thanks, thanks, that's perfect. Did you know this shirt cost more than my nicest work blouse?"

James snorted.

"Fair enough."

Casey brushed the worst of the hairs off her chest and led James into the cross-ties at the end of the barn. Sunlight was scattered across the floor, the sharp-edged shadows of palm fronds waving gently across the gleaming concrete. The light caught the ivory hoops around each of James's hind pasterns, the markings little scoops of white flecked with black specks of ermine.

"Goodness, even your anklets are perfectly clean," Casey noted, pulling her curry comb out of her grooming bucket. She bumped into a bridle hanging over the wall and knocked it down. "So messy," she muttered. "I guess no one uses the tack room anymore?"

The cross-ties were pretty messy; the boarders hung bridles all over the place, and the wall was a mish-mash of English and Western bridles. They left saddle pads to dry over the outside railing: fat Western pads with fleece backing and thin, diamond-pattern English pads. No one fussed too much about tack left in the cross-ties, or hanging along a horse's stall. Twin Palms Ranch was homey, not fancy. Which was fine, but Casey was used to everything being a bit more strict. A bit more clean.

She couldn't say she hadn't been *wa*rned. When she'd first signed the boarding contract, the owner, Liz—a sunburned, leathered, red-eyed woman—told her they weren't pretentious like the folks up in their fancy barns. And in her words, there'd been a warning: don't act stuck up, or you won't be welcome here for long.

So she'd tried to fit in, even though she missed her tidy tack locker and she secretly got very bothered when the barn aisle went unswept for a few days and dirt built up on the surface, the concrete obscured by chunks of dried mud and beaches of sand and a constant sighing of blowing hay wisps. She kept her things clean but did it in a low-key way, brushing the cobwebs off the front wall of James's stall with a broom, zippering her saddle into a fleece-lined saddle bag to keep the local spiders from considering it fair game for their next housing expansion; Casey was pretty sure if she lifted up her saddle and a long-legged wolf spider blinked at her from beneath the flap, she would die and that would be the end of all her troubles. She swept up after she cleaned out James's hooves, and she never left a mess in the wash-rack. She tried to be a good citizen, even though sometimes she felt like she was the only one who was putting in the effort.

And when things got too messy, Casey tried to remind herself that what really mattered was healthy, contented horses—but after coming back from beautiful, manicured Sungold Ranch, the haphazard approach to horsekeeping at Twin Palms made her grit her teeth.

"I was better off before I remembered what nice barns are like," she muttered. James tipped back his ear and listened to her. "Now I feel like we're really slumming it."

She finished grooming James, took a glance at the dirt left from picking out his hooves, and decided she had to sweep the mess up before she saddled him. As she brushed the dirt out of the cross-ties, Liz herself walked by, a pitchfork in hand. She was wearing Crocs and a long-sleeved fishing shirt over a pair of bike shorts. Her eyebrows went up as she noticed Casey cleaning under her horse. "You don't have to sweep that," she said. "Go on out and ride."

"Oh, I made a mess picking feet," Casey explained.

Liz paused and regarded her for a moment. Casey blushed and put the broom back against the wall.

"You sure like cleaning up," Liz observed. "I oughta hire you to run this barn."

Casey allowed herself a nervous laugh. She didn't know how to take the comment. Compliment? Complaint? She rarely saw Liz, who seemed to spend most of her time in the yellow double-wide trailer up near the front of the property. She only came down to the barn twice a day, to do morning and evening chores, and didn't own her own horse. Sky had introduced Liz to Casey as an old friend, but with an age difference spanning nearly thirty years and absolutely no resemblance in personality, Casey couldn't really see how a relationship existed between them. Chances were, she figured, Liz somehow knew Sky's mother, who was a prominent real estate agent in West Palm Beach. Even properties out here in the back of beyond were worth a lot in the scalding-hot Florida property market. Sky's mom probably had every farm owner east of Lake Okeechobee on speed-dial.

Liz was still surveying her with that mildly skeptical expression she seemed to save for Casey alone. "You like it here, Casey?"

The question seemed idle, but it struck Casey like a bolt from the blue. Liz might have some other boarder in mind for James's stall, someone who fit in better. That was all she needed, to get asked to leave! Casey plastered on a bright smile. "Yes, of course I like it here! This place is great! I wasn't sweeping out of, I don't know, *aggression,* or anything. I just don't want my horse to leave a mess for anyone else. You know, just trying to be a good boarder."

"Oh, you're a good boarder," Liz told her, a smile finally cracking her leathery face. "Just a little high-maintenance."

Casey nearly squeaked with shock. She was pretty sure she'd never asked for anything special as a boarder...not here, and not back at St. Johns, either. "I'm sorry—I—I'm high-maintenance? I certainly never meant—"

"Oh, you don't mean to be," Liz assured her. She leaned on the pitchfork, ready to dig into a dissertation about Casey's shortcomings. "Sky spoiled you up there at her place, that's all. Your little supplement containers and your blankets and your special hoof dressings and all that...you know horses don't *need* any of that stuff, right? It's just out there to take your money."

"I—uh—" Casey was at a loss. She seized on the first thing Liz had listed. "I didn't realize the supplements were a problem." James was on three different feed supplements: one for his hooves, one for his joints, one for his digestion. They came in little plastic containers—all a person had to do was peel off the lid and dump the powder over his grain. Literally, it took two seconds. And okay, he had two blankets, one for very cold nights and one for kind-of cold nights. But on the other hand, he *only* had two blankets. There were horses at St. Johns who had four different weights of blanket hanging on their stall doors all winter, with specific instructions for which temperature block corresponded to each weight. She didn't do anything like *that*. And yes, sure, he needed a hoof hardener applied when the pastures were muddy. But Casey did this. Not Liz. So she couldn't be accused of being high-maintenance for requesting someone else paint his hooves with hardener.

Anyway, Casey had thought all of these things were normal. Even Caruso had two different blankets, and she was pretty sure that Chico was on a vitamin supplement, too. And *all* the horses got electrolytes in the summer, although that was a barn wide thing, along with generic Metamucil once a month.

But maybe Casey was wrong about what she thought was part of good and normal horse-mom stuff...or she was giving the wrong impression. Either way, she couldn't afford to alienate Liz now. If she was told to find another barn now, when she was literally only home for a couple of weeks before flying off to her work assignments? She'd be in serious trouble.

She'd be in serious trouble either way, because she had no idea where else she'd keep James without breaking her budget.

"Liz, I'm so sorry if I've been causing you extra work," she offered, not sure what else she could say. She certainly couldn't change anything. James needed all of those things. She'd just have to watch her behavior, make sure there wasn't anything too prissy in the way she handled James or talked to the other boarders. "I'll be more careful in the future, I promise."

"Aww, you're alright," Liz said cheerfully, brushing away all the concern she'd just created. "Between you and Hannah, I got my work cut out, that's all. She's always had that horse show bug, but there wasn't much she could do about it. Then you came along and just encourage it. Gotta teach both of y'all to calm down a little bit, take life as it comes." Liz shrugged. "Hannah's just a kid, so she's gonna be a little foolish. But you, I've got hope for you."

Casey couldn't imagine what hope Liz might be holding out for her. She wasn't going to change. But since Liz wasn't, either, and since Casey was totally dependent on her—for boarding James, for renting her the truck and trailer when she did eventually get to a horse show —all she could do was smile and nod, then get back to tacking up, with one more worry piled on top of her already sagging shoulders.

"I'm sure she didn't mean anything by it." Brandon pushed a glass of water at her. "Here, drink this. You're all red and dehydrated. What is it, ninety degrees out there?"

"Something like that." Casey leaned on the kitchen island and peeled off her wet boot socks. "But no, it's not only the heat, if that's what you're thinking. Liz genuinely decided today, of all days, was the day to fix me. After I finished with James, she came at me *again* and told me I ought to stop wearing boots and breeches to ride in. Said to get a nylon saddle and ride in shorts."

"You can do that?" Brandon's face was alight with curiosity. "Nylon and shorts, sounds comfortable. I always thought all that leather you guys use was too much for Florida heat."

"Not a nylon *English* saddle, silly. Even a synthetic English saddle has the stirrup leathers on top, and it would pinch your legs to pieces if you rode in shorts. Liz means a Western saddle. For bopping around the arena like the other boarders do. Which would be really boring." She set her empty glass down, hoping Brandon would refill it.

He did—and served it to her with a side of confusion. "Wait. I think it's weird that you would consider riding around the arena to be boring. What's wrong with hanging out with friends, chit-chatting on horseback? I think it sounds cool."

"Riding is work," Casey said around a gulp of water. "It's hard, hard work."

He tipped his head at her. "Don't you get enough of that at your job?"

She rolled her eyes. "Now you sound like Liz. And Maria. My two self-appointed guardian angels, apparently. Do you guys want to get together and plan an intervention, come at me as a team?"

"Come on, Casey, you know I'm still new to this whole horse thing. I'm just trying to understand. And ever since you started taking lessons, you've been more tired and on edge. I'd heard horses were supposed to be, like, therapy."

"That's just for books in the self-help section. Horses are stress." *Horses are never being as good as a teenager who has been riding two years to your two decades. Horses are bad steps and awkward strides which take you thousands of dollars to figure out. Horses are anchors which keep you down when you want to get away. Horses are like oxygen, but it's oxygen you have to pay a fortune for. Horses are like a drug, and if you give them up to save yourself, only a shell remains.*

The thoughts sped through her brain until she put her hands to her forehead to stop them. Where was all of this coming from? James wasn't stress. James wasn't everything that was wrong with her life. James was just...he was just an enormous responsibility she barely had time for, and the omission was killing her.

"Maybe horses are therapy when you've got all the time in the world," Casey allowed at last. "But for me, right now, riding just feels like one more thing I can't seem to get right."

"But things are going to get better," Brandon said uncertainly.

"I guess." Casey refilled her glass. "I certainly hope."

A half-hour later, showered and lotioned, feeling much more human than she had when she'd come home, Casey opened up her email and found a reminder for her lunch with Raina on Monday. A smile tugged at her lips—she'd forgotten about Raina in all the work and travel craziness. Now the idea of having a friend in her own neck of the woods was a triumphant one.

Even if getting to this lunch was going to be a challenge with her current workload.

Oh well. That was Monday's problem. This was Saturday night, and she had all of tomorrow to enjoy before dealing with Monday morning's emails and phone calls and general drama. She tossed her phone onto the dresser, guessing she'd leave it behind while she joined Brandon in the living room. A moment later, she laughed at herself and picked it up again. Obviously, she would not leave her phone in another room. That was crazy-talk.

Chapter Ten

CASEY LIKED HER early morning Sundays at the barn. She liked using the arena without having to dodge around the other boarders getting in her way as she tried to school James. She also enjoyed the break from riding with Hannah. On Sunday mornings, Hannah handled the morning barn chores for Liz. As Casey groomed James and rode alone, Hannah cleaned stalls with her AirPods plugged tightly into her ears, singing softly while she scooped manure and wet bedding into the wheelbarrow. It was the most restful version of the teenager Casey saw all week.

Brandon always did something of his own on Sunday mornings, whether it was hanging out with friends or working on one of his coding projects, so there wasn't any question of half of the couple having fun while the other sat home and waited. He was often vague about his plans, and Casey had a suspicion that sometimes he went back to bed or played video games while she was gone, but that was his business. If he was getting more sleep, good for him. Brandon worked hard. He deserved some downtime.

She often wondered why she couldn't apply the same attitude towards herself.

This morning was hot and humid already, despite the early hour. She was already sweating like it was high summer. Palm Beach was more tropical than her old home; the stormy season usually began several weeks earlier than they did up in Cocoa, and the short winters rarely brought so much as a brisk night in the forties. That second, heavier blanket she'd brought for James hadn't actually seen any use since she'd arrived. Casey wasn't looking forward to her first proper summer here, which would somehow be even hotter and steamier than at home. This morning, she even found herself thinking fondly of the mild breezes back in southern California. What would it be like to ride at Sungold Ranch on a Sunday morning? Cool and pleasant, perhaps even jacket weather.

"And it's not like I want to go back," she told herself as she headed into the barn. "It's just different from here. Anyway, I'm going to wrap up that project and then tell Sharon and Phillip they've got to hire someone else to do their site work. I'm staying home and riding James this summer."

Even if it was a million degrees and storming, simultaneously, the entire season. She'd wasted too much time this spring. If she had to buckle down and ride all summer to get a handle on their problems, so be it.

James was inside his stall, finishing up his breakfast hay. He pricked his ears as she approached, putting his head over his door in hopes of treats. She smiled, a little surge in her chest reminding her it didn't matter whether he was happy to see her or happy to see the cookies in her hand—either way, he made her heart lift.

"Here are your cookies, sir," Casey told him, handing over a peanut butter cookie and a rub on the forehead. He crunched the cookie before shoving his chest against the top board of the stall wall, stretching out his neck and turning his head sideways to beg for more. Adorable, but Casey remained resolute. She wagged a finger at him. "You know the order! No more cookies until after your saddle is on your back, sir."

James soon recovered from his disappointment, distracted by a good back-rub with the curry comb. Soon, they walking around the arena. Sweat rose on James's neck; Casey felt a similar sheen on hers. A swallow-tailed kite wheeled overhead, wide wings and scissor tail floating on some hidden air current. "Sure," she told the bird. "*You* found some wind, but down here, it's perfectly still."

The bird tipped his wings and sailed away, leaving Casey alone with her thoughts. Well, and with James. But he seemed to have his own ideas to ponder this morning. Or he could simply be hot, and not interested in expending too much energy. Whatever the reason, he was quiet enough for her to ride nearly an hour without requiring too much concentration on their work. For once, James put his head down and did as Casey asked him without any drama.

Casey couldn't help but wonder if Hannah's riding had been a positive influence. This idea immediately hurt her own feelings.

"You aren't going well just because that light little thing rode you, right?" she asked him. James chewed at the bit, stretching his head towards the ground. Casey shook her head. "That's not an answer."

They circled the arena once more. Casey looked back at the barn. She could see Hannah inside, cleaning water buckets. She chewed at her lip, pondering. Was Hannah's loosey-goosey riding style really better for James?

Or was he behaving himself out of boredom? They weren't *doing* anything. Only schooling in big circles. Possibly, she was putting him to sleep with this kind of exercise, boring him into submission. "But I don't even know what we should be working on," Casey said aloud. "We did walk trot canter, we did some transitions, we trotted over some poles...that's it, right? For a day without jumping?"

James snorted and shook his head.

"Sky's right. I need to get back into a lesson program. I'm lost without a coach."

As they came to the arena gate, James suddenly stopped, his ears focused on the barn. He was making his case pretty clear: time to go inside. Casey felt her resistance crumble. They weren't *doing* anything. What was the point in taking another loop? Who cared if they put in a full hour in the saddle?

"You want to go in now, James? We might as well." Casey sighed and patted his neck. "I have got to get myself together. Find a way to make this all seem worthwhile." She considered the words she'd said aloud, and asked the still air around her the question that scared her most. "Do I really think this isn't worthwhile anymore?"

At Goldie's barn, the surrounding activity was energizing, and she'd charged back to work after her morning there, filled with motivation. But here, in this empty arena she'd once seen as the highlight of her week, Casey felt...nothing. No drive. No energy. No purpose.

"I think moving to West Palm broke me," she said. "This place just isn't doing it for me."

Her horse tipped back his ears, listening to her voice, but he gave no advice, and there was no one else to hear her.

"Hannah. Hey, Hannah!" Casey leaned over the stall wall, waving. "Helloooo?"

Hannah popped out an AirPod, grinning. She'd been shaking bags of shavings into the freshly cleaned stalls, and dust flew all around her. It stuck to her sweaty face, making Casey want to sneeze. "Hey, what's up? You looked nice in the arena."

"Thank you." Casey didn't really want to dwell on her ride. Fifty minutes in the saddle shouldn't have left her this hollow inside, but she figured the only way out had to be up. So she asked the question she'd been mulling over as she untacked James. "Hannah, you can't afford riding lessons once in a while, can you?"

Hannah shook her head. "It would be either shows or riding lessons."

"And you choose shows. But, are you sure? Because I thought we might find a trainer who would give us semi-private lessons. It would mean a break on the cost."

"No, that's okay." Hannah went back to spreading shavings. "Thanks for offering."

"You bet." Casey hoped Hannah didn't notice her disappointment. She shouldn't be relying on a teenager to get through this, whatever this was. But she didn't see any possibility of trailering off the farm to take lessons regularly without someone else's contribution. Renting the trailer, gas money, and private lessons all added up to a number well beyond her budget.

Hannah balled up the empty shavings bag. "We're still going to Hunter's Glen in a couple weeks, though, right?"

Casey imagined the two weeks she'd be in San Diego, not riding James. Then a week to get him in gear. Then the horse show. She wondered if she'd survive the day. "Unless things seem too crazy with James."

Hannah's head snapped up, her gaze fixed on Casey. "You *said* we're going!"

"I did. Before I got assigned another two weeks in San Diego. That changes things, don't you think?"

"Don't worry about that. I'll be handling James. He'll be ready." She took a pocketknife from her back pocket and zipped the blade through another bag of shavings.

Casey stood back, avoiding the worst of the sawdust drifting through the air. Hannah's words did not make her feel better. If James liked Hannah more than her, didn't that just make everything worse?

She was trying not to feel jealous. In fact, jealous wasn't even the right word.

What she was feeling was *freaked out.*

"Sounds like Hannah is a typical teenager," Raina laughed, putting down her latte. "Some of them have absolutely no feelings for other humans. I guess that develops later in life."

"If at all," Casey snorted, but she was grinning. Raina was a good lunch companion; she had a fork stuck into a slice of cheesecake in front of her, but she'd barely touched it since the server set it down. Too much to say. Their Monday lunch had extended well beyond the forty-five minutes she'd allotted in her calendar, into coffee and dessert. Casey welcomed the ruination of her schedule. She *needed* this. Something about Raina made her want to pour out all her feelings, and Raina seemed happy to eat her own slice of cake and listen, offering occasional observations along the way.

Possibly Casey had been talking *too* much, though. She still didn't know a thing about the woman sitting across from her. "I'm sorry to just blather like that. You caught me at a weird point in my life. Everything's changing and I don't have any idea where it's going."

"I know the feeling." Raina's eyes were soft and kind. "I went through something similar last year. I left Florida briefly, tried working for a big name trainer in upstate New York. Things got...

crazy."

Casey lifted her eyebrows. "Do I know who this trainer is?"

"Oh, yes." Raina laughed, shaking her head ruefully. "*Everyone* does. My dad told me not to go work for them, said he'd heard all kinds of stories, but who listens to their dad? I went. Thought I needed to prove myself away from my family, or something stupid like that. I ended up mucking stalls every day and didn't get in the saddle for the first three months. Then when I was allowed to ride, I was told to hack out retirees. It was a total bust."

Casey gaped at her. "But, Raina, you have all kinds of experience. How could they justify that kind of treatment?"

"Apparently there was a mistake with my application, or that's what they told me when I finally got up the courage to ask why I wasn't being treated like the other working students. Supposedly they thought I was there to learn to be a groom." Raina's chuckle was mirthless. "I think you can guess why, right?" She shook out her raven-black hair. "I don't roll my r's anymore, but the proof is in the mirror."

"God, that's so wrong. So what happened? Did you ever get anywhere with their horses?"

"No." Raina took a sip of her latte and gazed into the distance, which wasn't very far; the cafe was small and cozy. She was seeing something beyond the plain beige walls. "I put up with it for six months, and I came home when my contract was up. Such a waste. Never went to a single show, never jumped a single fence. I know, I know! I should have stood up for myself, I should have questioned them sooner when they didn't let me ride. It was obvious I wasn't being treated like the other girls there. And guys—there were two guys. But it's not as simple as just saying, *hey, you're being unfair.*"

"I get it. And that's a big program," Casey observed. "Sounds like it was easy to let them lose you in the shuffle."

"A lot of times, that's easiest, isn't it? Just get lost, let things happen to you. Let the blame go. They'd never have admitted they were wrong, anyway."

Casey considered Raina's words as she scooped up her cheesecake. Was that what she was doing? Letting herself get lost in the shuffle with Atlantic Horse Show Productions? Sharon and Phillip were making all the decisions; she was bearing all the brunt. They didn't seem to notice how much she was taking on or how disruptive their plans were to her real life.

She was well aware she had to stand up to them. She was planning on it! What she didn't know, of course, was how she'd do it. Raina's words rang true: it was so much easier to let things happen to you, then try to get someone else to admit they were wrong. Casey was a master of conflict-avoidance.

When she'd been unhappy at Bluewater Marketing, she'd taken a leave of absence to get away from the place. When she'd been unhappy as a groom at St. Johns, she'd simply declined to let Sky renew their agreement.

But she'd never actually requested a change in terms, or a more appropriate working arrangement. Did that ever even work? What boss would admit they were wrong?

"I'm sorry," Raina said after a few minutes of silence passed between them. "I didn't mean to make everything about my struggle. It's not really that big a deal."

"No, no—" Casey struggled to swallow the cake in her mouth. "It's not like that. You made me think about my job, and it's really stressful right now." She shook her head. "It's fine, really. Anyway, I have been talking your ear off about leaving James with Hannah, and how awful it makes me feel. That must have been pretty boring."

Raina's smile returned. "I think it's sweet. You love James a lot, and you're jealous when someone else gets to ride him. Someone you chose to ride him, that you're *paying* to ride him, but still."

"It's not only the riding, though. I mean, I am jealous!" Casey forced a laugh. "But it's everything else she does, too. It's the time she spends with him. It's how well he goes after she rides him. And then she's plastering him all over her social media. That's—he's *mine*. That's my horse on her page! I'm just...um..."

"Incredibly, insanely jealous," Raina supplied helpfully.

"Yes. That's pretty much it. I worked really hard to get James into my life and now I'm jealous of anyone else who loves on him."

"Well, I was going to ask if I could ride him when you got back from California," Raina declared. "But now, I know better. Don't worry—I'll be totally hands off your cutie-pie James."

"I appreciate that. Finally, one of my friends leaves my horse alone!"

"What about your boyfriend? Does he ever do anything with him?"

Casey snickered. "Who, Brandon? Touch a horse? Not on purpose. He's an ocean guy. Dolphins and coral reefs, all the way."

"Too bad," Raina mused. "Horses are such a nice thing to share in a relationship."

"Oh, I don't know. Seems like something else to argue about." Casey shook her head and finished up her cheesecake. Brandon at the barn, what a thought. Like she didn't have enough trouble balancing her life.

Chapter Eleven

"So, will you be bored while I'm gone?" Casey's voice was teasing, but she was serious. Her time at home was nearly gone, and her work clothes were back in the washing machine. She had to pack tomorrow; she'd already spread her suitcase across one corner of the bedroom, waiting to be filled. Casey avoided looking at it every time she walked through the room, choosing instead to look at the framed picture of James hanging on the wall above it.

"Probably a little bored, but I have some plans," Brandon said. "You don't need to worry about me. I can keep busy."

"Care to share?"

"Not really." He winked mischievously. "It's something I've been playing with for a while. If it works out, you'll know about it. If it doesn't, then it stays my secret forever. No reason to embarrass myself by sharing a failure if I don't need to."

Casey gave him an exaggerated eye-roll. "Fine, don't tell me what you're up to. Enjoy being mysterious. You know what *I'll* be doing."

"Having a good time putting on a horse show with a person you really like at a beautiful equestrian center in one of the world's few perfect climates?" He waggled his eyebrows.

"Stop making my job sound amazing with all those alluring details. I'm the marketing writer, not you, and I won't have my misleading work thrown in my face." She laughed ruefully. "Anyway, it's not that great. Obviously, I would much rather stay at home." All her prior interest in Sungold, and Goldie, had faded during the past week. She had enough problems here without having to jet across the country constantly. And what could Goldie really teach her about life? When all was said and done, she was just another horse trainer working herself into an early grave. Casey could find a dozen people exactly like her without leaving West Palm.

"Listen," Brandon told her, tugging her close. "If you hate your job, I have a simple strategy for you. Spend some time every day looking for a new one. Twenty minutes, tops. Drop a couple keywords in your resume and fire it off to every listing you like. Don't even do that customized thing. No one really cares about that."

"I don't even know what I'd apply for," Casey complained. She let Brandon wrap his arms around her, but she realized her body was stiff and angry, her muscles protesting his attempts to calm her. "Would I go back to email marketing? I'm a marketing manager now, but it's too small a company for my position to translate properly in a larger one. I'd have to take a step back at a bigger firm, and I don't want to do that."

"Well, Miss Manager, maybe you don't hate this job as much as you think."

"Ugh, it's not about the title." Casey shook her head fiercely, like a horse shaking off flies. Her hair brushed against his face. "I'm in such an awkward place right now, job-wise. Seriously, Brandon—if I wait this out, will things get better? Like they keep telling me it will? Or are they just being normal bosses and blowing smoke up my ass to keep me compliant?"

She remembered Raina's story. Treated like a groom for six months, when she was an experienced competitor looking to take her game to the next level. Waiting for things to work out really didn't seem to be the way the world worked.

Brandon kissed the top of her head. "I don't know, Casey. I wish I could tell you."

She supposed that was only fair. If she didn't know, how could Brandon?

San Diego slumbered under a stubborn marine layer on the day she arrived, making her reunion with the west coast a little underwhelming. Gray, heavy clouds blanketed the coast and hills, reflecting Casey's mood perfectly.

She couldn't stop herself from flicking through Hannah's Instagram as she stood waiting in the rental car line. The teenager's feed was already picture after picture of James being babied in the barn, first bathed and covered with bubbles, then grazing the bright green spring grass outside the barn as he dried. Hannah was taking to James as if she didn't already own poor Caruso.

"Not that I blame her," Casey muttered to herself. "James is ten times as nice as Caruso."

Another woman looked at her curiously before going back to her own phone, and Casey reminded herself that talking to oneself was great in the barn or in the car, but might be considered weird in long queues at airports.

She checked into her hotel and allowed herself some time to catch up on emails before heading out to meet Goldie. Most of her leads had agreed to work with the production company, but she still had her work cut out for her over the next two weeks: meeting with vendors, going over contracts, getting designs and copy ready for the banners she'd have printed and hung around the arenas and paddock fences. She had to dig deep into her graphic design skills, scant as they were, for this project—Phillip did most of their graphics, but when she'd asked who was handling the San Diego clients, he'd made it pretty clear he was busy with the shows Atlantic already had in motion.

"Spring is our busy month," he'd reminded her during their last check-in.

"Season," Sharon had corrected him.

"Sure," he'd agreed. "Season. Month. It all blends together."

Casey was beginning to see how this might be the case. "This isn't my usual job," she'd tried, a last-ditch effort, however low-key, to remind them they were sending a marketing manager off on an operation manager's job. "I'm not sure I'm the best choice for Sungold's show."

"You'll be amazing," Sharon told her. "Thanks for stepping up."

Casey couldn't make herself remind Sharon that she hadn't stepped up; they'd drafted her.

By the time she got on the road to Sungold Farm, schools were letting out and traffic was thickening with the afternoon routines of suburbia: grocery store runs, karate class drop-offs, dentist appointments. There was a decent amount of sprawl to fight through before the landscape opened up and livestock replaced strip malls, enough time for Casey to talk herself through several scenarios in which she found the perfect marketing job in an adjacent equestrian field—writing for a tack company's catalog came to mind—and gave her regretful notice to Sharon and Phillip. They'd be sad, of course.

Maybe they'd even offer to hire people to replace the California crew, and she could go back to just being overworked on the east coast, instead of on both. Would she keep her job, if they offered this concession?

"That would work, actually," she decided. "At least when I was just running all over Florida, I slept in my own bed at night. And rode James a few days a week, instead of skipping out on him for half a month."

Casey cheered herself up with this scenario for the last half-hour of the drive, and was so wrapped up in her dream world that she nearly missed the turnoff to Sungold.

When she parked in the crowded parking lot, she realized she hadn't yet seen the place during busy after school hours. Goldie's farm had been a lazy, sun-drenched place of refuge the last time she'd been here. Now it was a zoo that made St. Johns Equestrian Center look like a mountaintop monastery. There were people—mostly tweens and teens—*everywhere*. The arenas each had four or five horses in them. Two rings were hosting group riding lessons, with instructors standing in the middle or adjusting fences. The third arena had an individual lesson taking place, and as Casey walked closer, she saw the instructor was wearing a headset, speaking calmly into a small mic as the student followed her instructions.

"Whoa," she murmured. She'd heard of upper-level instructors using headsets instead of shouting across the arena, but she'd never seen it in use. "That's next-level fancy."

The rider nodded shortly at some unheard message from her instructor, and her horse gently rocked into a collected canter.

Casey's perfection-loving heart soared. No yelling! No confusion! Could a barn really run like this? She felt her long allegiance to St. Johns suddenly waning. Goldie's place was simply sensational.

Of course, the group lessons were the regular garden variety, with young instructors shouting to kids on a variety of horses, from slowly chugging lesson ponies to hot, half-trained ex-racehorses. Casey went into the barn without paying too much attention to them. She knew all about that kind of riding.

Inside the barn, kids and adults were bustling around: tacking up, mucking out, leading in, leading out. Casey looked around for someone she knew, and finally spotted Sharmayne in the feed room, serenely measuring out evening grain into small buckets. She stepped inside.

"Hey, Sharmayne, seen Goldie?"

Sharmayne looked up, tossing her tight braids back over her shoulder. "Hey, Casey! Back so soon? I think she's riding out on the ridge. Should be back in about fifteen minutes, I'd say."

Out riding? Now, with all of her clients here and the barn operating like a booming lesson factory? That seemed odd. "Oh, okay. I'll wait—do you think I could use her office? I have a couple emails to check on."

"Of course. Make yourself at home. Just stay out of the aisle at four fifty-eight or so." Sharmayne grinned. "When the four o'clock lesson comes in, it's usually like a stampede. They're advanced beginners, and you know what that means."

She did, actually. Mayhem. Over-confidence, under-confidence, and everything in between. Casey ducked into the office, a wood-paneled room which felt like old California, and sat behind Goldie's desk. She set up her laptop and was flicking through some emails on the barn's weak wi-fi when the four o'clock kids clattered past the door, and then a few minutes later, Goldie herself appeared, holding the reins of none other than Daisy, the mare Casey had ridden on her last visit.

She looked delighted to see Casey—Goldie, not Daisy. "If I'd known you were coming now, I'd have saved Daisy for you!"

"Oh, I really don't have time to ride," Casey assured her. "I have way too much to fit in this week."

"Nothing's ever too pressing that you can't fit in a ride. Come on, I'll have Sharmayne tack up a horse for you. Let me see, who is available..." Goldie leaned into the room and picked up the open lesson book, running her fingers down the names of horses. "Busy day," she observed, as if it was the first she was hearing of it.

"No no, it's fine, I promise you." Casey was becoming alarmed. If Goldie insisted she got on a horse, she wasn't sure she was supposed to decline...but she had a month's worth of work to fit into two weeks, and only a little experience in how to do most of it. Saddling up for a trail ride was definitely not on the agenda. Casey wondered how she could distract Goldie. Somehow, she didn't suppose just saying she had work to do would be enough. Goldie wasn't big on office work.

Luckily, Daisy chose this moment to push into the office, shoving her shoulders through the doorway, and nudged Goldie in the back. Goldie jumped and turned around so quickly the mare spooked and hopped back, nearly bumping her head on the doorframe. Casey jumped up, afraid Daisy might hurt herself, but Goldie didn't seem bothered.

"Silly girl, let's get you untacked," she told the mare. Then she looked over her shoulder and winked at Casey. "I'll be back in ten and we'll do some work, if that's what you *really* want."

"That would be great," Casey said. "Thanks."

But Goldie didn't come back in ten minutes. Or twenty. Or thirty. Once Casey had finished her emails and taken about as much of the slow wi-fi as she could handle, she zipped her laptop back into its bag and strolled into the aisle, hoping someone had called Goldie into some urgent barn business. That would make a better excuse than simply vanishing. But the wiry horse trainer was nowhere to be seen, in or out of the barn.

Casey found Sharmayne in the hay-shed, loading bales on the back of a Mule. "You seen Goldie?" she asked, giving the young woman room as she threw down more bales from the top of a towering stack.

Sharmayne climbed down the haystack and gave Casey a pitying glance. "She took out another horse. I don't think she even realized what she was doing. I offered to hose off Daisy, she got distracted by something a student was saying, and before I could stop her, she got on the student's horse and rode off."

Casey kept her mouth closed, but she could feel the muscles threatening to give in completely and let her jaw drop to her chest. Goldie was off *riding?* With difficulty, she got herself together. "I guess if the horse was causing issues, she has to put that first," she allowed.

Sharmayne's smile was thin. "That's generous of you. Listen. If you want to get this done on a quick turnaround, you're going to have to handle it yourself."

"But I can't," Casey replied, spreading her hands. "This is her show series. I can't make these decisions for her—"

"Tell her she okayed it, and she'll trust you," Sharmayne told her, coming closer and lowering her voice. "And if you really don't know what to do, ask me. Trust me, that's how things get done around here. Since before I got here, and probably long before that. Goldie doesn't focus on the business. She lets everyone else handle the details."

"And she takes the credit?" Casey guessed. She was beginning to see that the Goldie she'd met on the last trip had dazzled her with California sunshine and pretty views. "That sucks for the staff."

Sharmayne shrugged. "It's her farm. All the credit I need is a good reference when I leave here."

"Where are you planning on going?" Sharmayne's statement momentarily distracted Casey from her own problems. Here was a young woman who was heading off on an equestrian professional career. Doing what Casey had once proven she couldn't. She felt a stirring of envy. Women like Sharmayne were always so driven, so sure of what they wanted to do. Why couldn't she have that?

"I'm heading east," Sharmayne said, shoving hay bales into place in the Mule's cargo bay. "I've got my eye on jobs with a few jumper trainers. After this summer, I'm going to start looking for an assistant trainer position. I've been Goldie's working student for a decade, if you count all those years mucking stalls for a lesson every week when I was a kid. That's long enough. But she won't take me to Indio. I'm thinking that if I can't get A-circuit shows on my resume, at least helping put on a show series here should give me some clout."

"That should be more than enough," Casey agreed.

"It should be, but I have this one extra hurdle to get over." Sharmayne tilted her head and stretched her neck, as if to draw attention to her skin tone. "I don't want anyone refusing me because of the way I look, so I'm not giving them a chance. I have to come out swinging in any interview I show up for."

Casey nodded, suddenly acutely aware of the color of her own skin. Equestrian sports in the United States were overwhelmingly white-girl. It was tough enough getting a good job in the horse business without being judged for something so irrelevant. Casey made up her mind to help Sharmayne however she could. And it worked out for her, too, because she needed Sharmayne. "Well, whatever help you can give me, I'll take. I was expecting someone else's input. You know the property and the students and the local businesses who are sponsoring us, so if Goldie won't help me, I'm going to have to come to you."

Sharmayne nodded, her chin high and her eyes sparkling. "I'm counting on it, Casey. You've got an assistant in me. Whatever you need, just ask."

"I appreciate it," Casey told her, holding out her hand. "Really, I'm grateful."

Sharmayne's grip was firm, but light. "No problem."

Grateful didn't describe it, Casey thought, walking back to her rental car an hour later. Goldie had come back from her ride and handed off her horse, but refused to sit down with Casey to go over anything she had on the agenda. Instead, she nodded at Casey's questions, gave her a vague smile, and turned away, announcing that an instructor in the ring needed her help. Casey watched her go with a sensation of disbelief. Then she turned and packed up her laptop. She had a long drive back to the hotel, and the jet lag was already creeping up on her.

"You coming back tomorrow?" Sharmayne asked, passing the office door and glancing in.

Casey laughed grimly. "Honestly? Only if I run into problems I can't figure out on my own."

"I'll be here. Or call the barn line." Sharmayne dug into her pocket and pulled out a wrinkled business card. "I usually answer."

Casey took the card and looked at it for a moment while Sharmayne headed back to work. Curved and warm from resting in the other woman's pocket, it reminded her of the card Sky had given her, not long ago. Just a year ago. Something about horsewomen helping horsewomen...she tried to put it into a coherent thought as she drove up the long driveway, but nothing condensed in her brain. She figured the time change was making her foggy.

As she waited for the automatic gate (now fixed) to open, Casey glanced in her rear-view mirror and looked back over the farm she'd be spending so much time at over the next two weeks. Horses spun in the arenas, putting in their laps as their riders worked on their own equitation. From up here, it looked like a series of carousels. Around and around, getting worn out with effort, but in the end, right back where they'd started.

Chapter Twelve

CASEY'S PHONE WAS singing away at its FaceTime tune when she got out of the shower, and she raced across the hotel room with just a towel pinched around her hair. She glanced at the open curtain with embarrassment, but her room was on the sixth floor and she figured it was unlikely the drivers on the freeway a few hundred feet away could actually see her naked. And if they could, well, as long as she didn't know about it, she figured it couldn't hurt her.

"Hey, Brandon," she said as she answered the call, leaving the phone propped on the desk. She had to laugh at his expression. "Brandon, your eyeballs are popping out of your head, babe."

"Well, that's my kind of hello!"

"No robe in this cheapskate hotel, so I'm stuck running around naked."

"Well, no complaints here. But you look kinda cold."

"Brandon! Don't make me hang up on you."

"Sorry, sorry! Seriously, though, how cold do you have that room?

I know you like the AC turned down way too low."

"That's it, mister—" Casey dropped the towel and advanced threateningly on the phone. Brandon held up his hands.

"I'm sorry! Don't hang up on me. Tell me about your day."

Casey sighed and picked up her towel again. "Absolutely ludicrous, if you must know. I was just about to put on my comfy pajamas and order Thai food. *That* kind of day."

"I can order for you, if you want." Brandon propped up his phone, and she saw him opening his laptop.

"You don't have to do that," she protested. "I can order my own food."

"Drunken noodles and shrimp spring rolls, right?"

"Yes, please. And a tea?"

"You got it." Brandon typed for a moment, clicked a few times, then nodded. "Twenty minutes. That's fast."

"You're a lifesaver. I didn't even realize how hungry I was until this moment."

"Jet lag messed you up?"

"Big time. You'd never believe I was just here a week ago." Casey dug around in her suitcase for her pajamas. It really was freezing in here; Brandon knew her all too well. She loved cranking up the AC in hotel rooms, and she inevitably got the shivers after a shower. But the upside was that she got to wear cozy pajamas, which rarely got used in Florida.

"How did things go at the farm? Things progressing there?"

Casey debated how much she wanted to get into it. Not much, she decided. "It's in progress. The working student is going to be my biggest help, I think. Goldie is a little flightier than I realized."

"Typical horse trainer."

The observation caught Casey by surprise. She was never sure how much attention Brandon was paying when she had the occasional trainer-related meltdown. After a moment, she nodded. "It can be an ideal profession for the flighty and hard-to-pin-down, I guess."

"Their minds are on horses, business is an extra annoyance," Brandon guessed.

"That's definitely part of it." Casey tugged on her pajamas, which elicited a groan from Brandon. "Shut it. I set the AC on sixty-four, by the way."

"Oh my God, Casey, haven't you heard of climate change? Save the freaking planet, why don't you?"

"It's a very small space," she defended herself. "Speaking of saving the planet, what are you up to? How was your day?"

"I met with a dolphin conservation group. Want to hear about it?" Brandon's face lit up with excitement.

Casey understood how much he loved dolphins, so even though she was afraid she'd fall asleep during his story, she told him yes, absolutely. Then she got to work with all her post-shower lotions and hair-brushing while Brandon told a long, rambling story in his soothing voice, all about different types of dolphins and seagrass beds and ocean temperatures. By the end of the story she probably couldn't have repeated back much of the information, but his face was alight with pleasure and she had the sensation of being a good girlfriend from three thousand miles away.

It was the first time all day she'd felt really good at something.

She was listening for the knock at the door that would announce her dinner when Brandon took it into his head to show her the doormat the new neighbors had put out. "That's not necessary," she assured him.

"No, it's really weird," he insisted.

As he walked the phone through the condo, her eyes fell on

something strange in the foyer, where their most-worn shoes were lined up neatly. In the gap where her favorite work mules would have been, she saw something suspicious.

"Brandon, wait."

He paused, bringing the phone back to his face. "What's up?"

"Not you. Point the phone back at the shoes by the closet door." She watched a strange expression pass over his face.

"Why?" he asked. "You miss your shoes that much?" His head bobbed a little, and she realized what was happening.

"Don't hide them from me in the hall closet!"

"Hide what?" Brandon's face was all innocence. He pointed the phone back at the shoes. The gap for her work mules filled in by his running shoes. The shoes he'd probably been wearing until a few seconds ago. "Just shoes, honey."

Casey bit her lower lip and nodded. By the time his face was back on the screen, she was all smiles. "Glad to see you're going running in the morning."

She knew what she'd seen. Brandon might have tried to hide them, but those hadn't been running shoes in the foyer.

Those had been cowboy boots.

Cowboy boots. Why would there be cowboy boots in her English-riding home? Casey ate her drunken noodles in silence while she contemplated this extraordinary development. She had never, not even for fashion purposes, owned a pair of cowboy boots.

Not that she had anything *against* cowboy boots. And these weren't like flashy red leather or anything like that (Brandon could definitely not pull off red cowboy boots). They had been brown, and from the quick glimpse she'd gotten, she hadn't noticed anything shiny about them. They'd even looked a little slouched, as if someone had broken them in around the ankles.

As if someone went riding in them.

But that wasn't possible. For another thing, Brandon's interest in outdoor activities was pretty much limited to sports which could be mastered while wearing flip-flops or water shoes. Toss a Frisbee? Yes. Snorkel all afternoon? For sure. Ride a horse? No way.

So those boots weren't Brandon's? Was that the conclusion? He *had* hidden them from her, so something was going on. Casey imagined Brandon having an affair with a cowboy-boot-wearing madam and found she couldn't do it. His taste in women ran a little nerdy; she often suspected he'd given her a second look the first time they'd met based upon her oversized glasses and the short bang she'd worn back then.

So the boots *were* Brandon's.

But what could he possibly be doing in them? Casey tried to picture Brandon hanging out at a country bar, possibly learning to line-dance. This created such a ridiculous mental scene that she nearly spit out a mouthful of noodles.

"Okay, okay, get a hold of yourself," she muttered. "There's a rational explanation for these boots. Maybe they belong to a friend."

Except Casey knew all of his friends, and most of them wore All-Stars or Toms.

The boots were Brandon's.

"Brandon is becoming a cowboy," Casey said aloud. "My boyfriend, the cowboy. How do I feel about this?"

The answer was: she had no idea. It was possible she preferred the affair with a cowgirl theory. Should she run through that scenario again?

Nope. She shook herself all over and forked another pile of noodles into her mouth, chewing ferociously as if it would give her mind something useful to think about. She would not start jumping to ridiculous conclusions over a pair of cowboy boots! She would not go crazy on a two-week work trip!

She would just...take a bath. A hot bath. That would go a long way towards calming her crazy brain. There was a second towel in the bathroom. More hot water in the tank. A bottle of wine she'd picked up on her way back to the hotel earlier.

Sure, Brandon would go crazy if he knew she was keeping the air conditioning on sixty-four degrees *and* taking a shower and a bath within an hour of each other, but Brandon wasn't here. He was at home.

With his cowboy boots.

"I mean, yeah, I'd be a little surprised by cowboy boots in the house, too." Sharmayne tapped the page Casey had laid out on Goldie's desk. "This one. I like the font. What is it?"

"It's called...um...*Looking Flowers.* Very cutesy. It would be cute for pony classes, don't you?" The script was playful, not formal, with little curls on the strokes of every letter. "I bet the kids will love it."

"Perfect, we'll use that one on the junior champions and we'll use a nice plain font for the adults."

"Easy enough." Casey made a few marks on her checklist. They had been going over prizes and ribbons for the past ten minutes or so, and she was happy with how decisive Sharmayne was. She considered pros and cons in seconds, snapped out her decision, and was ready for the next question. "Okay. Last one. This is for the cooler for High Point Champion. The top prize for the entire series."

"Hmmm..." Sharmayne looked over the choices, then tapped an image. "This one."

"A classic." Casey marked her choice. "Well, we did it! I can get all of these in to the trophy company."

"Not bad! Did we set a record for time?"

"I don't know...this is the first time I've handled this." Casey gave Sharmayne a sheepish grin. "I *told* you I was working way outside my job description!"

"You and me both, right?" Sharmayne leaned back in her chair and looked at the framed photos on the office walls. They were mostly of Goldie, although a few students had made the cut. "This is a crazy old business, isn't it? No one does what they're supposed to, and a couple of people have to pick up the slack for everyone."

Casey glanced at the open door. Sharmayne saw her expression and easily followed her train of thought. "It's okay. Goldie's out on Sunny Jim. She always rides him for a full hour. I'd say we have forty more minutes of quiet before she comes in."

"Okay, then I can ask you. Is Goldie good to work for?"

"Define good."

"I mean, does she give you credit where credit's due? Does she build you up?" Casey remembered Raina's issues with her big name trainer. "She doesn't...you know, look down on you at all?"

"Ahh, I get ya now." Sharmayne shook her head. "No, I haven't had that problem with Goldie. I do believe she doesn't give me enough credit for what I *could* do, but when it comes to what I am doing around here, she's been good to me. Goldie's perfect in one respect: she knows what she does best. She's an amazing trainer, she's a fantastic rider, and she has great ideas. Everything else, she leaves for her team."

"That's a skill in and of itself," Casey admitted. "I guess that might be her secret to success. A trainer with no business skills running her barn into the ground...that's like the classic story, right?"

"I totally agree," Sharmayne said, nodding. "This place runs so well because people trust in Goldie and she gives them freedom to handle the everyday stuff she doesn't care about. Even me, the working student," she added with a shrug.

Casey wondered how to put her question. She decided she had to go for it. After all, Raina had been open about her issues with her big name trainer. "I just wondered, since you've been a working student for so long, if Goldie...you know..." It was harder to say than she'd expected.

"Holds me back because she's prejudiced?" Sharmayne grinned. "I mean, valid question. She's old-fashioned. But I don't think she sees me as different from the white girls. I think she just sees me as her special project and she doesn't want to give me up."

She got up and tapped a picture on the wall. It was an old one, judging by the faded colors, but still impressive. Goldie was jumping a sleek chestnut horse over a massive oxer. Her form was perfect, her face as aggressive as her horse's. "This is a Saddlebred mare. Gold Rush. The perfect name, right? She's retired now, having babies. Goldie got her at an auction and turned her into a Grand Prix jumper when everyone said a Saddlebred was good for nothing in the jumping ring. This is the kind of thing I mean. Goldie makes her own rules. She doesn't worry about anyone else."

Casey stoop up to get a better study of the picture. She'd noticed it before; she'd thought the horse had a strangely shaped head. Now she realized she was just seeing the Saddlebred blood: a bit of a Roman nose beneath a dished forehead, prominent eyes, a long upper lip. Nothing she hadn't seen before, just not on a top level jumper. Gold Rush didn't look the part, but conformation could tell just a tiny part of the story when a horse was born both athletic and aggressive.

"I guess nothing is ever what it looks like," Casey mused. "A Saddlebred jumping Grand Prix. A bustling farm with a checked-out boss. A pair of cowboy boots in my foyer." She tossed a cheeky smile at Sharmayne. "Am I what I seem?"

Sharmayne surveyed her with an amused expression. After a pause, she said, "You seem like a white girl experiencing one very long quarter-life crisis. And I mean that in the nicest way possible."

Casey threw herself back down in Goldie's desk chair. "You got me."

"You also seem like you need a break from all this heavy talk," Sharmayne suggested. "And so do I. Come on, I have a couple lesson ponies to school. You can get on one and save me some time."

Casey glanced at her checklist for the day, satisfied with the number of boxes she'd ticked. "You know what? Thanks to you, I'm ahead of schedule. So yes, I owe you one. Let's ride."

"You're getting Stinker Bell," Sharmayne warned her, heading into the barn aisle. "Hope you don't mind a couple bolts here and there."

Casey didn't love bolting under saddle, but Stinker Bell wasn't that bad a pony. About thirteen hands of patchy brown-and-white coat, with a hammer head and a pair of distrustful dark eyes, Bell—as Casey promptly called her, thinking the name *Stinker* would not get her anywhere with this pony—was a lifelong lesson horse. It was a rough fate for any pony, but, Sharmayne explained, Goldie tried to make it easy on the lesson horses by giving them plenty of time off. After their breaks, they had to be ridden back in for a few weeks before they were ready to rejoin the lesson program.

"She's had a month off to regroup," Sharmayne said, mounting her own pony, a chestnut beauty named Aurora, after the Disney princess. "Don't worry, I've been riding her all week, but she could use someone different on her back to change things up. Don't want to get her too used to one rider's way of doing things."

Casey shifted in the saddle, which seemed to wobble on the pony's narrow spine before settling over her much rounder barrel. "If this one's a lifetime member of the lesson herd, what's Aurora's story? I don't want to say she's prettier, but…"

"Oh, she's prettier." Sharmayne laughed. "Aurora here will probably sell in the next year. A couple girls have their eyes on her. You know how it is. Refined and beautiful gets all the money. Ugly and serviceable just put in their time."

"Sorry, Bell," Casey told the pony, and gently put her leg on, expecting the usual school horse resistance to moving forward. She just barely hung on when the pony took off at a full gallop.

By the time Goldie returned to the farm on a sweaty Sunny Jim, Casey had gotten Bell out of the bolting routine and the pony was trotting and cantering neatly around the arena. Sharmayne was jumping Aurora over a course of small cross-rails.

"Look at this!" Goldie cried, riding into the arena. "My girls on their ponies!"

Casey experienced an unreasonably warm and fuzzy sensation at being called one of Goldie's girls.

"I got our Casey ahead on her checklist so she could get out and do some actual work!" Sharmayne called, cantering past on Aurora. "Okay, Casey, let's see you jump that little troll!"

Casey patted Bell's neck. "They don't mean it," she told the pony. "You're not a troll. You're just…" she trailed off. She'd been about to say, 'You're just a very ugly pony,' but that was mean, and sometimes the truth was a little too raw to share, even when one was talking to a pony. "You're just *fast*," she amended.

With the reins loosened, Bell tossed her head and quickened her pace. Her little legs scissored beneath Casey as she trotted towards the first jump. Casey's breath caught a little as the cross-rail neared. She hadn't ridden a pony in years, and the whole sensation was strange—what was jumping going to be like? Oh God, if she fell off this pony in front of Goldie and Sharmayne, she could never come back. She'd have to fly back to Florida, quit her job, cut her hair, change her name.

For a moment, she hung back in the saddle, clutching the reins a little too tightly. Bell shook her head harder this time, demanding rein, and Casey realized that a school pony with ten years of experience probably would not accept any interference from the person in the saddle, no matter how much bigger and heavier she was than the usual student.

She opened her fingers, slipping the reins and giving Bell as much space as she wanted, and the pony responded with a graceful leap over the cross-rail, finding the perfect distance all by herself.

"Oh!" Casey realized, delighted. "You're a push-button pony!"

They cantered around the rest of the course like they were putting in a winning round in the Medium Ponies. Casey was certain she'd never ridden such a beautiful hunter course in her life. Bell found every distance and every spot, landing on the correct lead after every line. She even tugged Casey into a final circle after the last jump and broke down to the trot at the exact right moment.

Casey took a breath as the pony finally steadied to a walk. Then she laughed, looking up at Sharmayne and Goldie, who were sitting on their horses at the top of the ring. Both of them had knowing smiles on their faces. Casey suspected they had set her up, but she loved the trick. "You guys! This pony is *incredible!*"

"That's what I love about Stinker there," Goldie observed. "She's always good for a pick-me-up."

"Once you get over the initial bolting," Sharmayne added.

"Well, yeah. That's the price of admission."

Casey rode up to them, the ridiculous smile on her face getting wider by the moment. "She's so much fun. Thanks for putting me on her, Sharmayne. And thanks for getting so much done with me today. I feel a lot better about everything."

"Better?" Goldie's gaze turned sharp. "Was there a problem?"

"Oh no, no," Casey assured her hastily. There was no point in telling Goldie that her absence had given Casey serious anxiety. Goldie would not change, and Sharmayne was more than enough of a stand-in. "I was just stressed from the trip, and jet-lag, and being away from my horse. You know."

"And her boyfriend just bought cowboy boots, and he's hiding them from her," Sharmayne added.

Goldie's eyebrows went up. "Really!"

Casey nodded reluctantly.

"Well, now that's a mystery!" Goldie announced. "You better keep your eye on that one, Casey. Sounds like there's about to be two horsemen in the family."

"Oh no," Casey laughed. "Brandon wouldn't ride a horse. There must be some other explanation. Maybe someone thought I could use them and gave them to him, and he doesn't know what to do with them now." Suddenly, this felt like the logical explanation. Why hadn't she thought of it before? The ride on Bell must have cleared her head.

"If you say so." Goldie shrugged, unconvinced. "Well, I'm taking Jim in. Nice riding there, girls. See y'all inside." She turned her horse and headed back out of the arena.

Casey and Sharmayne looked at each other. Sharmayne's face was bright with suppressed laughter. "You know, I never did guess he might be learning to ride. But Goldie's got a point."

"No way," Casey shook her head, confident at last. "No chance."

Chapter Thirteen

"Excited?"

Casey blushed. "Does it show?"

She'd been practically twirling around the barn all morning, getting in Sharmayne's way, bugging Goldie for answers the woman rarely gave, and generally being as silly as a girl newly fallen in love.

Sharmayne shook her head, smiling tolerantly. "If I'd known inviting your boyfriend out here was going to make you so annoying, I'd never have suggested it."

"But you were right!" Casey brushed off Sharmayne's mock insults. "This is just what we needed. A mini-vacation. We'll spend all weekend at the beach, we'll swim, we'll watch the sunset, then we'll go out and have drinks and eat really outrageous desserts..."

"Sounds like the same things you could do in Florida."

"You'd think that, but we don't make it to the beach very often these days, and it's different there. Hotter, for one thing. No," Casey decided, nodding her head. "We definitely needed this. But listen, don't let the place burn down without me this weekend. On Monday, we put all this work together, and in two months, boom! Your first show!"

"It's going to be crazy." Sharmayne gave Casey an exaggerated grimace, but she was excited, too. Casey knew Sharmayne was more sure than ever that this show series would help her get a job in the east. With horse show management under her belt, she'd have more knowledge than most barn manager candidates—even if she didn't have the title from Goldie to put on her resume.

Casey was pretty excited about the upcoming series, too. She'd fallen in love with the project despite herself. Maybe it was the organization—all those checklists from Phillip and Sharon had kept her busy ticking off projects one by one, which felt deeply satisfying to her perfectionist soul. And there was Sharmayne, the perfect partner throughout the process of organizing sponsors and ordering supplies. The past week had gone beautifully, she had to admit, and this had been the hard week.

Everything they did next week would be procedural: setting up the order of events and tasks which Goldie (read: Sharmayne) would have to do running up to the show itself. Then she'd leave them...and in two months' time, she looked forward to hearing how beautifully the first show in the series had gone.

In two months' time, Sungold Ranch and Sharmayne (and, yes, Goldie) would be a distant memory. Casey was almost sorry for it; she enjoyed being around these energetic, passionate women. But at least she had Raina to go back to—that was a friendship worth cultivating.

"Hello, earth to Casey!" Sharmayne was laughing. "You better get out of here. With traffic you're *just* going to make the airport in time."

"Oh my gosh." Casey looked down at her clothes, which were not at all what she'd intended to wear to pick up Brandon. She'd abandoned her soft work suits after day one at Sungold, realizing that jeans and barn shirts were better suited to the work she was doing. Today she was wearing *very* worn jeans and a plaid top which made her look like she was going to take out a guitar and belt out a love ballad. All she was missing were the boots and buckle. Funny, those mystery boots in the foyer would come in handy right about now. "I meant to go home and change!"

"Forget it, cowgirl. You're going to get your man looking exactly like that."

"If he's wearing those boots, I'm going to lose my mind," Casey confided, packing up her laptop and the rest of the work she'd spread across Goldie's desk.

"If he's wearing those boots, I'm going to need pics *immediately,*" Sharmayne informed her. "Like, photograph him first, text me second, *then* greet him. Got it?"

"I promise," Casey laughed. "As soon as I pick myself up off the floor."

He wasn't wearing the boots. Casey actually took a deep breath as she saw him walking out of the secure arrivals area, his carry-on bag slung over his shoulder, his shoes blissfully normal.

If Brandon noticed her checking out his feet, he gave nothing away. He dropped his bag and wrapped his arms around her. They had just enough time for a hello kiss before a frowning security guard waved them away from arrivals.

"No more cinematic airport greetings in the modern era," Brandon lamented as they power-walked out of the airport.

"I guess we'll have to save that for the hotel." Casey gave him a sly grin.

"Sexy times at the Courtyard by Marriott. My, my." Brandon

squeezed her hand. "It would be a shame if someone booked a suite at a historic beachside hotel."

Casey turned her head so quickly, her neck cricked. His eyes were sparkling with mischief. "You didn't! Did you?"

"It's been a while since we went away together," Brandon said. "I thought we could use the treat."

"Brandon! Where are we going?"

"Where else? The Hotel del Coronado!"

"Oh my God." Casey stopped in her tracks. "You mean it? The fancy one on the beach? With the red roofs and the little dormers?"

"The one and only." Brandon grinned. "Although the room is something called a *studio* suite, and my inner travel agent tells me a place like this doesn't overstate with the word 'studio.' So I wouldn't get too overwhelmed before we see what they give us."

"Brandon, are you kidding? I can't believe it!"

All thoughts of cowboy boots were forgotten now. Casey drove them back to her hotel by the freeway, and he helped her throw her weekend clothes into a bag. Casey paused by the front desk to let them know that housekeeping wouldn't be necessary that weekend, and then they were back on the road, speeding towards the beach.

Well, not speeding, because Friday afternoon traffic in San Diego was something special to be savored. Or so Brandon told Casey when she got impatient and banged her hand on the steering wheel.

"You're supposed to be less tense after a week in the sunshine," he reminded her. "What happened to that SoCal vibe? I expected you to meet me in yoga pants and with your hands pressed together in greeting. Very disappointed by the blue jeans and rapturous kiss, if we're being honest."

"Emotion *is* distasteful," Casey agreed solemnly. "We should make a point to do less of that." A car slipped into the tiny space in front of hers and she felt such a shiver of rage, she thought the top of her head might actually lift off. "What is *with* you people?" she shouted.

"Emotion," Brandon chuckled. "The curse of the gods."

"If you don't keep your ironic mouth shut, I will push you out of the car and spend the weekend without you," Casey informed him tensely.

Brandon, to his credit, took her at her word and kept quiet until they'd gotten clear of the traffic jam.

Just another reason Casey knew they were soulmates.

Beaches were good for whatever ailed you, Casey thought that evening, her toes digging into the sand. Well, except maybe for sunburn. Probably not effective against most infectious diseases, for that matter. But for problems of the soul, Casey always found time spent on a beach provided her with some much-needed mental clarity. She'd been gazing out at the Pacific for about thirty minutes, and she already felt much better about life in general.

"If I could keep James at the beach and live in a little shack, I would do it," she declared, putting her empty cocktail glass to one side. The jaunty umbrella inside listed against the half-melted ice cubes, water soaking into the pink paper.

Brandon gave her a sideways glance. "What if you lived in a *nice* house at the beach, but you couldn't keep James there and you had to drive two hours inland to ride him?"

"Please tell me this is theoretical," Casey said quickly.

"Oh, of course it is. I can't afford a nice house on a beach. Not when I'm spending all our savings on extravagant weekends at the del Coronado."

"Thank goodness," Casey laughed, hiding a rush of relief. "Because no, I wouldn't do it. As much as I love the beach, James is too important to me to keep him that far away. Being around horses is too important to me. That's something I'm figuring out about myself. This week hasn't been half-bad, Brandon, can you believe it? Sure, yes, I didn't want to come, but being able to work out of Sungold, and spending all this time with Sharmayne, has been really great. I'm a little sad to be leaving next weekend, even though I'm also dying to get home and be with James."

"And me," Brandon suggested.

"And you, obviously." She wriggled her toes deeper into the sand. "It's invigorating, being with ambitious people who want to do a good job, make the horse world better. Sometimes I suspect that working in my home office alone all the time, and riding alone, or even with Hannah, isn't the best strategy. I may need a change."

Brandon nodded; she felt his head moving next to her, even though he said nothing. She took that as permission to continue her line of thought.

"I'm not saying I want a new job...but I want this one to work out better. I definitely need Sharon and Phillip to hire help for me...but in West Palm. Not out here. Someone I can work with a few days a week. I could use a colleague. Someone to talk with, eat lunch with, that kind of thing."

"That's...hmm." Brandon dropped his chin to his chest, brow furrowing. "That's an idea, for sure. It takes an investment they haven't been willing to make, though. Do you have any idea how you'll sell it to them?"

"No idea," Casey admitted. "This is the first time I've ever taken this thought to its conclusion, honestly. I guess the waves and the drinks are helping me work it out creatively."

"Yeah, alcohol and oceans can do that," Brandon agreed. "Well, if you need a partner to work with, that makes sense. You figured out your problem. Now all you have to do is come up with the solution."

She laughed. "Sure. That's it."

"In the meantime, I have a question for you."

"Oh?" She kept her tone light, but she couldn't help giving him a sidelong glance. He wasn't planning...*that*...on this beach weekend, was he? It would certainly explain the splurge, but...they didn't really need the change right now, or the expense of a wedding. She hoped he was planning to leave well enough alone.

"It's not that serious."

She tried to rearrange her face. "Did I look like it was serious?"

"You looked like you thought it was serious."

"No, I'm good. Nothing's serious. Life's a beach. Ask your question."

"Will you go on a ride with me tomorrow?"

Casey pushed herself upright, sand falling from her elbows, and stared at Brandon. "A ride? Like a *horse* ride?"

"Yeah." His grin was sheepish; his gaze cast around as if he was too embarrassed to meet her eyes. "I...well, I booked us a ride tomorrow morning. On the beach. They don't bring the horses up here—something about not running over tourists, I didn't follow completely—but it's a short drive south. You've never ridden on the beach, right?"

"No, never." Casey remembered the boots. "Hey, Brandon, be honest. Have you been learning to ride?"

"Who, me?"

"Yes, you."

"Look!" Brandon pointed at the ocean. "Dolphins!"

"Big deal," Casey snorted. "Like I've never seen a dolphin. Don't change the subject with me."

"*Three* dolphins! What a sight!"

"Brandon! What's going on? I saw the boots."

"In my bag? But I didn't unpack them—"

Brandon's face, as he realized she'd caught him, was absolutely priceless. Casey forgot to be irritated with him for keeping something so massive from her and rolled back on her towel, shaking with laughter. He thought he was so clever! That was a boyfriend for you.

"It was supposed to be a surprise," he grumbled eventually.

Casey propped herself up on her elbows and gave him her most skeptical expression. "Why on *earth* would you learn to ride in secret?"

"In case it didn't work out. But I hoped we'd hang out more if we both rode! And if I can ride, you won't always have to ride with Hannah."

"What's wrong with Hannah?"

"She seems to bum you out. She's always pushing you to do things you don't really want to."

"She doesn't—" Casey interrupted, but Brandon was getting warmed up now.

"She *does*. She's the one obsessed with going to horse shows. She doesn't let you have fun with James. You come home depressed after you ride with her. And look at the way she makes you feel when she's taking care of James for you! Now, I'm not staying *I* could ride James instead of her while you're away—"

"Thank God," Casey muttered.

"But I had already started thinking that if I learned more about horses, when you're on trips I could go out and brush him, give him baths, do all the stuff she's doing like she owns him. And if she's riding him, I can supervise, so you're sure she's not running wild. But I'd have to know what I was doing. So, yeah. I started taking riding lessons. It was actually a few months ago. I just wanted to be good enough to ride competently before I told you."

Casey gaped at him now, her hilarity all laughed out. He'd been taking riding lessons for months, at who knew what expense, when she had been going without instruction for so long? Where was he finding the money? And if they were talking about finances and the things she wasn't spending their savings on, how about this hugely expensive hotel he'd booked for the weekend without consulting her? She had a perfectly good hotel room, albeit overlooking the freeway instead of the ocean, sitting empty!

Casey rolled over and pushed herself up from her towel, suddenly in need of some space. She was afraid she'd say something she'd regret. He was just trying to be nice—but he'd gone about it all wrong.

Brandon looked up at her with alarm. "Wait, where are you going?"

She brushed sand from her arms and legs, careful not to let it fall on her towel. She'd be back. Probably. "I need another drink," she said tersely.

"I'll get it—"

"*No.* Sorry. I just need a moment alone to process this." She turned on her heel.

"Casey, stop. Casey, wait, are you *mad?*" Brandon's voice was utterly bewildered. Both sides of Casey flared up at that—the loving side longed to explain things to him; the angry side supposed it was just typical that he didn't get what he'd done wrong.

So, to avoid choosing one side over the other, Casey kept her mouth shut and stalked away.

The pool bar was only a short walk; Casey slid onto a stool at the bar, making sure there were people on either side of her, just in case Brandon decided to follow her. A young and frankly glamorous woman in a bikini sat to her left, a deeply tanned and going-to-seed middle-aged man leaned over the bar to her left, his elbow dangerously near a bottle of Bud Lite. Neither of them looked over at her; they were too busy with their own conversations. Casey gave a weary smile to the sun-kissed bartender, who smoothed back her black hair and placed a napkin in front of her.

"What's a pretty girl like you doing alone on a fine drinking evening like this?"

"Just a mojito, thanks," Casey said, ignoring the bartender's obvious interest.

The paper fluttered in the sea breeze and Casey slapped her hand on top of it, making a loud sound which seemed to startle everyone— even the bartender. *Jumpy crowd,* she thought, irritated, and turned her attention to the TV playing baseball in one corner. Brandon watched baseball, but Casey only knew the basics: man hits ball, man runs bases. It didn't seem like enough to be a sport, not compared to the lifelong logistics of dressage or even nailing the perfect hunter round, but Casey knew better than to say this out loud. Only other horse-people would understand. That was why she needed more horsewomen as friends.

And not Brandon?

She couldn't answer the question satisfactorily. Not yet. She figured the rum would help.

Her mojito came in a tall, narrow glass, crushed mint leaves pressing against the ice, and she drank down half of it without really realizing what she was doing. The glamorous woman beside her left, presumably to do a photoshoot or star in a movie, and a much older woman filled the stool. She had a coif of iron-gray hair and a lavender cover-up. Casey liked her immediately, and she was pleased when the woman turned and said hello.

It was just a polite greeting, the type anyone might use when throwing themselves into someone else's close quarters, but Casey jumped on it. "Hi there," she said cheerfully. "I'm Casey. Isn't this place beautiful?"

The woman lifted a slim eyebrow briefly, taking in Casey's over-eager face. Then, as if sensing that Casey needed someone to talk to, she settled a little more comfortably onto her bar stool, held up a finger to the bartender, and turned her full attention to Casey. "It is beautiful. I try to make it over here once a month, just to remind myself of what heaven is like."

"Once a month! You must live nearby?"

"I live in Seattle," the woman said, a grim smile playing on her lips. "Which is a lovely place to live, but the wet and cold seeps into my bones and I have to come here to thaw out."

Casey was leaning forward, fascinated already. She wanted to know what made this woman tick. What made her keep a place like this at arm's-length, living instead in a city where she shivered? "Can I ask you something? Have you considered just moving down here? If you love it here so much, why not make this your home?"

The woman shook her head, her smile broadening. "Listen to you! That's what all young people say. You go on one vacation and you want to remake your lives to look like your trip. But then your vacation spot loses its magic. How much would I love it here if I had to drive to work every day, pick up things for dinner at the market every night, buy vacuum cleaner bags on Saturday afternoon while I'm out running errands instead of sitting at this bar enjoying the view and the sea breeze?" The woman wagged her finger. "Listen to me. Save vacation for vacation, real life for real life."

Casey took a contemplative sip of her drink.

"I don't mean to preach," the other woman said, suddenly apologetic.

Casey held up a hand. "No, you didn't. It's just interesting. I don't know that I've ever talked to anyone who felt that way. I live near the beach in Florida—well, I used to live closer to the beach, and I was there all the time. I definitely took it for granted. But then I kind of replaced it with horses, and I guess that makes being here now feel a little more special."

"That's it," the woman agreed. "You already know what I'm talking about." She accepted a margarita from the bartender—it must have been her usual—and said, "Enjoy your vacation, and enjoy your real life, but don't confuse them for each other. Now, what you *can* do is take some of the ways you behave on vacation, and apply those to your real life. Think about that."

Casey considered this as the bartender began making a second mojito for her—unasked for, but definitely appreciated. Her trip to San Diego wasn't exactly a vacation, but it seemed like she could learn from what she was doing differently out here, and find the changes which made her happy.

The answer seemed obvious. *It's Sharmayne,* she thought. Sharing the work with Sharmayne makes me happy. *Just like I told Brandon. I want to work with someone else.*

She spent so much of her time alone. It was a problem for her, and it needed to end.

And that might mean starting with the guy back on the beach, who seemed to understand her problem better than she had. Casey had been leaving him alone a lot lately...and when he tried to get closer to her, she got mad at him and stormed off. Definitely not the reaction he deserved, poor man. She couldn't even be angry with him about the money. Brandon was learning to ride so they could be together, so he could help her, for heaven's sakes. Her need for riding lessons was all tied up in the complicated horse show life she was still trying to live.

Casey leaned forward and asked the bartender to mix up one more mojito. "I'm taking it to my boyfriend," she added, tilting her head back towards the beach.

"Plastic cups, then," the bartender said tonelessly, taking back Casey's drink and dumping it into a new cup. She slid it across the counter with bothering with eye contact and shook up Brandon's drink. Casey left a generous tip to make up for whatever she'd done wrong, then took them both down the beach, where her boyfriend was waiting for her judgment.

"That was an awful reaction, and I'm the worst," she said, sitting down next to him.

Brandon took the cup from her and carefully wedged it into the sand at his side. "That was a perfectly reasonable reaction, and you're the best," he told her. "I should have been honest with you from the start."

Casey closed her eyes, a sudden burning behind her eyelids telling her that emotion was going to spill over in its usual, annoying way. "I should have realized that you were spending too much time alone, because I have been, too. It would be better if we could do things together. Even ride," she added, unable to keep a little skepticism from her tone.

"*Even* ride?" Brandon laughed. "Casey, you don't think I can do it."

"No, it's not that. I mean—I don't think you can ride the way I do. That's the only problem I see. Riding is such hard work, and it would take you a really long time to catch up, and we don't have a horse for you anyway..." She trailed off, catching the disappointment in his expression. "What? I'm sorry, these are just facts."

"First off, never let facts get in the way of a good time. Second, off," Brandon paused, studying her face. "Casey, you know you're a perfectionist. When are you going to start dealing with the fact that you never allow yourself to enjoy anything?"

"What?" Casey blinked. "I mean, yeah, of course I am, but what makes you think I don't enjoy myself?"

"You're exhausted all the time, you're reaching for goals you can't get to, you tell me you're not enjoying yourself—which I thought was the number one giveaway that things weren't working out..."

She looked back out at the ocean. Evening was descending upon them, diffuse golden light dancing off the waves. The setting sun silhouetted distant sailboats against the yellow backdrop of sky, and people were pausing their beachcombing strolls, shading their eyes to take in the sight. She suddenly remembered the sunset celebrations in Mallory Square, their weekends in Key West, other mojitos in plastic cups. Before James. Before horse shows. Before her job ate her life. Before there was nothing left of her to give to good times and vacations.

Had her life been better without horses? The question had popped into her head before. She'd always managed to shove it aside, but now it demanded her attention. If she couldn't even have fun anymore, what was the point of all this drama?

There were no easy answers to that, though.

"I don't know what to say," she sighed. "I love having a horse. But when I ride, I want to improve. I want to show. It's part of my personality...you *know* I'm a perfectionist. This is how I'm wired. I'm sorry that it takes away from everything else."

"And I don't want you to be less of who you are," Brandon said tenderly. "I just want you to find a way to relax. You *need* to relax. I'm worried about you."

She nodded. She could accept that she had a problem. She just couldn't blame the horses for it. That wouldn't get her anywhere.

"Let's start tomorrow, okay? With a beach ride? Tell me how that makes you feel, and we'll work from there."

"Okay," Casey agreed. "Tomorrow, I'll get on a horse and just relax."

Surely, on a beach, such things were possible.

Chapter Fourteen

CASEY WAS HAVING the time of her life. She couldn't believe she'd never done this before! How could she be a Florida native, raised within fifteen miles of the ocean, and never once taken a gallop down a sandy beach, with the sound of waves crashing in her ears a glorious backdrop to the rhythm of her horse's hooves? This was like heaven!

Of course, she wasn't exactly galloping. She'd just nudged her rented horse into an easy lope when the guide wasn't paying attention to her. This was most of the time. The poor woman had to focus on the crowd of civilians clustering their horses close to her, fearful of what their big, scary livery horses might do to them. Casey spotted this behavior as soon as they'd ridden out and she'd hung back from the herd strategically, her horse pulling at the bit as his buddies got farther away. Once they were a few hundred feet behind, she'd let go and encouraged him—okay, she bumped his sides with her heels, because even then he wasn't in a hurry to break out of his slow jog— to stretch out and catch his buddies.

Brandon kept glancing over his shoulder, aware of what she was doing, an approving grin on his face. He remained happy to stay somewhere in the middle, close to the pack—although not in the cluster of frightened newbies.

This was an interesting perk to her ride: the chance to watch Brandon in the saddle, and see that after just a couple months of weekly riding lessons, he had already found a comfortable position on his horse. Brandon sat easily in the center of his Western saddle. His heels were down, his back was straight. And although he occasionally lost his balance, usually while the horse was sidestepping a clump of seaweed or a tide pool left by the retreating ocean, the jostling was always minor and Brandon bounced right back into position.

Like a Weeble, Casey thought, almost exasperated at how easy riding seemed to come to her boyfriend. *He wobbles, but he doesn't fall down.*

Besides the very slight irritation she felt at Brandon's apparently innate ability to sit a horse, Casey was having an excellent morning. Some might even call it a perfect morning. Being a born perfectionist, of course, Casey saw a few things she might change. For one, the marine layer of heavy clouds had returned, and the ocean to her left was awash with fog. San Diego had an interesting way of either providing perfect weather or depressing weather, with nothing in between. A land of extremes, and yet without extreme temperatures or rainfall or wind or anything else which the rest of the world experienced. The opposite of Florida, in short.

The other thing she would change would be her horse, who was round and slow and not particularly interested in his job. But she couldn't blame a livery horse for being bored at work, even if his office was a long, sandy strand. No one liked to do the same thing over and over every day. She remembered the woman from the pool bar, telling her that moving to her favorite vacation spot would remove all the joy. Repetition ruined things. Something to consider, when she was drilling twenty-meter circles or canter transitions with James.

Her horse finally caught up to Brandon's and immediately slowed his gait to match his stablemate's slow jog. She glanced over at Brandon, who was bobbing gently in the saddle, evidently working hard at keeping the bounce in his legs—and doing pretty well at it.

"This was a good idea," she told him. "Except now I want to do this in Florida."

"With James?" Brandon grinned. "You want to take your ex-racehorse out on the beach?"

"Well..." Casey tried to imagine what James would be like on the beach. Something told her he'd have a serious case of the zoomies. She'd seen enough fail videos to know that horses didn't always react well to their first glimpse of ocean. "Maybe something quieter, to start. A horse just a few notches up from this guy." She gave her horse a pat on the neck, to let him know she didn't think he was bad or anything. Just not the right mount for her. "I want to gallop, but I don't want to set any track records, if you know what I mean."

"Well, as I hear it, speed was never James's forte."

"Wait and see what happens if he decides he has to run away from the surf to save his own silly neck. Personally, I think James's old trainer would be pretty impressed if I took that horse to the beach."

"Is it really that hard to get them used to the waves?"

"Well, you know I've never tried it. But I've definitely heard stories. And seen some pretty hilarious videos. Hilarious because I'm not the one in them, screaming my head off or spitting out seawater."

"We'll have to see what happens," Brandon decided, evidently sharing none of her nerves.

Well, that was the nice thing about being a new rider, wasn't it?

You didn't have a rich store of horror stories and personal experience with near-misses to keep your imagination running at full-tilt all the time, providing a running tab of all the ways you or your horse could die at any given moment?

Brandon must have seen the skepticism on her face, because he reached out and patted her knee comfortingly. "Don't spend all your time worrying about hypotheticals, Case," he reminded her. "This is supposed to be fun."

She shook herself and smiled back at him, then turned her attention to the horses ahead of them, the faintest suggestion of sunlight glinting off the ocean to their left, the high dunes rising to their right. She breathed deep and tried to absorb the salty air deep into her senses. Tried to do all the things that meditation masters and relaxation apps told her to do every time she felt like she was losing control and heading down an anxiety spiral. As usual, her results were mixed, but her mind eventually started to slow, its catastrophe reel playing a little less loudly. She was on a quiet horse, on a quiet beach, riding alongside her boyfriend. In a week she'd be going home to her horse and her home (and her boyfriend). Everything was fine.

Everything was fine.

"Honestly, it was an incredible ride," Casey told Brandon. "Ten out of ten, would do again."

"We will," he said. "In Florida."

She gazed out across the ocean. The hotel's studio suite was as small as he'd warned, but the view of the Pacific was worth whatever he was paying for it—Casey had made a mental vow to avoid looking at the bank statements for the next month, to let Brandon keep his surprise a secret—and she was already lamenting her return to the freeway cloverleaf where her California home would be for the next week.

Brandon gone, this view a memory, and her last week with Sharmayne...she definitely had mixed emotions about going home.

"Why the long sigh?" Brandon asked.

Casey hadn't even realized she'd made a sound. "Just the beautiful beach," she hedged. "Maybe we should get a really big-screen TV and run a 24/7 loop of the beach on it."

"Now you're talking like a tech guy's girlfriend," Brandon laughed. "Don't tempt me, or you'll come home to a simulated Pacific sunset every night."

"Do you think it would cure seasonal depression?" Casey asked, only half-joking.

She had to run to Sungold in the afternoon—Goldie had left some files unsigned, despite Sharmayne's best efforts to take care of everything herself, and she wanted to fax them to the Florida office before Monday morning emails started flying in from the east coast. Brandon chose to tag along, despite Casey's suggestion that he'd have more fun hanging out at the pool.

"You have to leave tomorrow, so this is your best chance to get a tan on that pale bod," she reminded him, poking his chest. Brandon was never good at getting tan; it usually took until late August and a summer of playing at watersports with his friends to get even a faint glow going. And even though they both knew sun exposure wasn't exactly the most healthy idea, living in Florida with a ghost-like pallor wasn't in the cards, either. People either thought you were a tourist or a shut-in. Plus, Casey was fairly certain it was tougher to get a burn once you had a good base layer of tan—although she wasn't sure if that was actual medical science or it just seemed that way. "And since when do you want to come visit barns with me? This is a first."

"Maybe since I just became a rider, myself?" Brandon gave her a lopsided smile. "Okay, I'm not trying to steal your position as the equestrian in the family, but could you accept that I'm trying to learn about horses properly, and seeing this farm you've been talking about so much would be great for me? I'd love to see the differences between a Florida barn and a California one."

"This is like the difference between a shanty and a spa, if we're talking about Twin Palms," Casey grumbled. "But sure, come on. This will be educational for you."

She probably wasn't being fair to Twin Palms, she told herself as they drove down the winding driveway to Sungold. Sure, there was no comparison between the two farms. But the horses were happy either way. James was in good condition and got a lot of turnout, and the other boarders were nice enough, even if they weren't particularly stimulating. Sungold just had the amenities she'd gotten used to enjoying at St. Johns, and then some.

Plus—Sungold had Goldie for an owner and head trainer. And as useless as Goldie was about business, she was fun and interesting, and her outgoing nature was all about empowering the riders under her care.

Or really *any* rider, it turned out. Goldie greeted Brandon, who was wearing his cowboy boots, with extreme friendliness. Too much friendliness, in fact. She trampled right over Casey's plans for the day.

"So you're the famous boyfriend! And you're dressed for a ride! This is perfect. Let's go check out the view from the ridge today. Sharmayne? Who should Brandon ride? Let's find him someone quiet—he's new to our sport, we don't want to over-face him too soon! Casey will never forgive us, will you, Casey?" Goldie belly-laughed.

"Oh, we weren't staying," Casey hedged, holding up a hand as she could slow down the runaway Goldie train before it left the station. "I really just need these pages signed. If you could just put your signature here and here—"

"You didn't drive *all the way* out here to just get my name on some papers! Not with this fella in tow! He could be sitting by the pool right now! But no, he came all the way out here with you. If he was waitin' on ya, I'd send you right back and tell you to stop working on weekends, you workaholic you! But with you both here, dressed and ready to ride? Come on, don't tell me it won't be fun!"

Casey resisted the urge to glare at Brandon's cowboy boots. *They* were responsible for this mess. All she wanted was to go back to the del Coronado, order a drink, and perhaps slip into that beautiful pool one more time. Not get on a horse. For once, she didn't want to get on a horse!

But next to her, Brandon was nodding eagerly. "I've never ridden twice in one day. Thanks so much for the offer!"

"Oh, today's the perfect day for a lotta firsts," Goldie declared. "Sharmayne? You pick a horse for our cowboy here?"

Sharmayne gave Casey a sympathetic look, but they both knew her hands were tied. She had to play along with the boss's whims. "I'd put him on Peanut Butter. He's a good novice horse, and he doesn't have any lessons until five o'clock."

"Perfect choice! I'll get Jim ready, and Casey? You want to ride Daisy? Good. Sharmayne, grab a groom and get those two tacked up, but don't worry about Sunny Jim—I got him. And Casey, we'll go sign these papers of yours real quick, so you can get that frown line out of your forehead."

"I'll help Sharmayne, if that's okay?" Brandon glanced hopefully her way. "I'm still getting the hang of tacking up."

"Of course you are! Go with Sharmayne, she'll take care of ya." Goldie directed a conspiratorial smile at Casey, as if to congratulate her on her horseback-riding man.

Casey smiled wanly in return.

Was it jealousy? Frustration? Or was she just tired and maybe a little PMS-y? Casey sat on her second horse of the day and tried to figure out what had her in such a snit.

Whatever it was, she knew she had to get over it in a hurry.

Brandon was trying, and that was more than Casey could say for herself right now. He glanced back at her now, his face alight with the beautiful view from the ridge. Casey smiled back at him, trying hard to put her whole heart into the cause. She wanted Brandon to be happy, to enjoy riding as much as she did. It was a gift she'd never expected, a boyfriend who rode.

She just had to get used to the idea, that was all.

She just needed a little more time with this.

Chapter Fifteen

AFTER TWO WEEKS in California, Florida's humidity hit like a slap in the face.

Casey paused for a moment when that thick air slid over her skin —a moment just long enough for the crowd of fellow travelers behind her to mutter in irritation. A few suitcases were rolled rather aggressively into hers. But Casey wasn't too surprised by the critical attitudes surrounding her. Most of the people flying into West Palm's airport were coming from cold, northern climes which weren't exactly known for producing friendly faces. (Yes, Casey was thinking specifically of New York City when she made this allowance for bad behavior. Reputations are earned, not granted.)

And anyway, the humidity was going to surprise them, too, even if they insisted on rushing headlong into that cloud of steamy air hovering just outside the airport's sliding doors, rather than giving their bodies a chance to acclimate, as Casey was doing. As much as a body *could* acclimate, anyway. She wondered suddenly if anyone ever really got used to summer in Florida—even natives like herself.

And yes, it was summer now. When she'd left, things had been rushing rapidly towards the tropical summer season, but some traces of Florida's dry spring had still remained. Now it was all gone. They were still a week away from Memorial Day, but this wasn't picnic weather.

Casey rolled her bag onto the concrete sidewalk and the doors slid closed behind her, taking their air-conditioned comfort with them. Out here in Arrivals, the heavy air curdled with diesel fumes and cigarette smoke. She walked along the pavement for what felt like forever, trying not to breathe in the cancerous soup that passed for an atmosphere, glancing between the waiting cars and the line of thunderclouds rising in the west, their white caps spreading out as they grew over the hot peninsula.

Finally, she saw their familiar blue Prius, and as Brandon hopped out to grab her suitcase, relief flooded through Casey. Not just relief at seeing him, but at the way her *heart reacted* when she saw him. That surge of love and affection, that certainty there was no one else in the world she wanted to see right now. She welcomed the feelings, letting them wash over her, not wanting to admit how profoundly frightened she'd been that they might not come.

The fact, the *secret* fact, it must be emphasized, was that she'd been a little glad when Brandon had left San Diego last Sunday. A little, tiny, guilty bit of glad. As he disappeared through the morass of airport security, she'd felt as if she'd gotten something back that was all hers, and she didn't have to pretend she was happy about sharing it anymore. She couldn't quite explain what that feeling was, anymore than she could explain how irritated she'd been on that ride up the ridge with Goldie and Brandon. All she knew was that it was irrational, and unnecessary, and she needed to get over it. And she also knew she had been very afraid it wouldn't go away.

"Brandon, I missed you," she said, meaning every word.

He closed the door on her bag and pulled her close, kissing her for such a long time the airport police officer patrolling nearby got mad and told him to wrap it up. "Get a room, kids," he growled, sounding like a character from an old detective show. "The sign says *No Standing.*"

Casey laughed as Brandon hustled her into the car. "Let's try not to get arrested before we get home, okay?"

"No one better get between us and home," Brandon growled, climbing in on the driver's side. Then he gave a friendly wave to the police officer, who rolled his eyes and kept walking.

"You put on such a tough show," she observed.

"I'm turning into a cowboy," he told her, winking.

"Oh, please don't."

They drove through the sprawl of West Palm with the radio on and the air conditioning blasting, and when they finally got to the condo, Casey opted for a long, lukewarm shower to get the travel grime off. When she turned off the water at last, thunder was growling outside and the light in the window was dim.

"I guess I'm not riding James this evening," she sighed, coming into the kitchen.

James opened a beer for her. "Then I guess you can have this."

"Thanks." She watched as the first fat raindrops hit the kitchen window. "So when did summer start?"

"You mean rain every day around three o'clock? Two days ago, actually. I'm not sure if it will stick or if we'll get a little dry spell before June, but it seems pretty content to stay."

The rain drummed against the window with gusto now.

Casey remembered how hard it had been to fit in rides around the rainstorms last summer. She wondered if she could rearrange her life so that she rode first thing in the morning. There would be no one else at the barn; well, maybe Liz, mucking out. For the first time, the idea struck her as terribly lonely. She'd been spoiled at Sungold Farm, with Goldie and Sharmayne and the great crowd of students around at all times. It was going to be tough to go back to riding alone.

But she'd make it work. And there was Hannah—not the best riding companion, true, but the best one she had. Maybe she could convince her to get up early and ride a few mornings a week… although asking a teenager to get up and ride at six-thirty in the morning all summer didn't seem like a proposal with a high success rate.

Well, she'd float the idea and see what happened. And either way, she'd get up early and ride in the morning.

No—Monday morning. She'd forgotten she'd promised Brandon they'd go out on a friend's boat tomorrow, and they were leaving early. Casey plucked at the beer bottle's label, fighting the urge to tell him she couldn't come after all. One more day would not make a difference to James. Not when she'd already been gone two weeks.

She twisted the label off and crushed it in her palm.

"This isn't cute!"

Her warnings fell on deaf ears. James wiggled as she groomed, bounced as she saddled up, and tossed his head irritatingly when she tried to bridle him. Casey was out of breath and red-faced by the time she had him tacked up. She reached for her helmet, half-afraid of what was waiting for her when she mounted up, and then James did something so astonishingly rude, she couldn't even react at first. He reached out one hoof and *pawed*. His shoe left a white streak on the concrete, and his shoulder shoved her to one side.

As she stumbled away from him, she dropped her helmet and winced as it landed on her grooming kit. Hopefully, that was better than hitting the concrete floor.

"James!" she shouted as soon as she had her voice back. "What on *earth?*"

Her voice echoed in the empty barn. It turned out that six-thirty on a Monday morning was so early, she'd even beat Liz and morning chores. That was probably the issue, of course—James never came into the barn before everyone else, and he hadn't had his breakfast yet. Everything was strange for him right now...and she could just add in whatever trouble Hannah had been letting him get away with, Casey thought darkly.

James shifted from side to side, nipping at the reins. Casey realized she was in for serious trouble out in that arena. She considered putting taking off his bridle and giving him some grain. Surely if he had a little breakfast, that would help steady his brain. Casey looked at the calendar on her phone, hoping to find some wiggle room. She had an eight-thirty call with Phillip and Sharon. It was their usual Monday morning meeting, but this one would place an extra spotlight on her, since she had to report back on the preparations for the Sungold show series. She absolutely couldn't be late, although she *could* be unwashed and unchanged.

Still, if she put James away to eat something, it would take at least fifteen minutes. She'd only have twenty left to ride. That was barely enough time to get him warmed-up.

Casey sighed and decided. She could manage this ride if she hustled. If it didn't work out, well, she'd try feeding him first tomorrow.

Assuming she lived that long. Casey buckled her helmet and gave the strap a little tug, tightening it against her chin. Time to go to war.

A few minutes later, she was standing James up near the mounting block inside the arena. More wiggling, more nipping at the reins. She sighed, her breath coming out like a rush of frustration. He didn't want to wait for her; he was bursting at the seams with nervous energy. Why was he so bouncy? Had Hannah even ridden him while she'd been away? He'd been so quiet when she came back from the first trip; she'd thought maybe Hannah had done him some good, but this behavior was the complete opposite.

With a sudden burst of determination, Casey launched herself into the saddle, gathering the reins up close to her chest as James immediately scooted forward. She felt herself grabbing for her right stirrup, but it was okay—she could ride without stirrups, even if it had been more than six months since her last lesson without them. *You know how to handle this,* she told herself as James skittered around the arena like a half-drunk spider. *Sit deep and—*

And spit out the dirt.

She looked up at the hazy blue sky, dazed. How had she ended up here, her shoulder digging into the deep gray sand of the arena? Casey couldn't think of what happened. She got up and saw James standing across from her, looking just as astonished as she was.

Well, that was okay. He hadn't meant to dump her, judging by his expression. She brushed herself off, noting that nothing actually hurt. It was an easy fall. Easy mount, easy fall, right? No problem. He'd be better now. He'd get himself together and behave.

But he was still a squirmy worm to mount, and she still found herself fighting to get her stirrups—but this time she ran him right into the high, slatted walls of the arena so that he was forced to stop, just long enough for her to nudge her right boot into the stirrup where it belonged at last, and choke up on the reins—taking a little handful of mane while she was at it.

Here I am grabbing mane again, she thought ruefully, turning James's head to the left so that he could stride out again. "Walk," she said firmly, hoping the addition of voice commands would remind him who was in charge. Then, as he began to jog, she deepened her tone. "Just walk. Whoa, James. Whoa—whoa—*James!*"

He chose the opposite tack and took took off, his hind end scooting beneath him. Casey's first thought was that a particularly vicious fly had bitten him, maybe right above the tail. She'd seen the big black "mud wasps"—awful creatures that no one seemed to know the real name for—land right above his tail and hang on tight before. In the pasture, the horses actually had to drop to the ground and roll to get the bloodsuckers off. She hazarded a glance over her shoulder, but there was nothing on his dark hindquarters. Well, other than a sheen of nervous sweat.

"Enough, James, slow *down,*" Casey shouted, giving up any semblance of nice, measured voice commands. He was ripping at the bit, trying to tug the reins right out of her hands, and she was leaning back against him, placing her weight against his. She knew this was a losing battle, but at the same time, she didn't know how to change the stakes. James had started this fight, not her.

He ran two tight circles around the arena, his legs scrambling for purchase in the deep sand as he shaved off the turns, avoiding the corners. Casey's head was awash with fears about strained tendons and torn ligaments. The footing was much too heavy for these kinds of shenanigans. This arena wasn't designed to make a horse's life safer and more comfortable. Like everything else at Twin Palms, it just wasn't good enough when the stakes were high.

As if reading her mind, James stumbled hard, his hind legs nearly flying out from beneath him as he tried to take another tight turn, and Casey felt herself tumbling backwards from the saddle. Not even her death-grip on the reins could save her. This time, she landed on her back, and as the wind smacked out of her lungs, she closed her eyes against the glaring morning sun and had a moment's fleeting thought.

I'm too old for this.

But she wasn't, of course. She was thirty-four, as of five days ago—a day marked only by a lot of social media messages she hadn't acknowledged. Thirty-four: that was still spring chicken in horsewoman years, right? Great riders didn't hit their strides until they were in their forties and fifties. Olympians regularly kept on medaling into their sixties and beyond. She wasn't even asking to be great—she was just trying to get her horse around the arena without too much bloodshed.

Casey slowly pushed herself upright. James stood at the gate, gazing across the grass, past the barn, to where his buddies were clustered near the pasture gate. They were waiting for breakfast. Liz would be here soon, Casey thought. Embarrassment rose through her, heat flooding her cheeks. She couldn't let Liz see her floundering like this. And she was running out of time…Casey checked her watch, brushing sand from the face. Twenty after seven. She had about fifteen minutes to get things right, and then she'd have to take James back in, to give him a shower and cool out properly before he could eat. As things were, she'd be sitting down to take her hour-long call with arena sand still stuck inside her bra.

She got up again—a little more slowly this time, as some things were definitely sore now—and stomped across the sand to catch James.

This time, he wasn't quite so eager to be captured. He'd evidently decided they weren't having a good morning, and he saw no reason to continue their misadventures. Casey stumbled after him, slopping through puddles, and baking in the rising sun. She felt like Florida was torturing her, and her mind flitted back to San Diego. She knew her thoughts were traitorous: she was a Floridian, through and through, and anyway, James and Brandon were not part of San Diego, or Sungold Ranch. She'd been alone there, making friends with new people and riding new horses who had nothing to do with her real life. She couldn't be seduced by the allure of a fresh start, of a place where no one knew who she really was. Where no one had seen her coated in sand and drenched in sweat, trying in vain to catch her horse.

Finally, James stood still long enough for her to snag his reins, and even though he jumped backward immediately, nostrils flared and eyes wide as if he didn't even recognize her, she held on until he stilled, then dragged him back to the mounting block. She was grim this time as she set about wedging him between the block and the wall, and she barely noticed the way he stepped away from her as she slammed one boot into the stirrup and swung aboard. Her body was sore, but warmed up, and there was little he could do that she wasn't already prepared for at this late stage in the game.

James jogged unpleasantly beneath her, tossing his head while she glanced at her watch. She had five minutes to make something out of this ride. She didn't love her chances.

"James, let's just get this right," she muttered, wiggling her fingers on the reins to try to get a soft jaw out of him. He threw his head up and down, but finally he left it lower than he'd started. She counted that as a win.

They were trotting with almost recognizable rhythm, and Casey was relaxing into the tack, when the roar of a truck startled them both. She looked up—so did James—but the arena walls were six feet tall, meant to keep in cattle during sorting, and they couldn't see the source of the noise. Casey figured it must be Liz arriving. She tensed up a little despite herself, hating to think she'd be seen in such a bedraggled state. It was just so obvious she'd fallen off. James must have recognized the sound of Liz's truck, because he picked up his head and whinnied. The horses in the pasture behind them echoed the sound.

"Fine. You can go in," she told him, reining back. It would be impossible to get his attention back now, when he was thinking about grain and his friends were heading inside. Anyway, she was probably running up against the clock. She'd have to get going—

A flock of ibis suddenly appeared over the arena walls, long red beaks and white bodies and black-tipped wings flapping furiously against the humid air, and as they struggled to attain altitude, their dangling orange legs nearly brushed against the top of Casey's helmet. James literally seemed to have a heart attack—he seized up, snorted with a sound like a gag, and then threw himself sideways to escape the aerial assault.

This time, when Casey came off, she hit the arena wall, and it hurt.

Behind the closed door of her office, Casey allowed herself to sag in her chair.

She had put on a tough girl act for the past hour, and she was tired. She'd been covered in sand and mud when she'd led James into the barn, which had caused Liz to stare and make several remarks about riding with no one else around. Since Liz rarely cared if her boarders rode alone, without helmets, or barefoot, this was a particularly insulting line of conversation. Sure, Casey could have said, she definitely shouldn't have been riding alone, and it was a damn good thing she hadn't actually hurt herself when she'd gone flying into the fence—or any of the other times she'd gotten dumped this morning

—but despite her lapse in good judgement, it stung that Liz singled her out to be the first person in Twin Palms history who couldn't be trusted to ride alone.

So she'd disguised any hint of a limp or a hitch in movement while she'd hosed off James and put him in his stall to eat, and while she flipped her saddle pad to dry in the sun and hung her bridle on its usual peg. She'd even managed to bend over and put a clean saddle pad on the seat of her car before she sat down, trying to protect the upholstery from her muddy bottom, and while the movement had felt like she was trying to break her back in two, the triumph in performing it while Liz looked on and not giving away a hint of her agony was enough to get her home in one piece.

She'd lurched inside her condo's front door hoping that Brandon would have gone into the office today, but no, he was on the sofa, sipping coffee and typing away at something. She waved away his look of alarm, said she didn't have time to talk about it, and gathered her own cup of coffee before she bolted the office door behind her. Then she placed the saddle pad on the office chair, sat down, and allowed herself to cry for precisely three minutes.

That was all she had time for. Her office calendar pinged, her laptop lit up, and she had to dial in to her call. Casey wiped her face, adjusted her bra so that the worst of the sand wasn't rubbing against her cleavage, and put on her professional smile.

"Sharon, Phillip, good morning!"

Chapter Sixteen

"So, HOW WAS your first morning back?" Brandon asked. "Ready to grab some lunch?"

Casey spun slowly in her chair, trying to think how to answer that question. She was still wearing her dirty riding clothes, and an ache in her back and left shoulder was making sitting upright and typing extremely difficult. The eight-thirty call lasted until ten, with a full inbox of emails waiting afterwards, plus her usual Monday morning ad tweaking. All she wanted from life was a shower, and maybe for Brandon to stop smiling at her as if everything was great.

Still, she managed to infuse some very realistic regret into her voice when she told him, "I don't think I've got time to go anywhere. I'll be using the next twenty minutes to get all this grime off. And there's a pile of work backed up thanks to the San Diego trip." A pile, a mountain, a same difference. Enough work to bury her, whatever you called it.

Brandon nodded, his eyes rounding as he took in her messy state.

"I didn't realize you never escaped the office long enough to change. How about I order us some lunch instead, and have it waiting when you're ready?"

"That would be great." Casey stood up, not without a little difficulty. "The saltier, the better. I'll be in the shower."

Under the pounding hot water, things usually felt better. But not today. Casey had been trying to push the morning's trauma out of her mind so that she could get through her Monday routine, and so far, the work had really helped. But without a screen in front of her face, her brain found plenty of room to roam, and the situation with James was screaming for her attention.

She'd fallen off three times! In one morning! Three times in three days was bad luck. Three falls in one ride was a serious situation unfolding. She knew a lot of things went wrong this morning—she'd changed his morning routine without warning, and James was a horse who thrived on patterns. The feeding situation was front and center; she should give him some grain before their next morning ride, obviously. Unfortunately, that would mean getting up even earlier, and what was more, that would mean doing getting up early every single weekday, without fail, so that the routine made sense to him. Casey thought of a five-thirty alarm every morning and sighed.

Not exactly the stuff she'd been dreaming of when she'd started riding horses again.

And then there was Hannah. What exactly went down with Hannah and James while she'd been out west? Had the girl been riding him or just playing with him on the ground—and which scenario was actually worse? Casey wasn't sure. Her only reporting on James's behavior was Hannah's Instagram pictures. Her feed was peppered with scene after scene of James getting pampered like a modern-day Bucephalus. The baths, the primping, the grazing, the cookies—James would definitely have thought himself the reincarnation of Alexander the Great's very spoiled horse.

And Casey did have to admit that James looked pretty great. His coat was soft, if still a little sunburned, but that would pass now the horses were on night turnout during the hottest months. His mane was trimmed to a perfect four-finger length, his bridle path was clipped close, his fetlocks were clipped cleanly. Hannah had turned show grooming into a social media circus, providing video or photo clips of every act involving a comb or a clipper.

But Casey hadn't seen a single picture or video to prove any rides had taken place.

What if Hannah had been afraid of James—or worse, what if she'd gotten thrown from him at some point—and instead of owning up to Casey, she'd simply decided not to ride him? Maybe he was okay with a week off work, but two weeks right after that vacation was simply too much.

Casey was inclined to lean into this theory. It would explain a lot. It would certainly explain how he'd gone from a kind of tough horse three weeks ago to an explosive mess this morning. Casey had been riding James for almost a year now, and she knew: even if he was pissed about breakfast, even if he was confused about a change in routine, none of those things would have been enough to create the massive shift in temperament he'd shown her this morning.

But combine anxiety and a long vacation without a single lunge session to get the bucks out? Oh, that was cause for trouble, all right.

Casey heard the front door close and realized she'd been in the shower for a solid twenty minutes. Lunch had already arrived. She stepped out and started toweling her hair, her mind still on the problem of Hannah. How could she get the truth out of the girl? Was it even worth confronting her? Or should she just try to move on, start the morning rides with a lunge line session for a few days until James had the hang of working again, and just pretend none of this had ever happened?

Her shoulder twinged with pain, reminding Casey that pretending things were okay was rarely the right choice with horses. And anyway, she could still be wrong about the whole thing. It was possible that Hannah had been riding James and things had just gone very wrong. Or that Hannah didn't even realize she'd done such a terrible job. Look at the way Caruso behaved daily. Hannah didn't have any problems with that.

Casey knew if didn't get all the details, she would face a very uphill battle to get her horse going right again. A battle which might involve her ending up in the dirt, again and again.

Casey wasn't sure how many falls her frail, thirty-four-year-old body could be expected to sustain before she ended up in the hospital, or worse, at the chiropractor.

No, she'd have to talk to Hannah. In person, so the girl couldn't lie to her easily. She'd have to go to the barn tonight and get the details, rain or shine.

Thunder rumbled outside as Casey tugged on a clean t-shirt. *Rain, then,* she thought wearily, and for just a moment, she let herself remember the sunny, golden days of Southern California.

Then she went out to the kitchen and sat down to eat lunch with Brandon.

The rain was clearing when she drove out to Twin Palms that evening. Casey couldn't help her annoyance as she looked at the gray skies. It would be a heck of a lot nicer riding now, under the shade of all those clouds, than it had been this morning with nothing to filter the glaring sun. "Naturally," she muttered, turning down the barn drive.

"You get up early, the rain clears up. There's no winning in Florida."

She felt a little better when she saw the other cars parked outside the barn, and the slow parade of riders circling inside the arena. With their heads tilted towards each other as they talked, the other boarders liked to ride in tight couples or trios, their hands loose on the reins, just taking up space. Trying to get any actual work done around them was nearly impossible.

"Score one, early morning," Casey admitted, perking up a little. She hopped out of the car and started looking for Hannah.

"Casey!" Hannah came out of the tack room, her bridle in one hand. It looked damp and oily. "I should have waited longer. I rode in the rain, while everyone else was hanging around in here. I figured you wouldn't come with the weather so bad."

"Oh well, you know." Casey waved a hand vaguely. She didn't want her questions to seem urgent, or mean. "Just wanted to ask how you got on with James. If he was good to ride, what you guys did, that kind of thing."

"It was fine. He was fine." Hannah held up her bridle and squinted at it. "I think I oiled it too much."

"But what did you guys do?" Casey persisted. "How many times did you ride him?"

"Oh, I don't know. Like...a few times. Yeah, there is definitely too much oil on this. I gotta sop some up." Hannah retreated into the tack room.

Casey ran her hand through her hair, tugging at her loose ponytail. Hannah had better own up. What was a few times? One? Three? None? "Hannah," she called. "Talk to me, please."

She went into the tack room, where Hannah on her knees, rummaging through a big rubber storage container. "What aren't you telling me?"

"Nothing," Hannah insisted, her voice muffled by the piles of saddle pads and equipment she was tugging at. "Nothing happened."

"Something happened. Tell me."

Hannah flung herself backwards so quickly she nearly toppled over. She righted herself and stood up, but kept her eyes trained on the concrete floor. "I fell off him, okay? I didn't ride him for a couple of days and then when I did, he dumped me. I hadn't fallen off in a while and it scared me."

Casey let out a breath. "Hannah! Were you hurt? You should have told me!"

"I wasn't hurt. I was just freaked out. So, I knew not to ride him alone again, but I was embarrassed to ride him in front of everyone else. In case he did it again. So...I didn't ride him again." She clenched her fists at her sides. "I'm sorry."

Casey tugged the girl close and gave her a hug. "No, I'm sorry. I shouldn't have asked you to ride him."

Hannah pushed away from her. "I should have been able to ride him! I'm not good enough." She shook her head. "It's embarrassing."

"Don't be embarrassed. I fell off James three times this morning." The admission hurt a little. She had told no one, supposing she'd prefer to take that dismal of a stat to her grave. But Hannah felt worse than she did. The kid could use a little commiseration. "He's having a tough phase, I guess."

"Three times—this *morning?*" Hannah quickly forgot her own embarrassment. "Man, what did he do? And why were you riding in the morning?"

"He was just giving me his general foolishness." Casey waved away their worthless ride. No point in rehashing it now. "Listen, I'm glad you didn't get hurt. I don't know what's going on with James right now. He's clearly going through something."

170

"It might be the whole traveling thing," Hannah suggested. "Maybe you should send him to a trainer the next time you go away."

Casey imagined how much money that would cost. "Sure," she agreed, but she knew there was no budget for professional training.

She was going to have to figure James out on her own.

Chapter Seventeen

THE NEXT WEEK fell into a pattern. An early ride, with so-so results. She stopped falling off every time James spooked, which was a plus. James did not stop spooking at everything he saw, which was a minus. Casey was at her wit's end with him. She was almost ready to ask for help on social media. *That's* how serious things were getting.

Luckily, she didn't have time to poke that particular hornet's nest. Because, in addition to handling everything left undone during her trip, the bosses had asked her to handle Tildy's upcoming show. And Sharon and Phillip made it clear they were expecting the same level of attention she'd put into setting up Goldie's series. To Casey's own chagrin, she didn't put up a fight when the order came down. As it turned out, she was still susceptible to a pat on the head from the bosses. They'd told her she'd done a wonderful job with Goldie's show set-up.

"You did better than we would have done," Phillip had assured her, earning himself a throat-clearing from Sharon. That bit of praise alone made her absolutely want to nail Tildy's show. She'd felt a satisfying little thrill at a job well done, and now she craved a repeat.

Plus, she was already looking forward to meeting up with Raina again. Casey hoped that she and Raina might have the same working relationship she'd enjoyed with Sharmayne—and that, even better, it would continue in person after the show set-up was complete. Raina was a trainer, too, which meant she might have some input on how Casey should deal with James.

As soon as they got together. It turned out both of them were having a bit of a hairy week, scheduling-wise. Casey tried a few times to set up a lunch. But Raina couldn't make any of her dates, and asked if they might try again next week.

By Friday, Casey was back in the weary grind of working alone. At least this time, she told herself, she had hope. Setting up her workstation for the morning, Casey let herself daydream about having a local friend again—someone closer to her own age, this time. As soon as she and Raina got together, things would start going smoothly—

"What's this?" Casey squinted at her screen. One of her spreadsheets was corrupted and wouldn't open. "Come on, buddy, don't do this to me."

She tried everything, but it quickly became clear that she was going to have to redo everything in the file. She'd simply lost miles and miles of data, along with tables and formulas she'd built herself. Gone.

Casey gave herself a moment to hang her head before she shook herself off and got back on the horse.

"Thanks, life," she muttered, tugging out a diary from her work bag. She had at least two hours of extra work to sort out now.

She'd gotten through a dozen rows of data when her phone buzzed. Casey picked it up, then put it down again without replying. Of course, it was *Hannah*. Wanting to know why she'd ridden alone this morning, why she hadn't waited for Hannah like she'd said she would. Had Casey made that promise? She flicked her eyes to the ceiling for a moment, trying to remember. But nothing came to mind. How was she supposed to remember *anything* outside of these mountains of work, anyway?

She glared at her phone screen again, the emojis and teenage drama written there in digital ink. Another bubble popped up. More complaints. Casey's fist tightened around the phone. Suddenly, she couldn't deal with the idea of Hannah. All of her baths and trims and cute selfies, while Casey had been working her ass off in California. *And* having some fun and riding, sure, but mainly working her ass off. To come back to what? A horse who had left her bruised from collarbone to ankle. The sad truth was, she was better off without Hannah. Had they ever really been friends? Or had Casey just been desperate for someone to ride with at Twin Palms, someone who seemed to get her a little bit?

"No, Hannah," Casey muttered, flipping her phone over. "You will not produce the guilt thing with me today. I'll deal with you later." And when the phone buzzed insistently again, she dropped it into her bag where it couldn't bother her anymore.

"Finally, some peace," she muttered, digging back in to her spreadsheet. For a moment, she relished the silence. Then she heard the front door open and close, followed by a hum of low voices. There were visitors in the living room.

Casey's head came up, and she looked around at the office door suspiciously. It wasn't a large condo; the office was at the end of a short hallway, so there was very little buffer from any noise in the living room or kitchen. But since it was just Casey and Brandon, two very quiet people, there had been no need to block sound when the other person was working.

"Who could he be having over?" Casey murmured, then scolded herself for being nosy. It was Brandon's house, too. If he wanted to have someone over to watch a game or something while she was still bent over her work, that was better than him sitting around, waiting for her. She should be a better girlfriend and remember that. And put in some earbuds. She picked up her phone once more, swiping *Do Not Disturb* so that Hannah couldn't butt in again, and put on some music to drown out the living room noise.

Then she didn't look up from her work for another two hours.

At five o'clock, as thunder rumbled outside and rain began to rattle on the curtained window, Casey straightened her neck and blinked. Coming out of a work trance was never easy, but at least she'd gotten the spreadsheet recovered and had rolled a little way into the vendor list. This part was easier than she'd expected—she'd overlooked the fact that their Florida vendors and sponsors were established customers, and they didn't require anywhere near the handholding that the newcomers in California had needed. She was feeling better about organizing Tildy's show series. It might not even take the full two weeks they'd given her to put it together.

"Which is good," Casey said, pushing back from her desk. "Because I have a ton of new ads to create at the end of next week. My *actual* job, marketing horse shows, who'd have thought?" She decided to make a pot of coffee. She'd do a little more work, then make it up to Brandon with a nice dinner somewhere.

Casey opened the bedroom door, stared for a moment, and gasped.

"Surprise!"

The roar went up from the living room, competition for the

thunder and heavy rain currently battering the windows. Casey stared at the crowd in her little condo and her hands flew to her mouth. Beneath vintage-style paper banners and pennants, with balloons crowding the corners of the room, a group of people were waving their hands and cheering for her. Noisemakers popped and shrilled. Next door, a dog began to bark, either in exasperation or because he wanted to be part of the fun.

Alison was the first to realize Casey didn't know what to make of the scene before her. She stepped forward and tugged Casey into a firm hug, her red hair falling over Casey's face like a curtain. "Brandon invited us down for you," she whispered into Casey's ear. "It's to make up for your missing your birthday during your trip."

"Oh my God, Alison, I don't even know how to react. He should have told me—look at me!" Casey stepped back as Alison's arms loosened around her, and she indicated her outfit: loose black leggings, a long blue shirt with a saggy neckline. "I don't even wear this shirt outside anymore."

"That's the danger with surprise parties," Alison agreed. "Come on, let's get you changed." She nudged Casey towards her bedroom, while calling over her shoulder, "Be right back!"

Alison was familiar with Casey's closet, and she'd tugged out one of her favorite sundresses before Casey had even gotten her old shirt tugged over her head. "Put that on and don't worry about anything else—you look fine," Alison instructed. "Well, tug a brush through your hair. I'm glad you kept those long bangs, it lets you do a messy chic thing even when you aren't thinking about it."

"I can't believe you drove all the way down here in this weather for a party in my living room," Casey moaned, pulling the dress on. The rain was hammering against the window with all the intensity of a hurricane. "And Heather, too? You guys are too good to me. Seriously.

You shouldn't have come."

"But you're glad we're here, right?"

Casey looked at her friend. All the loneliness and uncertainty of the past months welled up in her, and her throat seemed to close. She nodded, blinking back tears.

Alison sat on the bed next to her, tugging her close, and Casey gave in readily, tipping her head onto Alison's shoulder. "First of all, this was supposed to be down in the party pavilion, which would have been adorable. And if this rain ever stops, we'll take all the decorations down there and just keep the party going. Second of all, before we go home tonight, you're going to tell us what's going on, and we're going to fix it."

"It's too big to fix," Casey sighed.

"Nothing's too big to fix," Alison informed her. "Nothing."

And so, with a little help from her oldest friends, Casey enjoyed her surprise party. The rain did eventually stop, as Florida rain almost always does, and the party made a big game out of dragging the decorations down to the party pavilion. Soon the damp air was swirling with smoke as Brandon started one of his signature cook-outs, and everyone was swinging to music, topping off drinks, and generally having a wonderful time.

After a while talking to the guests—mainly Brandon's work friends —Casey settled down in a quietish corner with Heather and Alison. Heather had brought sparkling wine and procured a bottle of orange juice from the fridge. She set them in front of the birthday girl with a flourish.

"It's time for mimosas and problem solving," she declared. "I'll pour. You spill."

"I don't even know where to begin," Casey confessed.

Alison rolled her eyes. "I bet I know where to begin. He has four legs, and big brown eyes, and a snotty nose—"

"He does not have a snotty nose! You're thinking of a cow." Casey laughed despite herself. "But you're right. James is where it begins. I'm having a tough time with him. *And* at work. And the two things are not gelling at all. When work takes me away, I can't get anything done with James. But work pays me just enough to keep James here. There's no money to pay for help with him. And it shows, believe me."

"Shows how?" Alison put a mimosa in front of her.

"Well, I'd show you the bruises, but the sundress you chose is a little tough to pull up and everyone would get flashed."

"And you're not wearing cute underwear. I see your point." Alison nodded. "So you fell off?"

"Three times. In one morning." Casey took a deep gulp of her drink.

Heather whistled. "Three falls in one ride is..."

"Painful," Alison supplied.

"Embarrassing," Casey said. "And emblematic of a deeper problem which I don't want to face, because I can't do anything about it. I've ridden four times since then, and I've fallen off once, and I can't say he's improved much. I'm just more ready for his tricks now. I don't have a fix to actually stop them."

"Well, I mean...I'm sure you'll..." Out of her depth, Alison floundered for words.

Casey shook her head. "No, it's a problem which requires money to fix, trust me. And time. Neither of which I have."

There was a moment of silence, during which *Under Pressure* began to play on the boombox, and the rest of the party began to whoop and sing along. Brandon, bouncing away to the beat, waved at her with his spatula. Casey managed a wry grin.

"How are things with Brandon?" Heather asked suddenly.

Casey shrugged. "Things are fine."

"Just fine?" Heather didn't have an innocent voice, so the question came out as if part of a broader interrogation.

"Fine is fine," Casey insisted. "Brandon's not the issue here, believe me."

"It's all work," Alison confirmed. "Work and James."

"Yup. So, how do we fix it?"

Casey's two best friends in the world gave each other uncertain glances.

Casey sighed and tipped back her cup again, drinking every last drop of her mimosa. She couldn't expect two women, one of whom hadn't been near horses in more than fifteen years, and the other who had never been around them in her life, to fix an equestrian problem. And since Casey worked in horses, all of her problems were equestrian problems. This wasn't the work of civilians. "You don't have to solve it, guys," she said, holding her cup out for a refill. "Just knowing you're here and you care is enough."

And that was enough, for the rest of the evening. In fact, by the time they'd worked through the barbecue Brandon had prepared, and wiped the sauce from their faces, and done a little more dancing to work up their appetites for the cake, Casey was feeling like things were fine. Under control, even. Of course, she'd handle things. All the things.

She'd get James sorted out. She'd get through this rough period at work. She'd get her show schedule nailed down. She'd figure out what Brandon wanted from her with the whole learning-to-ride thing. She'd set up regular lunches or coffees with Raina. She'd even make up with Hannah.

Hell, maybe in six more months, her life would be so under

control, she'd get Brandon a puppy for Christmas. Why was she denying him a puppy? What kind of girlfriend stood in the way of a boyfriend who wanted a puppy? Not a girlfriend like her, that was for sure. Casey accepted another refill of her cup and swayed to the music. She had it all figured out. Well, not the details. But those would come to her.

Things were fine.

And then her phone buzzed.

She left the pavilion, walking across a few dozen feet of grass and pine needles to take the call. The evening was stretching lazily towards sunset, and although the sky had never properly cleared after the storms had rolled through, the gray layer above was shot through with cotton-candy pinks and gumball yellows. It would be a pretty evening, a perfect ending right before the mosquitoes showed up and broke up the party, Casey thought dreamily.

"Hello," she said into her phone, far too buzzed to achieve a professional *Hello this is Casey speaking.*

"Casey, this is Goldie."

"Goldie! How are you? I wish you were here. We're having a party, well, it's my birthday party, I didn't tell you but my birthday was two weeks ago while I was working with you, so my boyfriend threw me a surprise party—"

"Casey, we have a huge problem here. I'm looking at these invoices and I didn't agree to any of these costs. And who okayed these sponsors? I won't have anything to do with Victor Swanson, so he can take his trailer dealership straight to hell. He's not putting banners up in *my* arena. And—"

The list went on, Goldie's voice tearing apart every scrap of work Casey had done during her time in San Diego. She listened in stunned silence, her lips occasionally forming words of protest or defense, although the sounds didn't actually rise from her throat. As the party throbbed on a few dozen feet away, and people began to shout for cake, she saw Heather and Alison looking in her direction, gesturing to her. She shook her head, holding up a hand. *Stay away.*

She didn't want her friends to overhear any of this.

When Goldie had raged herself out, Casey thought she'd have the opportunity to refute the woman's claims. But Goldie didn't give her the chance. "I'll be speaking to your bosses," she snapped. The line clicked, and Goldie was gone.

Casey looked at her phone until the screen turned black. Then she looked up at the sky, the pink and yellow streaks spreading across the gray clouds. A whole horse show, planned with the working student because the trainer wouldn't do the work. How had she thought that was okay?

"And now I'm going to lose my job," she told the radiant sky.

"Casey! Cake!" Brandon was calling.

Casey looked back at the party. Her friends were still huddled close, watching her with concern.

But how could she explain the way equestrian problems worked? In the real world, her story wouldn't make any sense. No one would take threats from someone like Goldie seriously. She'd signed off on the work, or certainly her name was there, and the contracts were legal and that was that. If she didn't like it, if she had buyer's remorse, too bad.

If only things were that simple in the horse business. Goldie could *wreck* her with just a few sharp words. A few stories spread at feed stores. A few insinuations posted online. She could be branded untrustworthy, a know-nothing, a charlatan. And that was just the personal consequences. Goldie could do plenty of damage to Atlantic Horse Show Productions, too. The horse world was tightly bound, and all its connecting threads were made of gossip, as shiny and gossamer as a spider's web.

Casey wasn't about to burden Heather and Alison with this. Tomorrow, she'd call Raina. At least she had one ally in this strange, crazy world she'd made her home. For tonight, she had to put it aside, enjoy the party, and eat cake.

She swallowed and put on a smile. "Here I come!" she called. "Time for cake!"

Chapter Eighteen

WELL, THERE WAS one useful thing about riding first thing in the morning. It let Casey put off her work problems.

Somehow, she got through the weekend without hearing from Goldie again, which gave her hope—a tiny, winking star of hope which she clung to with all her being—that Goldie had gotten her outrage out of her system and it would not come up again. Perhaps it was a drunken rage, or a bad reaction to paying bills. After all, what did Casey really know about Goldie? It was possible she was completely impossible to deal with on a business level, like a lot of professional horse-people were, and behaved that way about every invoice she received.

Casey could only hope this was the right conclusion. She'd have to bring up the phone call on Monday morning. But until then? She woke up at five o'clock, shut off her alarm, and poured coffee into her travel mug. James first. Everything else later.

The other nice thing, she thought, pulling into the barn lane, was that she didn't have to deal with the Hannah problem yet. Casey wasn't sure how she wanted to work her relationship with Hannah going forward—were they friends? Riding buddies? Was neither a better choice?—because Hannah still rode in the afternoon, after school.

The barn lane had one little twist. Casey steered around it one-handed, sipping her coffee, and nearly turned right into the ditch when she saw Hannah's battered old car in front of the barn.

"It's six o'clock in the morning!" she shouted, slamming her mug back in the cupholder. "Why are you here?"

Hannah walked out of the barn and stood, arms folded, as Casey pulled up. Her chin was jutting, her shoulders were set.

Casey resisted the urge to turn the wheel, do a quick u-turn, and go home. Or go to the beach. Or go deep into the Everglades and never return to human habitation. Anything to simply not have other people and their needs clawing at her throat anymore. When had everyone gotten so needy? When had she become the person who could solve (or exacerbate) everyone else's problems? This was a worrisome trend. She didn't have any answers; people couldn't expect that of her. She should become a hermit, and soon.

Of course, she just parked the car and got out, coffee in hand. Of course, she just waved cheerfully, and said, "Hey, Hannah, good morning," as if nothing was wrong. Of course, she just walked right past the girl, who stood there silently, with her folded arms across her chest, staring into the distance as if she had decided to give Casey the cold shoulder and would remain a statue until Casey's ride was done, her horse was hosed off, and she was heading home.

Casey decided this was fine. Anything to avoid a predawn confrontation.

But no; Hannah followed her into the tack room. Casey gritted her teeth and put down her coffee mug, waiting for it to begin.

"Why don't you want to ride with me anymore?"

Hannah's voice cracked a little, knocking Casey off-balance.

"Of course I want to ride with you," she lied. "Why wouldn't I? Are you crazy?" *Stop doubling down on this, Casey.* "But I have to ride in the morning before work right now. And it storms so much in the evening. This is because of my crazy schedule and the weather. It's nothing personal." At least that much was true. Riding without Hannah was a perk, but not a major reason.

"Oh. But you stopped coming out at night. I didn't think you were riding at all until I asked Liz if she'd seen you." The hurt in Hannah's face was excruciating to look at. "She said you were riding five days a week. I felt so stupid."

"I thought you worked late nights," Casey improvised. "Aren't you allowed to work later now that you're sixteen?"

"I'm working dinner right now. My shift is seven to eleven, so it's easy to ride either morning or evening." Hannah's gaze dropped to the floor. "I thought you didn't want to see me."

Casey wanted to sit Hannah down and explain adulthood to her. Didn't Hannah understand adult friendships weren't about seeing each other every day, or even every month? Couldn't Hannah guess Casey was so busy trying to keep her head above water, she had no time to consider how a schedule change might affect someone else? Didn't she realize that most women in their thirties didn't *have* friendships outside of people they were forced to see daily, at offices or school pick-ups or kid events?

No, of course she didn't. Hannah was still living a life fraught with personal rivalries and shifting alliances. Forced proximity could breed high emotion, and high schoolers were definitely forced into one another's company. She didn't know all that stuff, all those big emotions and betrayals, just got wedged into professional nonsense later. Stuff that didn't really matter. Stuff like horse show sponsors for one freaking unrated series in the middle of nowhere, California.

Welp, so much for not thinking about work.

Casey sat down in one of the tack room's creaking lawn chairs and stared hard at Hannah until the girl met her eyes. "Hannah, listen to me. You know I like you. This isn't about finding someone else or wanting to be alone or anything like that. It's just about work being crazy and the weather being bad and needing to ride in a quiet arena without the other boarders in my way. But, if you want to ride with me in the morning, that's fine. Come ride with me. I'm happy to have you. Just understand that if I don't make it one day because I'm underwater with emails or something, that's not personal. I can't have you thinking things are like a roller coaster with us, okay? That's too stressful. My life is too difficult right now for you to need me holding your hand all the time. Make sense?"

Hannah nodded. "I won't do that. I promise."

Her words were so innocently passionate. *I promise.* Casey wanted to tell her nothing was that serious. They were just agreeing to ride together.

But Hannah would grow up in her own time. There was no point in trying to rush things. And maybe this could be a positive. She would test her progress with Hannah in the ring against riding alone last week. An A/B test, like she did with email subject lines at work.

"Okay," she said, standing up. "Let's get our tack and ride. I have to get out of here by eight-thirty."

James had always preferred the company of other horses. So it did not surprise Casey to find out he was immediately more steady with Caruso nearby. Even if Caruso was a bit of a psycho. She wished

Hannah had a quieter horse, one who could be a good influence on James. But she had a feeling that even if Hannah rode a push-button pony, by the end of the ride she'd have the thing leaping and rushing like a fire-breathing dragon. She had that effect on horses. Which was why she wouldn't be riding James again anytime soon.

Overall, though, the return to riding with Hannah wasn't so bad. Casey was able to mount without difficulty, and James moved around the arena with only a touch of extra spring to his stride. Sure, he spooked repeatedly at the pile of jump poles in the corner, and he almost unseated her when Hannah cantered by without warning and he bolted after the other horse, but all in all? A solid ride, nothing like the rodeos they'd put in last week. Casey felt heartened. Perhaps riding with Hannah was for the best. She gave James a pat and started to think about cooling him out.

Suddenly, Hannah was dismounting and handing her reins up to Casey to hold. Caruso touched noses with James and squealed. "What are we doing now?" Casey asked, trying fruitlessly to separate the two horses.

"Just setting some jumps really quick," Hannah called, bolting across the arena. She started dragging out jump poles two by two.

"Hannah, come on. The arena is really deep. We can't jump today. Let's wait and see if it dries out by tomorrow."

A rumble of thunder punctuated Casey's suggestion. *Really, bad weather this early?* She looked around and saw some storm clouds slowly rolling their way from the east. Storms off the Atlantic. She shook her head. Rain from inland in the afternoon, rain from the ocean in the morning. There was no winning here. "We should completely abandon riding for the summer," she muttered. The clouds grumbled their agreement.

"Crap, we have to hurry!" Hannah hustled back for more jump

poles.

"Hannah, no." Casey tugged on Caruso's reins as the horse nibbled flirtatiously along James's neck. "We need to cool these guys out and head in. Even if it wasn't going to storm, the footing here sucks. We can't be jumping on it when it's this soggy. Look, you're literally splashing in puddles just to get those standards set up."

Hannah barely glanced at her muddy riding boots. "We have to jump or we're *never* going to be ready to show," she insisted, placing the jump poles into their cups. "These aren't even that big."

"It's not the size that matters, it's the motion." Casey heard herself and grimaced. "I mean, it's the motion of taking off and landing. We need to be kind to their legs. Come on, Hannah, you're acting like a child. This is your horse's health we're talking about here. You can't play around with that."

"I'm not being a child. I'm taking my riding career seriously. Which is something you should do, too."

Casey stared at the girl. Then she sighed and shrugged it all off. "You know what? No. I will not argue this with you. It's thundering, I have a life to attend to, I have a million other things which need my attention. Thanks for riding with me, Hannah. Now take your horse and do what you want. I'm going in."

Hannah took Caruso's reins back without looking at Casey, or even thanking her for holding the horse while she set up jumps. But Casey decided she couldn't let that bother her. Hannah's temper tantrums were really the least of her concerns right now. She nudged James into a walk and they headed out of the arena, leaving Hannah and Caruso to do whatever the girl decided to do.

Hannah wasn't her responsibility, and thank goodness. She had more than enough of those.

Casey gave James a quick shower, her eye on the sky as the thunder grew louder. When the storm seemed to hold off, she gave him a few minutes of grazing before she put him in his stall. The other horses were already inside, eating their breakfasts.

Liz held up his grain bucket. "Can he eat now? Or is he still hot?"

Casey took the bucket. "He's good now, thanks. Giving him a little handful before we ride seems to keep him from getting too breakfast-crazy." She poured the grain and James slammed his nose into his feed-bin, rattling the stall front. "Mostly."

"Did Hannah think to give Caruso a nibble?"

Casey followed Liz's glance towards the arena, where Hannah was cantering Caruso over the jumps she'd set up. "I think so? I wasn't paying that much attention. She might have missed that step, honestly."

"Having a kid run wild here is trouble," Liz grunted. "They don't *think*. I like it better when she's here in the evening, when everyone can keep an eye on her. Is she going to ride with you in the mornings now?"

Casey considered the way they'd left things in the arena. "I really don't know," she admitted. "We just had argued about jumping in the mud, and, well, as you can see..." Thunder rolled overhead, rattling the metal barn roof. "Plus, she shouldn't be out in that weather, and I mentioned that, as well."

"So she doesn't listen to you anymore, either." Liz shook her head. "She's entered the terrible teens. Now we're in for it. This isn't the right barn for her. I ought to tell her parents that, but they can't afford to move her."

"Maybe she could get a job at another barn? She's already working here on Sunday mornings and she's got that busser job at JJ's, by the interstate. It could be time for her to just get a weekend job at a bigger barn, you know? She'd learn a lot if she could work off board with a trainer."

Liz just shook her head again, her mouth turning down grimly. "Barns don't hire kids like they used to. I could find her a job at a friend's place with lots of other kids, but they don't jump, and if she tries to run barrels with that scrawny little Anglo of hers, she'll snap his weedy legs. Well, just have to hope for the best. With any luck she'll get a boyfriend and forget all about horse showing."

That didn't sound like the best-case scenario to Casey, but she supposed she could see where Liz was coming from. Hannah had big dreams and high hopes, but she didn't have the sense or the knowledge to get where she wanted to go on her own, and she didn't have the money to buy the help she needed. Maybe the notorious "discovering boys" stage that derailed so many show careers was the only solution.

It was a sad thought.

Lightning flashed, startlingly bright, and Casey realized the early morning sunshine had been completely blotted out by the approaching storm. "Starting way too soon today," she said, picking up her damp saddle pad to move it to a more protected spot. "I better get going before my road floods again."

"Ah, Florida," Liz mused, gazing up at the threatening sky. "Wouldn't trade her for the world, but my, she's wet."

Wet isn't the half of it, Casey thought half an hour later, slopping up to her front door through a puddle which seemed to have overtaken the entire yard. It wrapped around the building like a moat. "We now live on an island," she announced as she stepped inside, "and it's not the tropical kind with lots of rum drinks."

"What a shame." Brandon was on the couch, typing away at his laptop. "I could use a rum drink to get me through these emails."

Casey didn't even want to think about her emails. But it was almost nine o'clock, and if she didn't start plowing through her Outlook inbox in the next fifteen minutes, she was bound to fall behind before they took their Monday morning call. She tugged off her wet boots, saying, "I have to take a thirty-second shower and skim my inbox." Thunder punctuated her words. "So pray the water main isn't struck by lightning."

"I'm always praying for that." Brandon looked up at last. "Holy cow, you got drowned on the way in here."

"Brandon, I'm not exaggerating when I say we live on an island right now. If this is going to be an all-day thing, we might want to sandbag the front door."

He looked concerned at that, setting down his laptop and standing to take a look.

Casey left him to enjoy his Mr. Fix-it persona and peeled off her breeches and riding shirt before stepping into the shower. She could have stayed under the hot water all morning, except for all the thunder booming around the building, and the pesky feeling that Goldie had sent some very choice emails to Sharon and Phillip on Friday night. She'd ignored her inbox all weekend, but now she was out of time.

Towel around her shoulders to keep her wet hair from soaking through her shirt, Casey flipped open her laptop and started scanning emails. There they were. From Goldie, at eleven twenty-three Friday night—it would have been just sort of late on Pacific time, but too late to capture anyone's attention on the east coast before morning. Then the concerned send from Sharon's box at eight-twelve this morning—someone got up early!—that was going to be a demand for an explanation, a reassurance that everything was all right, or a request for a resignation.

Which one would it be? Casey bit her lip and opened the email.

"She wants me to go back and fix it." Casey spread peanut butter on toast. The moment she'd read the email from Sharon, she'd gotten a powerful hunger for peanut butter. She'd read the email a second time, for good measure, then she'd gotten up and headed into the kitchen. She took down the jar of Nutella. The second reading had given her a craving for chocolate.

Sometimes comfort food was the best and only way to tackle an unsolvable problem.

"Back to San Diego?"

"Back to San Diego," Casey repeated. "They've delayed the call until ten so they can strategize damage control, but Sharon's first idea is simply to send me back out there."

Brandon was leaning on the kitchen island. "Obviously, she's not thinking clearly. It would cost them at least a thousand dollars to send you back out there and cover lodging and transportation and everything else included. Give it a few minutes. Let Sharon sit down with Phillip and talk it out. They'll probably call Goldie and tell her she needs to live with the sponsorships you've set up."

"I would love it if things were that straightforward. But this isn't the real world, Brandon. This is the horse world." Casey gave the Nutella-coated knife a careful lick before she tossed it in the sink. "Goldie will do something crazy, like tell everyone in California that Atlantic Horse Shows are no good and won't work with businesses and are setting her up for failure. And people will believe her. Horse people don't use Yelp. They just gossip with each other and repeat vicious rumors. The entire industry is founded on distrust."

Brandon gave her a skeptical look. "And this is your chosen profession?"

She rolled her eyes. "I only wanted to write ad copy and monitor social media budgets," she reminded him. "I never meant to be this hands-on."

"I guess that's your reply."

"What? That I don't want to do it?" She filled her mouth with toast. He had to be crazy. The Nutella stuck to the roof of her mouth and she closed her eyes, content for a moment.

"Well, you don't, and it's not in your job description, so technically..."

Casey swallowed. "*Technically* doesn't pay the board bill."

"So you're going to let James hold you hostage to this job that's making you crazy?"

"This isn't James's fault," Casey reminded him. "And anyway, I know what I'm going to do. The chocolate and peanut butter are fixing my brain. I'm going to nail Tildy's show series, and then I'm going to tell them to hire someone else to handle these things. I'll stay the course through Tildy's show. It's my way out of this."

"How is that different from what I just said—"

"Because I haven't succeeded yet," Casey said, shrugging. "I need a bargaining chip before I can go in and make that kind of demand. I need a win."

"And what makes you think Tildy will be a win, and not just Goldie, Part Two?"

Casey considered his question around another bite of toast. Suddenly, she had it. "Because Goldie acts like she doesn't care what goes on around the barn, but she really wants everyone to know she's the boss. This is her acting out to show Sharmayne who's in charge."

"You think."

"I know. Tildy, on the other hand, genuinely doesn't care as long as everyone is happy and everything looks pretty. So I can work with

Raina on this to make things look great, and she'll be fine with that. More than fine. It's what she wants." She popped the last of the toast into her mouth, feeling a surge of triumph. This was going to work out. A couple of weeks with Raina and the show would be on track, Tildy would be singing her praises, and she'd be able to walk up to Sharon and Phillip at their next in-house meeting and say: *Guys, I did my part. Now, fix this or I'm out.*

Brandon rubbed his hand over his face. "If you're sure," he said finally.

"I'm sure." Casey took out her phone and texted Raina. They had to have lunch immediately. No more excuses. "And anyway, this is going to be their last chance."

He smiled at her word choice. "*Their* last chance, not yours. I like the way you're thinking."

Casey gave him a sly smile in return. "Well, I have a good guy backing me up. It's easier to be strong when you've got someone on your side. Even if they don't know how crazy the horse business is."

Brandon reached for the peanut butter jar she'd left out. "By the way, I may not have mentioned it to you before, but my riding lessons are moving from Sunday morning to Mondays at five o'clock. So you'll have to find your own amusement tonight."

She lifted her eyebrows. "Does that mean I'm not invited to watch your ride?"

He grinned and stuck his finger in the peanut butter. "That's exactly what that means. I don't need your knowing looks or your criticism."

"Or my wincing, or covering my eyes with my hands?" Casey felt her face break into a grin. "That's fine. I always have a lot of work to catch up on, anyway." She started to head back to her office. "I gotta get on this call."

"Just wait and see!" Brandon called after her. "Before you know it, we'll be trail riding together! I expect casual, light-hearted fun on horseback!"

Casey just shook her head, still grinning as she threw herself back into her work chair. Casual, light-hearted fun on horseback. Apparently, Brandon had just met her. Only a stranger would think she was capable of such things.

Chapter Nineteen

RAINA WAS UP for lunch, so they met at a hole-in-the-wall diner in a strip mall near Tildy's farm. It was a good half-hour from Casey's place, and the rain was still falling, which made traffic snarl. She ran into the diner ten minutes late and full of apologies, but Raina was just sitting placidly in a booth, two iced teas and a dish of lemon wedges on the table already, and waved away Casey's need for approval.

"I haven't sat down since six a.m.," she laughed, pushing an iced tea glass towards Casey. "Every minute you buy me here is a reprieve for my tired feet." She stretched out her muddy boots for Casey to see.

"Well, that's good, because the more we can get done today, the better. I'm on a tight schedule to turn this around." Casey dropped a lemon wedge into her tea and grinned at Raina. "Are you ready to make a horse show happen?"

"I'm pumped! You know this is a dream come true."

I hope this goes better for you than it did for Sharmayne. Casey couldn't help but feel a wave of guilt wash over her when she thought of Sharmayne. Goldie had thrown her under the bus, judging by the way Sharon and Phillip presented things on their phone call. She'd done everything but blame the working student for California's current drought. Casey stood up for Sharmayne, explaining that Goldie had refused to work with her, but she knew her bosses found the situation pretty hard to believe.

If Goldie really chose to turn this sponsorship issue into a power play with her working student, it could easily signal the end of Sharmayne's career—or at least a massive setback. Without a reference from Goldie after years of work, the young woman would be hard-pressed to find a barn of equivalent size and volume to hire her. She'd have to start at the bottom again.

Then again, it was possible nothing came of it. They were still working solely based on last Friday's intel. That was the last time Goldie had contacted anyone. Casey used that fact to put her potential trip back to San Diego on hold.

"Casey?" Raina's head was tilted, her gaze questioning. "You with me, girl?"

"I'm all yours," Casey assured her, pushing Goldie out of her mind. She tugged a portfolio from her bag. "I'm glad you got the big table. Because we have a lot of stuff to go over."

Their working lunch stretched past the allotted hour, but Casey was in no hurry to go back to her desk, and a quick skim of her inbox told her nothing new had come up on the Goldie front. So when Raina suggested they go back to Tildy's farm to look over the facility again, Casey agreed readily.

By the time they arrived, the afternoon riding lessons were showing up. The driveway was full of expensive cars dropping off girls wearing plaid skirts and white shirts, slinging bags stuffed with their riding clothes and boots over their shoulders. "This is like a much more high-end version of my old barn," Casey laughed as they went into one of the tack rooms. "Just upgrade the cars by fifty thousand bucks or so."

"And all the drivers are nannies or personal drivers," Raina added. "Whereas you probably saw actual parents."

"Most of the time, yeah." Casey glanced around. Wooden locker doors surrounded them. A bench ran down the middle of the room, and there was a tack hook by the window. Otherwise, the room was spare and clean. "Nice tack room."

"This is the one I share with the staff." Raina opened a locker and started pulling out spare paddock boots and half-chaps. "The other stable wing has a boarder tack room with lockers, and there's a lesson tack room, too, but no one uses it except for the grooms—the students don't tack up here, obviously. This is a hands-off barn."

Casey wondered if Brandon was learning to tack up on his own. He'd continued to keep surprisingly close-lipped about his riding lessons, and she knew she'd have to wait him out. Brandon usually talked about things when he was ready, and not a moment before.

Raina pulled out a second set of boots. Casey raised her eyebrows. "This doesn't look like a barn tour."

"You know what the barn looks like," Raina said. "How about we go for a ride and look the place over?"

"This keeps happening to me," Casey joked. "Every barn I go to, they want to mount me up. Are you going to let me tack up on my own horse?"

"I might make you tack up mine," Raina laughed. "I told you, you're giving me a big break from work!"

"But your job is riding," Casey pointed out. "So you're still ending up in the saddle."

"Horse-people," Raina said with a big mock sigh. "No one ever accused us of having any sense."

Casey had to agree. She slipped off her flats and pulled on the boots Raina offered.

Once they were dressed to ride, Raina led Casey down the barn aisle. She stopped in front of a stall housing a bay mare. "This is Margarita," she said. "One of my father's horses. You can ride her, and I'll take out one of the horses I'm riding for Tildy."

Casey eyeballed the mare, who was watching them from within the stall with pricked ears. She was a huge warmblood, with a gleaming bay coat and rippling muscles. This was not a lesson horse who needed a tune-up. This was a proper show horse. "Um, what does Margarita do for a living?" Casey asked, picking up the mare's leather halter.

"She's a jumper," Raina called over her shoulder, already heading to get her own horse. "Does the one point two meters. Nothing too crazy. She's not Grand Prix yet, obviously."

One point two! Casey paused, her hand frozen on the door latch, trying to remember her jumping tables. If she recalled correctly, that was nearly four feet. Casey hadn't jumped that high since she'd been in school—and even then, she'd been fooling around, doing naughty teenager stuff, and probably shouldn't have been doing it. This mare was in serious work, even if Raina brushed it off because it wasn't Grand Prix yet.

Not Grand Prix *yet*—Casey stared at the mare, who was now pressing her nose against the stall bars, eager to see if Casey had brought any treats. "I'm pretty sure this horse is too good for me to ride," she called.

"Oh, just give her a carrot and get her out," Raina replied, not bothering to turn around. "I have the utmost faith in you."

"It's misplaced!"

"I promise you, it isn't."

"My father always tells me a self-esteem problem is the worst problem you can have in the saddle," Raina said, her hands loose on her horse's reins. "And I believe it feeds into everything else. You must believe in yourself first and foremost. You can't always worry everyone else is better than you, or further ahead than you, or knows something you don't."

"But sometimes those things are *true*," Casey argued. She tried to emulate Raina's effortless style in the saddle. Margarita had a long stride and a powerful walk, and she was wider than James. When she'd ridden new horses at Sungold, she'd been nervous, but not out of her depth. But Margarita worried her. "I can't ride this mare the way you can."

"But when does it really matter? You tell me you can't ride a horse like Margarita. But did I send you out here to jump a one point two meter course? Or did I say, let's go for a nice little ride around the farm to get a look at the place?"

"The second one," Casey admitted.

"Look, I'm not telling you to go into therapy for five years so you can think you're the equal of everyone around you," Raina said. "But I am saying you put a little too much faith in that Goldie woman, and when she double-crossed you, it hit you in the self-esteem feels. So you better just forget her."

"That's tough to do when she's still a client I have to deal with."

"Not much, though. Because you aren't going back to San Diego. We know you aren't. Your boyfriend was right when he said they wouldn't spend the money. So your part is done, even if she wants to cry about the bill. All you have to do now is run her social media campaign, right? And she's not part of that." Raina had absorbed an impressive amount of information about Casey's job and problems, which told Casey just how much talking she'd done over the course of the afternoon. That in itself was embarrassing...but Casey had to remind herself that being embarrassed probably wasn't what Raina wanted for her, either.

Raina was just being a friend, and she was so, so lucky to have her.

"Well, now that you solved my work life, want to fix my horse life?" she joked.

Raina turned in the saddle, her expression interested. "Sure. What's the problem?"

Brandon got home from his riding lesson well after seven, looking about as dirty and disheveled as Casey usually did after a tough ride. A smear of mud on his right ear, and another streak across his shirt on the right shoulder, made her suspect he was going to need the Epsom salts. "Take a tumble?" she asked sympathetically, giving him a careful kiss as he came in the door.

"I sure did." Brandon rubbed his arm. "It's slick out front."

"Riding can be really tough—wait, what? You fell out front?"

"Yeah." Brandon tugged off his boots. "Why, did you think I fell off in my lesson?" He grinned at her. "No such luck."

"Well, I didn't *hope* you fell off," she said defensively, although she had a sneaking suspicion that she had hoped, just a little.

"Don't worry, falling off is your thing. I won't take your thing."

"What a thing to say!"

He laughed and rubbed at his sore elbow. "I'm just kidding, and you know it. But seriously, I'm barely learning to lope. I'm not going to fall off anytime soon. When I do, I'll let you gloat as much as you want."

"Lope?" Casey couldn't believe her ears. "It's *canter*, Brandon. This is a cantering household."

"Why are there two different words for the exact same thing?"

She shrugged. "I have no idea."

"And jogging and trotting? It's the same thing. You're really telling me that if I say jog instead of trot, I'm going to be in trouble with you?"

"Brandon, don't try to renegotiate the terms of the horse world! In this house, we trot and we canter. Keep your jogging and your loping out at your own barn, you crazy person, you."

He laughed and planted a smacking kiss on her cheek. "I love it when you go all horse-girl on me," he told her, and then he headed off to the bathroom to shower.

Casey stared after him for a moment, her hand involuntarily resting on her cheek. He'd never said he loved the horse-girl in her before. In fact, he usually made her feel as if it was a level of crazy she needed to temper around him.

Brandon was changing, and she suspected it would not be long before the words *jog* and *lope* weren't the only equestrian themes they were having minor disagreements about.

"I guess I should have gotten him into lessons with Sky," she muttered, going into the kitchen to check on dinner. "Who knew? Most men never become horse husbands. I never would've guessed it was going to be an issue."

Chapter Twenty

SHARON CALLED BEFORE nine on Wednesday morning, while Casey was still at the barn. She'd enjoyed a fairly good ride, and her mood was sunny, although Hannah hadn't shown up, and Casey was half-hoping, half-worried that she'd broken their friendship beyond repair. She reached for the phone and grimaced a little when she saw Sharon's name on the screen.

"Hey, Sharon." She realized she didn't sound at all enthused to speak to her boss, so she tried to perk up her phone voice a little. "Hope things are great up in Merritt Island! They're sunny and warm here."

"Pretty much the same," Sharon replied. Casey tried to detect any hint of frostiness in her voice, but couldn't pick up on anything unusual. "You know, summer days. Florida. All kind of the same. I was just calling—um, what's that noise?"

Casey glanced at James, who was digging into his breakfast with the sort of violence usually attributed to lions or tigers at feeding time. "Uh, just the plumber working on the sink in the kitchen."

Liz, cleaning a stall nearby, looked at her with a rare grin on her leathery face, but said nothing. Casey shrugged elaborately. *My boss,* she mouthed.

Sharon accepted the explanation. "Oh, got it. Well, I wanted to update you on the Sungold show situation."

Casey was at attention. "Yes?"

"We talked to Goldie yesterday. And things seemed straightened out. We offered to have you go back to renegotiate some of the contract—"

Casey ground her teeth together, a motion her dentist had strictly forbidden.

"—but Goldie insisted that wouldn't be necessary. She said she will handle replacing the deal she doesn't like."

"Excuse me?"

"She has a personal issue with one vendor. She's going to cancel that contract and bring in a replacement sponsor herself."

Casey took a breath and walked out of the barn aisle. She turned her face up to the watery sun. "Sharon, I don't think that's a good idea."

"You don't! Well, it's what we have, and—"

"No, listen—we have our name on top of this show. Every piece of literature and every advertisement says *Atlantic Horse Show Productions Presents* above the farm name. Above the series name. Above everything. What if she chooses some completely inappropriate business to sponsor her?"

"Like what?"

Casey bit her lip. There was a lot she could say right now that might not go over well with Sharon, simply because of their age gap. But Casey hadn't been working in social media for the past seven years for nothing. She knew how to vet companies and make sure they weren't problematic. It was second nature for her to dig into internet histories and really do a deep dive into what founders, owners, and official business statements were putting out there. And she'd nixed more than a few companies as potential sponsors because they'd allied themselves, even if it did not seem deliberate, with people or groups guilty of hate speech. The people who showed horses didn't exist in the same vacuum as their trainers. They had causes and morals they cared about. Things which might not be on the radar of a sixty-something-year-old woman who ate, breathed, and slept the horses on her farm, and nothing else.

Casey didn't see the divide as a political one. She saw it as a kindness gap. Some people were kind and embraced everyone. Some people were not. She made sure they only did business with people who appeared to be on the kind side of the gap. That way, she figured, no one's feelings got hurt, and everyone felt welcome at the horse show.

But Sharon didn't know about any of this.

"I'm not saying any one business in particular is problematic," Casey replied, choosing her words with care. "I am just saying that I put every potential sponsor through a rigorous process to make sure we don't accidentally step into any internet landmines. And there is absolutely no chance Goldie is going to choose a sponsor with the same level of care. And then there's the simple fact that Victor Swanson runs an important trailer dealership in the region, and he's going to be offended when his contract is canceled. So we're going to lose him for future events."

Sharon sighed into the speaker. "How did this happen? You said before she was good people. Can you explain what went wrong?"

"She was completely hands off until she decided her working

student was stealing her thunder." Casey shrugged her shoulders. "It's as simple as that, in my opinion. Now she's showing that she's the one in control."

"Well, it's done," Sharon said briskly, washing her hands of the problem. "I told her to go ahead. You concentrate on Tildy's show and the marketing. And I have one more request."

Casey held her breath, squinting up at the clouds overtaking the sun. She couldn't take on anymore.

"Can you go to the Sheridan Farms show next weekend and just—hold Mrs. Sheridan's hand, please? It's a one-off show and it shouldn't create any issues, but she's nervous, and I promised her we'd send a representative to deal with any problems as they arise. We have to go to Jacksonville."

The Sheridan Farms show was about an hour away. Casey shook her head at the sky. *Unbelievable,* she thought.

"Casey? We really need this. Sorry to infringe on your weekend plans, but we have the Jacksonville series kicking off, and we have to be there. You know it's huge. Our biggest of the year."

Casey knew. Three arenas, four days, hundreds and hundreds of competitors. The company's biggest brag. The Sheridan show, on the other hand, was one day, one arena, at a boarding stable. It was really just a schooling show. There was almost no chance anything would go wrong, unless a hurricane blew it away. And the ten-day outlook was in her favor, there. She'd go, but it would be a waste of day, just hanging around a horse show with nothing to do. Sounded awful...

And suddenly, Casey had an idea. An absolutely brilliant, fantastic, amazing idea.

"No problem," she told Sharon. "You guys go to Jacksonville. I'll handle everything here."

Liz was mucking out around James when Casey slipped her phone into her pocket and meandered back into the barn. She glanced up. "You know, you remind me of why I don't want a job," Liz told her. "Sometimes I need that."

"Happy to be of service." Casey grinned. "You remind me of why I need my own truck and trailer." She lifted her eyebrows suggestively.

Liz sighed. "Yes, you can use it. Weekend after next?"

"Yes. Just Saturday."

"It'll be parked here Friday night. And what about Hannah?"

Casey shrugged. "I haven't figured out what to do with Hannah," she said. "But this is the perfect chance to take James to his first show in a while, whether or not I bring her and Caruso."

The plan was perfect. She didn't have to show James; she'd just bring him over, put him in a stall—Mrs. Sheridan would give her a stall if she asked—and when the show was running like clockwork, as she knew it would, she would take him out for some walks, maybe saddle him up, maybe ride him, maybe put him in a class. All depending on his reaction, of course. She wouldn't push him. The plan wouldn't work if she got carted off the property in an ambulance. Sharon and Phillip would find out about *that*.

And if she put a little extra emphasis on their schooling rides this week, well, it would be good for both of them to ramp things back up. She'd been taking it easy on him over the past week or two, trying to get his head straightened out. Now he ought to be used to their morning rides, and ready to work hard.

Yes, it was a perfect plan.

Naturally, the moment Casey decided she was going to take James to a show, Brandon began to talk about going on trail rides. It quickly became his number one topic of conversation, morning, noon and night, and Casey wished he had more meetings to take him into the office. It was a little annoying to walk out of her office for coffee and find him in the kitchen, wanting to talk to her about her weekend plans.

"Annoying in an incredibly gratifying way," she had to amend when Raina cocked her head, smiled, and asked how it could be annoying to have a boyfriend who was learning to ride horses just so he could spend more time with her. "Annoying in a, 'Wow, this is going to take some time to get used to,' kind of way."

Raina just laughed and went back to the sponsor proposals Casey had pushed her way.

Things were going well with Tildy's show—almost too well. In fact, Casey's entire week was going really well, aside from the whole Brandon situation. So it didn't really come as a surprise late in the week when she was untacking James after a morning ride and looked down at her buzzing phone to see a San Diego number. Of *course,* someone would call her from San Diego, she thought. Just when she'd thought she could wash her hands of Goldie and her drama.

"Hello?" she asked cautiously, strongly considering hanging up if it turned out the caller was Goldie. She tucked the phone under her ear as she lifted the saddle and saddle pad from James's back.

"Casey? It's Sharmayne."

"Hey!" Relief flooded through her, coupled with an odd, new tension: she was still worried that their partnership had threatened Sharmayne's job with Goldie. Was Sharmayne calling to tell her she'd been fired? Casey felt her stomach perform a nervous little flip. She settled the saddle on a nearby sawhorse. "I've been thinking about you. How are things out there?"

"It's...a little weird," Sharmayne confessed. Her voice was low; she must be worried Goldie or someone else around the barn would overhear. "Goldie's totally acting like we did the whole show behind her back. I feel like—like maybe things are coming to their natural end, out here."

"Oh, no. Isn't that always the way?" Casey sighed and rubbed at her hair, loosening her ponytail. She dug into her pocket for a cookie and handed it to James, who gobbled it up. "Why are so many horse trainers like this?"

"I don't know, I really don't. But I guess it's okay. These jobs don't last forever. We all know that. And I was here a long time. It was past time to find something of my own."

"So, what's next? Are you job hunting? Still looking at those east coast barns?"

"Thinking about it. Actually, I'm thinking about Florida."

"Oh!" Casey imagined Sharmayne living nearby. Two friends in town? Was this what winning the lottery felt like? "That would be great! You'd be fantastic here. I'd love to have you in South Florida, honestly."

"Well, I like that reaction! Any leads for me?"

"I like how you get right to the punch," Casey laughed. "But I'd have to talk to some other people. I'm a little isolated, just dealing with one or two barns at a time. Not really in the whole show culture here, as crazy as that sounds."

"Well, it makes sense. You're planning behind the scenes, not getting out there to a new show every weekend."

"Exactly." Casey was glad Sharmayne understood. It could be hard when friends came seeking suggestions. She was happy to give a reference, but an introduction would be tough to come by. "I'll let you know if I hear anything, okay?"

"That would be great. And, Casey?"

"Yeah?"

"Don't hesitate, okay? Day or night."

The urgency in Sharmayne's request nearly broke Casey's heart. That's how bad it was for her out there. Waiting by the phone, day or night, hoping for a chance to get out. "I'll see what I can do," she promised.

Once she was off the phone, Casey wrapped her arms around James's hot neck and gave him an enormous hug. "I used to spend a lot of time regretting not being a pro in this business," she told her horse. "But now I'm seeing just what being a professional looks like. And it's not the rainbows and unicorns that Sky made it out to be."

James shook his head and ducked his nose to her pocket, unconcerned with her human problems. He just wanted food. As usual.

"We'll see who's ignoring who this weekend," Casey warned him, handing over another cookie.

"Want to ride with me this weekend?" Brandon asked.

Casey paused, halfway through tugging off a boot. She stared up at him through her bangs. "Brandon, I just came in the door."

"Well, I'm sorry, but it's Thursday and if I'm going to borrow Chico, I need to let Maria know." There was a touch of defensiveness in his voice. "She said I can ride him on Saturday morning, if you're willing to go with me." Brandon had gotten Maria's number somewhere, heaven only knew where, and she was delighted to offer Chico's services to Brandon. Casey suspected this was Maria's way of insisting, once again, that James needed time out of the arena. The notion put her back up.

"It's not a question of being *willing,* Brandon. I'm taking James to a show in a week. I'd like for him to be ready to go into the arena and go around like a gentleman. That means work." She bent over her boots again. "No time to waste, unfortunately."

"It always means work," Brandon scoffed. "So that's it? I take horseback riding lessons for months so that we can have fun together, and you're not going to ride with me?"

Casey threw herself onto the sofa, heedless of her sweaty, horsey clothes. Surely this wasn't really happening. What was her life coming to? Her boyfriend was mad at her for not having time to ride the range with him? Casey could honestly say she had not seen this coming. "I didn't say I wouldn't ride with you."

"Well, it sounds like it."

"Can you *please* just let me get through the show in one piece? And then we will talk about riding together?"

"Fine," Brandon huffed. "But I like riding. I'm not going to quit because you don't want me around." He stalked into their bedroom and closed the door behind him.

Casey looked at their closed bedroom door. She wanted a shower and a change of clothes before she sat down at her laptop. And now both were behind that door, with Brandon, who was planning on staying in their room and pouting for goodness knew how long. He needed his own office to hide in, she thought.

"We need a bigger place," she sighed to herself, and somehow that made things even worse. They couldn't afford a bigger place. It was one more thing on the list of things they couldn't change. The condo was too small. The traffic was too snarled. Her friends were too far away. Her barn was too basic. Her goals were impossible. Her boyfriend was probably going to tire of her and break up with her. She balled her fists and looked up at the ceiling, suddenly disheartened by everything.

Coming to West Palm had been a mistake.

Everything had been a mistake.

Her phone pinged, and she picked it up with an exasperated sigh.

"What now?" she muttered. Then she saw the text message and laughed.

Sorry I'm being such a big baby, Brandon had written. *Love you.*

"You dork," she said aloud, and then she went into the bedroom to call him that in person.

Chapter Twenty-One

SETTING A SHOW date weeks or months in the future was scary enough. Setting one for the following weekend was absolutely crazy. And yet, Casey thought, I did it. And here I am. Sitting on James, waiting for my class to be called.

Well, *sitting* on James was a bit of an understatement. Casey was technically in a seated position in the saddle, but she was working her butt off on James. The show-ground atmosphere had her horse anxious, confused, and flighty, and Casey was trying to keep him settled and give the appearance of a cool, collected, *trained* horse with every muscle in her body.

"Stand up, buddy, everyone's looking at us," she breathed desperately, as he tried to launch himself forward once again. He was the only one acting like a fool. The theme of the Sheridan show could have been "School Horses Step Out." It was a regular day for most of the quiet, experienced horses standing around the arena or trotting around the warm-up. Their easy-breezy demeanor made James stand out like a zebra in a field of buffalo.

A *dancing, hyperactive* zebra.

But it was early yet, Casey reminded herself again. She told herself this every time James did something else foolish, like spook at a paper number flapping on another rider's back, or careen backwards when an overhead loudspeaker had the temerity to make a gargling announcement. All this was fine, Casey told herself. This was good experience for her silly little ex-racehorse, and he would calm down as the day wore on. She was so determined to manifest good things that she entered him in a few classes. When she had asked Mrs. Sheridan about the possibility of bringing her horse along for the day, that kind woman hadn't just offered her a free stall, she'd given her carte blanche to enter as many classes as she liked, free of charge.

"I'm sure everything will go smoothly," Mrs. Sheridan assured her, a tiny quaver of age in her voice—she was another senior member of the horse community, although not wealthy like Tildy. Lorraine Sheridan had been teaching riding since the early days of the great winter migration to south Florida, and her prices hadn't kept up with inflation. "I'll just feel better with you here, in case we *do* need any help. So bring your horse, have some fun, and we'll call you if we need you."

Energized by the way her plan was coming together, Casey submitted a few entries ahead of time. She'd chosen classes which were spread out a bit, starting early with some walk-trot to warm him up; later, as the sun grew higher, and the day really heated up, she'd try him in some low jumping classes. Not that she wanted to wear out poor James by riding him during the heat of the day, but... No, Casey had to admit, that was exactly what she wanted to do. At least the jumping was in a covered ring. He would not get heat stroke or anything, but he wouldn't have a lot of excess energy to spend on making her crazy. And it would make it a lot easier, she reasoned, to finish on a good note for the day.

James spotted a discarded napkin on the ground and nearly went up on his hind legs.

"You're giving me gray hair," Casey groaned, putting her leg on and pushing him forward.

Nearby, a child on a sleepy-looking Appaloosa gave her an interested, appraising look. "That horse doing okay?" she asked Casey.

"He's fine." Casey tugged James in a circle, insisting he look at the napkin. Boy, was he going to be embarrassed when he realized he was freaking out about a piece of paper! "It's been a while since he was at a show."

"Where's your trainer?" The child asked. She put a hand up to check the big blue bows on her pigtails. "You want me to find her for you?"

Oh boy, do I ever. "I'm fine, thanks," Casey said, trying to keep her voice from sounding too shrill. "We just need to warm up a little more!"

James plunged to a quivering halt and tipped his nose towards the offending napkin. He snorted—that long, reverberating snort horses use to indicate their extreme skepticism of an object. Heads turned; there were a few chuckles as other riders saw the equine/napkin face-off.

Casey's cheeks warmed. Now she really hoped no one required her assistance today. It would be incredibly embarrassing to show up as the organizer and be recognized as the girl on the horse who was afraid of paper products.

Just her luck, really.

The loudspeaker overhead crackled, gathering itself to call the next class. With a start that made her clutch the reins in a minor panic of her own, Casey realized they were calling her walk-trot class. James skittered beneath her as she gathered the reins, tearing him away from his napkin dilemma. Maybe he'd be good, she thought. He liked being in the arena with other horses. Maybe that was where he'd focus.

Miracles happened, right?

After the class, Casey wasn't sure which gods she should be thanking. All she knew was, miracles *did* happen.

She clutched her ribbon so tightly she was afraid she was going to crease the satin. But seriously, what a triumph! To take James into a show-ring for the first time since last fall, without a trainer's help, and get him around nicely enough for a ribbon! Even a green one! Even in walk-trot! Even against a bunch of kids!

"Sixth place is really pretty," she muttered, admiring the little green ribbon as she guided James through the pack of horses surrounding the arena gate. The color would pop nicely against his dark coat. She only wished she had someone to take a picture of them with it. Maybe if she'd told Brandon what she was up to...but she'd instinctively known Brandon wouldn't approve of her taking James to a show she was technically working. She'd admit it tonight—no, she'd *announce* it tonight, describing the show as the triumph it would be. And in the meantime, a selfie would have to do. Casey dismounted, held the ribbon just out of James's grasping teeth, and grinned for her phone camera.

They had a long break before the afternoon jumping classes. Casey untacked and put James into his stall. He'd gone straight back to being a rubber ball after the class, and the stall didn't seem to help. For a moment, she watched him alternate between grabbing bites of hay and spinning in anxious circles. But there was nothing she could do to calm him. Casey sighed and headed off to check on the show secretary. Time to make sure everything was still going to plan. They'd made it to ten o'clock without calling her for anything, and she felt pretty good about that.

As she walked across the show-grounds, the clouds slowly covered the sky, and a long, low rumble of thunder in the distance served as a reminder: this was Florida in June, and just because they thought they could run a show in tropical weather didn't mean the sky had to cooperate. A few riders were glancing at one another, then up at the clouds, shaking their heads. But most ignored the impending storm. That was the thing about riders: they put riding, and showing in particular, ahead of everything else. Even when it was incredibly dangerous.

Casey ducked into the large white tent serving as show office, where a queue of junior riders were leaving with their packets tucked against their chests. Laura, the fresh-faced barn manager who had taken on secretary duties, greeted her with enthusiasm. "Casey! How is your morning going? I heard your name over the P.A. system earlier. Congrats on getting a ribbon already!"

"Thank you! I left it back on his stall," Casey added, noticing a lot of the younger set were wearing their ribbons on their belts as they ran around the show-grounds. "Green is pretty, but it makes my hips look wide."

"Totally understandable," Laura laughed. "Well, things are going great here. We almost had an issue when the engineer didn't show up this morning, but luckily Vance knows all about setting up the P.A. and everything else was ready to go."

"The engineer didn't show?" Casey's eyebrows came together. "That's odd. Sharon told me he's very reliable."

"It's no problem. He'd just be hanging around all day, anyway. Our arena lighting is new, and, like I said, we figured out the P.A." Laura shrugged it off. "Sit down and have something to drink! You look hot."

Casey accepted the chair pushed her way and a can of iced tea from the cooler. "I usually have a steadfast rule against showing in June, and this is why," she grimaced. "It's so humid I could melt right out of the saddle."

"But you got a ribbon," Laura said knowingly. "So you'll be mounting up again, in, what?"

"About two hours." Casey laughed begrudgingly. "I'm a fool for ribbons."

"We all are." Laura turned her attention to a tall trainer in gleaming boots, who requested the show packets for twelve students.

Casey leaned back in her chair, determined to enjoy the cool fan blowing on her and the cold iced tea in her hand for as long as she could. The thunder outside was growing more insistent, and she hoped it would pass while she was sitting here under shelter...even if the shelter was just a tent.

A half-hour later, Casey was promising herself she'd never take a storm for granted again. If she survived. Was she being dramatic? She gripped the flapping canvas above her head, wincing as the wind tried to peel the tent away from the ground. It wasn't easy to convince herself to hang on—the thunder crashing around, the blinding lightning flashing through the fabric, and the pounding onslaught of rain were all conspiring to make her feel like the best place to be right now would be under the table. And she was pretty sure that wasn't just a feeling. That was the damn truth.

No, she wasn't being dramatic. Things were bad.

Laura cast her a desperate look from the other side of the tent. "Casey, the tent isn't going to hold! We have to get this stuff into bins! Can you hang on alone?"

Casey wanted to put herself into a bin. But she just nodded, hanging on grimly. Laura started packing the laptop and packets into the waterproof bins stacked in one corner. The edges of the tent lifted as wind wailed around them, and a blinding flash of lightning coincided with an ear-splitting crash of thunder.

This is scary, this is fine, this is scary, this is fine. Casey's internal voice was not providing her with a lot to hold onto. She watched Laura pound the last lid onto the bins before sliding them under the table. Another flash of lightning caused spots to dance before her eyes, and she wondered with increasing worry if everyone had gotten to a safe shelter. Surely no one had remained out in the storm? Everyone had stalls, or at the very least, had gotten their horses back into their trailers?

And none of the horse trailers could flip over in this wind, right? That wasn't a thing, was it?

Things had been going so well. She'd been sitting there, drinking her iced tea, listening to Laura talk about the different trainers at the show. Thinking to herself about what a great job they'd all done with this weekend. Thinking that she really was doing some interesting, useful work at Atlantic Horse Show Productions, and considering the possibility that she should stop beating herself up about the time her job took from her and simply embrace the chaos for a while. Sure, it was thundering outside, and the wind was picking up, but this was Florida. No one expected a day without a thunderstorm.

Then everyone's phones went off at the same time.

Not a ringtone, but that high-pitched government alarm which was built into every smartphone: it blared like a siren, from the inner pockets of show coats and the cupholders of golf carts and the back pockets of jeans and the hidden compartments of grooming bags. It sounded like the end of the world. Horses snorted and shied, hysterical kids screamed, parents and trainers shouted for everyone to calm down and *shut off their phones.*

Casey had dug her phone out of her breeches pocket with difficulty, nearly slapping it to the ground in her blind urgency to shut the damn noise off, and next to her Laura was doing the same thing, poking desperately at the screen as if she'd forgotten how to disengage her own screen lock. All around them, the squeal was replaced by silence.

Silence, and the low, ominous rumble of thunder. For half a second, a long breathless half a second, there was quiet, only the sky daring to speak. But as people finally registered the messages they'd received, they began to read aloud, a low chant of discordant voices. *A Severe Thunderstorm Warning has been issued...wind gusts of sixty-five miles an hour...a brief tornado is possible...*

Casey looked at Laura, her eyes round with shock. "We need to get out of this tent."

Then the storm rushed over them with a howl of wind and the rattle of tropical raindrops.

And so here they were.

As the tent tore itself from her fingers at last, Casey dove under the table with Laura, and the entire structure sagged over them, flopping over the table. She clutched a table leg with one hand and a bin of heavy files with the other, certain they were her only anchors to the earth. The wind was deepening its voice, dipping from a howl to a roar. Casey did some quick assessments of the way she was living her life. If this wasn't a tornado, and they weren't blown away, she'd make some changes in her life. She'd stop showing in summer, for one thing. She'd have a talk with Sharon and Phillip about her role in the company. And she'd spend more time with Brandon. She'd go on trail rides with Brandon, for heaven's sake! He was just trying to see more of her! Maybe they'd get a dog. It was time they got a dog. She was being selfish. The canvas flapped around her legs, and she was getting soaked through, and the table was lurching in her grip...this was it...

With a gasp and a blast of chilly wind, the storm suddenly began to let up.

Chapter Twenty-Two

THE WIND HAD dropped to a friendly breeze, and the rain pattered gently on the tent-draped table over her head. Casey still wanted to stay put, though. And she thought Laura felt the same way. Right here, under this table, nothing would get to them. There was no telling what was going on outside, not with the collapsed tent folds blocking out the daylight. But eventually someone would let them out —she already heard voices, as the rain dissipated and the thunder drew away—so she was sure that soon, someone would notice the show secretary's tent was in a pile, and think to check and see if the show secretary might be underneath all that the mess.

Huddled across from her, Laura had her eyes tightly closed, still gripping the table leg with both hands. She slowly opened them, saw Casey watching her, and blinked a few times, like an owl waking up from a deep sleep. "I've lived in Florida my whole life..." she began, her words trailing off as if she'd run out of air.

"And I've never been so scared of a storm," Casey finished for her.

"Same. I hope someone—oh, here we go." The tent was lifting—people were talking, men with sharp voices. Horse show dads, she thought. Thank goodness for horse show dads.

"And *up!*" The tent lifted away from them, showering down a waterfall of cold water. Casey gasped, and Laura shrieked, and a few of the men swore in astonishment.

"You were in here the whole time?" The closest one asked. He was drenched to the skin, rainwater soaked through his classic horse show dad outfit of race-car jersey, khaki shorts, and unfashionable sneakers. "We figured you'd run into one of the barns. Or the covered ring, although it's kind of full."

He gestured, and as Casey stood up on shaking legs, she saw that the covered arena was jam-packed with horses and riders, most of them still looking pretty wild-eyed. A few were leading their horses from the arena, yelling for moms or trainers. A couple of the kids, she noticed with a pang, were crying.

And that wasn't the only activity. Wet competitors milled about the barns, where they'd taken refuge under the overhangs but still gotten drenched by the blowing rain. Kids were hanging over the stall doors where trainers and parents must have hustled them as the storm blew in, asking if it was safe to come out yet. Trainers and grooms were desperately trying to salvage stall drapes and camp chairs which were scattered through the muddy puddles around the barns. And in the outdoor arena, Casey was astonished to see, every single jump had been blown over, the poles rolling away and the silk flowers scattered across the clay footing.

Beside her, Laura brushed dirty water from her paddock boots and straightened her top. "Do we think anyone got hurt?" she asked the dad.

"Honestly, it doesn't look like it," he replied. "Paramedics are making their way around, checking for any problems. But everyone got to shelter. Thank goodness for that phone alert. It was literally just in time. Okay, I would have appreciated getting it a few minutes beforehand and missing out on this soaking." He plucked at his wet shirt. "But the high winds could have really hurt someone. You guys are lucky."

Casey remembered the eerie sound of all those phones shrieking at once and shivered.

"You cold? We can find you a dry hoodie somewhere, I'll bet. These trainers with a lot of kids know to pack everything but the kitchen sink." The dad started towards the closest barn before Casey had a chance to stop him. She turned to Laura, who was already taking charge of the other men and their muscle.

"I need to go check on James," she said. "And then I'll be right back."

"No problem," Laura said distractedly. "But can you try to find some members of the ground crew and get them setting up jumps? The radios don't seem to be working."

"Sure." The loss of communications was mildly concerning. What would cause that? A lightning strike? She wished the engineer had shown up to put things right. Still, they could run a horse show without radios. The farm wasn't that big. They'd just have to recruit some kids to be runners between the judge's stand and the announcer's booth. Assuming she could find some kids who weren't too shell-shocked for the job.

Casey left Laura to oversee the tent-raising and set off across the wet ground, sidestepping puddles at first until she realized there was no keeping her boots dry, then just sloshing through them. The barn where James was stabled was just a few hundred feet away, and she was pleased to see that despite the storm and chaos, he had finally settled down, only occasionally glancing over the stall door when another horse walked by.

"You're a real Florida-bred, aren't you?" She gave him a scratch on the neck and let him get back to his eating. Her tack had gotten wet, but if she was going to ride again this afternoon, all she could do was let it air-dry. It would have to wait until tonight for a good oiling. Or, more likely, until tomorrow. Casey wasn't sure how much extra time she was going to want to spend at the barn tonight. She didn't have a change of clothes.

Reassured that things would be back to normal soon, she rooted a towel out of her tack box and draped it over her saddle to soak up some of the water. As she started back towards the arenas, she saw the jump crew was already working to get the jumps reset, and the tent was taking shape. Everything was going to be fine, she told herself. Well, once all these kids stopped crying.

The storm clouds lingered, leaving the midday unusually dark, with occasional bursts of rain. Casey consulted her phone and found a tropical low had spun up out of nowhere near the Bahamas. Every meteorologist in the area with a Twitter account assured her that the afternoon would be squally, with sudden downpours and gusty winds. Nothing as nasty as that first line, she read, feeling a rise of relief in her chest. Just disruptive, fast-moving rainstorms. She could handle that. They could all handle that.

She was thankful the rest of the day's jumping classes were in the covered arena. While the gusting wind might still be an issue, the arena footing would stay mostly dry. As long as the competitors who had gotten beat up by the storm decided to stick around and finish the show-day, the Sheridan show would continue—and perhaps even be considered a success.

Casey walked over to the covered arena to watch the jump crew rake out the footing around the fences, which had been torn up by the sheltering horses during the storm. It was dark, and she glanced up at the shadowy rafters. The big lights in the ceiling weren't switched on. Possibly, they just hadn't gotten to it yet. Those lights were expensive to run.

She watched a member of the crew walk over to the light switches on the wall. He started flipping up the covers and turning the switches.

Nothing happened.

But that didn't matter, Casey told herself. It took a minute for those lights to warm up. They'd be on in a minute.

The guy who had flipped the light switches was looking up at the ceiling expectantly.

Nothing happened.

He put his hands on his hips, growing impatient. Still nothing. He called out to the crew and pointed up.

Casey felt her heart rise into her throat. It was too dark to ride in the arena; the clouds were thickening again, another squall was on its way. No one's phones were shrieking again. Just rain, and as soon as the lights switched on, they could use this arena, so rain was fine...

She felt her phone buzzing in her pocket and experienced a new level of anxiety when she saw it was Sharon texting.

Where are you? Lorraine Sheridan is looking everywhere for you. Laura told her you're showing and probably in the saddle, but you wouldn't be doing that when you're working a show? Would you?

Oh God, Casey thought. She'd been caught.

Pulling James up at one side of the arena, Casey quickly dialed Mrs. Sheridan.

"Casey! I didn't have your cell phone number. My God." Mrs.

Sheridan's voice was high-pitched, panicky. "We need an engineer, fast. Laura tells me that the one you contracted didn't show up this morning? And you knew? Did you follow up with him or get another one?"

Casey's tongue seemed to grow too large for her mouth. Laura had thrown her under the bus. But she couldn't really blame her—Laura was the one who had said they didn't need the engineer. She was just trying to save her own ass in this.

"Casey? Are you there?"

"I'm here. I'm—I'll find us an engineer," she promised. "Is this about the arena lights?"

"Yes, it's about the arena lights!" Mrs. Sheridan was rapidly progressing towards hysterical. "We can't hold the jumper classes without lights, and it's getting darker again. I think we're in for more rain. That arena is pitch-black in a storm, and we're already an hour behind. If you don't figure this out, we're going to end up owing refunds to nearly everyone here!"

"I'll find an engineer," Casey said again, her lips numb, her hand trembling as she lowered the phone from her ear. She looked out at the warm-up ring. Horses and ponies went splashing by, prepping for their jumper classes. But there was no way they'd go on. Because where on earth was Casey supposed to find an engineer to fix the lights in the next, what, fifteen minutes? How long would it take for the trainers to get restless and start demanding refunds? Rain splashed on the roof of the arena, and a few children on horseback shrieked at the fresh onslaught. They wouldn't last long in squally weather. They'd go home.

Casey thought about James eating hay in his stall, the risk she'd taken in bringing him, which had seemed so calculated. What could go wrong? And now Sharon was on to her, the afternoon classes were going to be canceled, and the refunds would wipe out any profit they'd stood to make on the show. She was definitely going to lose her job.

"I guess that solves some problems," she muttered. "But it will create some bigger ones."

She had to fix this, now.

Chapter Twenty-Three

THE SUN WAS sinking in a fiery sunset, and the barn, trees, and horses of Twin Palms Ranch seemed like nothing more than a series of black statues against all that blazing color. Casey looked at the show-off sky and snorted. Where had all that sun been earlier today, when she'd been dealing with the worst crisis of her career?

Indeed, Casey had made her own sunshine today. When things went wrong, she'd flicked through her contacts in horror, knowing she had no one to call. Finally, in desperation, she called Raina. There was no way Raina could get the lights on, but at least she'd have someone to cry to.

"Casey," Raina interrupted, shocked at her frantic tone. "Calm down, sweetie. I'll send my dad out."

"Your *dad?*" Casey sputtered.

"He'll fix the lights," Raina explained, her voice a pool of calm. "My dad fixes everything around the barn. Just give me the address and I'll get him there as soon as possible, okay?"

"I had no idea." Casey floundered for the words to thank Raina. "There's no way I can ever thank you enough."

"That's what friends are for, honey. Now, you just calm down and tell everyone help is on the way."

Raina hadn't oversold her father's electrical prowess. Casey didn't know what he did, but after an hour of fiddling with wires and boxes, the lights came on. A small cheer rose from the competitors waiting by the arena. By now, the only people left on horseback were hardcore teens who would never give up a horse show opportunity, or Sheridan Farm boarders who didn't have to trailer home through the flooding roads. Casey had studied their faces as she waited for Raina's father to finish his fix, in part because she wanted to keep her gaze away from the line of angry trainers queued up for refunds at Laura's reconstructed tent; in part because she was wondering what separated her from them.

While Raina's father was cleaning up, Casey dragged herself over to check on Laura and give her the good news. Laura was asking a trainer in Wellingtons and cut-off shorts to keep her students around a little longer. "We're going to run the jumper classes momentarily," she was promising.

"Lady, come on. Give me my money," the trainer snarled. "You can't expect us to wait around all day in this weather! And trust me, we'll think twice before we come to another show here."

Casey watched helplessly as Laura handed over a disconcertingly large wad of cash. The trainer left, still grumbling.

Laura shot Casey an exasperated look. "We can't really help that we had a tornado or whatever that was! What do they expect from us?"

But Casey knew what they expected—everything to be perfect. It was the same thing Mrs. Sheridan expected when she booked them, spending well outside her league for a good show experience. It was the Atlantic Horse Show promise. They'd handle everything. Even tornadoes, Casey supposed, even tropical depressions which popped out of the clear blue sea. But even if expecting them to manage the weather was absurd, everyone could reasonably expect the lights to stay on. And if she'd made sure an engineer on hand as she was supposed to, it wouldn't have taken two hours to get the afternoon classes underway.

This was on her.

There was no showing after this for her. Casey didn't show James in the over-fences classes when they eventually went on; she just let him eat hay in his stall until the last class had finished. Four horses competed in the final jumping class. The show-grounds were nearly deserted as Casey splashed back to the barn. She loaded up her horse and her damp tack in her borrowed trailer, and cautiously drove James home on a roundabout route, avoiding flooded roads.

And now here she was.

The barn was empty at first glance; it wasn't until she led James inside that she saw Hannah sitting in the tack room, flicking through her phone. She paused outside the open door, and James continued into his stall without her. She tossed his lead-rope over his back, letting him turn around to eat the grain she knew Liz would have dumped in his bucket, and continued into the tack room to face Hannah. She'd gone to this show without a single hint to Hannah; if the girl had skipped Saturday at the barn, she wouldn't even have known Casey had gone. No such luck, Casey thought, bracing for another tantrum.

But Hannah wasn't mad. *Just disappointed,* Casey thought wryly, as Hannah turned a tragically sad face to Casey. "I can't believe you took James to a show without me," she said brokenly. "And didn't even tell me about it."

Casey heaved a sigh that had her entire day's disappointments in it. "Hannah, did you even notice the weather today? It was a disaster. We had a freaking *tornado*. At one point, I was literally trapped under a collapsed tent. Also, there was so much flooding around here, the interstate was closed for like two hours. Traffic was completely stopped. Do you really think you missed anything worthwhile today?"

"That's not the point."

And Casey had to admit that Hannah was right. None of that really was the point. Shame the girl had to recognize that, though. Blaming the weather was a lot easier than taking responsibility for ducking out on her when she knew all Hannah wanted was to horse show with her. She took a breath and started again. "No, you're right. I went to a horse show without telling you. I'm really sorry about that. The truth was, my going at all was complicated and I shouldn't have even gone. I might have lost my job today."

Now Hannah's eyes widened. "What did you do?"

"I wasn't on top of things like I should have been, and when lightning knocked out the arena lights, there was no one there to fix them. We had to give a ton of refunds and the farm lost money on the show. Which means the company will lose money, and look really bad in the process. And that's all on me."

"I thought you did social media and stuff," Hannah said, puzzled. "How is making sure the lights work your job?"

Casey had to laugh at that. A bitter, exhausted laugh, but a laugh nonetheless. "I've been wondering that myself. I guess I got suckered into it. And now I'm going to get fired because I let my bosses talk me into doing something above my pay grade." Or adjacent to it, Casey thought. Either way, she was doing a job she didn't really fully understand, even with all the checklists and binders they'd handed her before she'd gone off to San Diego. She'd been bound to fail at it before too long.

And so here she was, facing down another work fiasco. Casey's laughter trailed off. She really was going to get fired—no doubt that it. And she deserved it, for not standing up to her bosses, for agreeing to do work she wasn't trained to do. She'd painted herself into this corner, stroke by stroke. She threw herself down on the bench beside Hannah. "A word of advice, don't ever assume you have to do something just because your boss says you do, okay? There's such a thing as a job title, and a job description. Stick to them or ask for more money to do more work. But don't ever give in and hope it will work out in the end. You can't work a job on hope."

Hannah nodded gravely. "I'll try to remember that. Luckily, there's not much at JJ's that isn't in my job description. It's basically 'do restaurant things.'"

"That does help. My thing was a little more complicated than that. And I screwed it up."

"What will you do now?"

Casey thought about her tiny savings account. The prospect of asking Brandon for money to help with James didn't sound appealing at all. They pooled their income for most things, but she set aside money for James. There was probably enough money to keep him for two months, assuming he didn't do anything idiotic like colic or lose his shoes. After that, though, the horse fund would be depleted to the point where she'd already have to be pulling another paycheck, or asking for help. Two months wasn't much time to get a job and start earning a paycheck. She could get a callback tomorrow and it could still take that long just to get to a second interview. Casey closed her eyes against a rising wave of panic and tried to push all of it from her mind. There was nothing she could do about it right now.

"I'll wait and see what happens before I panic about money," she decided. "Maybe it will be okay."

"If you need help with James, I could half-lease him from you," Hannah said. Was there hope in her voice? "With the extra shifts I'm getting at JJ's, I could afford to cover his board, anyway."

"Thanks," Casey said, closing her eyes against the possibility of losing her horse. "It won't come to that."

She wished she were as confident as her words.

Casey was still sitting in the dark barn two hours later, watching the moonrise and thinking about what to do next. She'd outlasted the evening mosquitoes, and even Hannah's constant presence. She'd seen an owl swoop over the dark arena, and watched the International Space Station float through the sky. Brandon had texted, and she'd told him to eat dinner without her. She promised to bring home milkshakes for dessert, hoping that would keep her out of the doghouse. She wasn't avoiding Brandon; she just needed some alone time. With a little quiet time to think, she might figure out how to get out of this mess.

She was startled when a pair of headlights appeared in the driveway, bouncing over the rough patches in the road. When Liz got out of her car, Casey breathed a sigh of relief, her shoulders dropping two inches. She'd been really nervous about who might pay a dark barn a visit this late in the evening. She should have known it was Liz, probably wondering where her truck and trailer were.

"Figures you'd be sitting out here all alone," Liz said, coming into the barn. She leaned against the nearest stall. "Rough day today?"

"Did you hear about it?"

"I heard something about it," Liz said wryly. "Also, the weather was terrible, so either way you were in for trouble. You want to talk about it?"

"Not really."

"Okay. You want to talk about anything? Or should I go?"

"You know any jobs opening up?"

"That bad, huh?" Liz gave her a sympathetic grimace.

"I'd say there's a 99% chance I'm getting fired first thing Monday."

Liz nodded slowly and sighed. "That's bad for me, isn't it? I tend to get late board payments when my clients get fired."

"I'll find something," Casey assured her, although her bravado was completely fake. "And I have some emergency horse savings."

"Aww, we'll manage. I was just joking. Mostly."

Silence fell across the barn, with only the sound of crickets and the occasional alligator grunt on the night breeze. In the field, a horse snorted. It might have been James, telling his friends about his insane day.

Casey had been pondering her life—well, mainly her past year—and she was tired of her own issues. She decided now was the perfect time to ask Liz something she'd been wondering for a while. Someone else's journey would be so much more interesting than her own. "Hey, Liz, can I ask you something?"

"Sure."

"What makes you run this place? You don't ride, you don't spend time with the boarders, you don't even have your own horse. Why run a boarding stable?"

"Do you hang out at your job when you're not working?"

"Well, no."

Liz laughed, a sound like rocks rattling in a bucket. "I'm just picking on you. I know what you mean. Most people, they run a barn and that's their whole life. It eats 'em up. I didn't want that for myself. I got kids, I got grandkids. I say to myself, 'Well, I like horses, but they can't be my whole life.' So I have this barn. I get in early, I feed, I spend some time with the horses, and then I get out. I move on. I take Sundays off and let Hannah run the show. And it works for me. The thing about horses is, they want everything. But life wants balance. It's up to us to learn to budget what we give our horses, or they'll take it all. And we'll have nothing left."

Casey considered this speech, the longest one Liz had ever made in front of her. There was a certain honor in being the recipient of that kind of life advice. It made her really want to take it to heart. It made her want to change her life for the better. To learn to balance things the way Liz did. But she didn't see how she could do it. "It seems like no matter how hard I try, James always outweighs everything else. When I'm up against the clock, I pick James and what he needs. Every time. I don't know that this is *wrong,* though, right? I have to put James first. He's my responsibility."

"Think about that," Liz cautioned her. "Are you putting what James *needs* first? Or are you putting what *you* want from James?"

Casey had no reply to that. She remembered talking to the girls back at St. Johns, the way one of them had said she'd be letting James and Sky down if she didn't show James. And she'd replied, so sure of herself, that all James wanted to do was eat, and so there was only one way to let him down, and that was to feed him dinner late.

And then what had she done? She'd convinced herself that showing James was the only way to prove she was doing right by the two of them. Doing the right thing with the money she spent on him. Doing the right thing with all the time she lavished on him.

Casey wondered if she'd just spent the past eight months trying to wedge the two of them into the wrong shaped hole.

"I think I got what we want and what we need mixed up," she said slowly. "Or what *I* want and what James needs, I guess."

"And what you need," Liz reminded her. "Which is balance."

"I still don't know how to find it," Casey said. "James always gets everything. Then work. Then Brandon."

"Figure out what you really love about horses," Liz advised. "Then just do that. Nothing more. And be honest with yourself. Don't say, 'I really love jumping three-foot courses with horses, and that's what I love the most.' That ain't true. And we both know it. You can love jumping courses, but that's not the main reason you get up and drive here so early every morning."

Life advice dispensed, Liz pushed off from the stall wall and stretched. "I'm heading home. You can leave the trailer here tonight. After you get it cleaned out, just drop it by the house, okay?"

"No problem," Casey said. "Thanks, Liz. For everything."

"You're welcome." Liz gave her one last grin. "Remember, be honest with yourself, okay? Don't lie to yourself, or you'll just end up with the rug coming out from under ya again."

"I got it," Casey replied. "Thanks."

She decided not to leave right after Liz; she was already so late going home, what was another half an hour? Trusting the moon to light her way, Casey walked through the wet grass and leaned on the pasture gate.

She could see a mist creeping through the pasture, and the horses were captured in black silhouette against its silvery glow. Casey whistled, and laughed to herself when she saw the horses lift their heads, their pricked ears forming sharp triangles. They were too far away for her to pick out who was who, but she thought the horse on the far right, the one who watched her the longest before going back to his grazing, must be James.

Would she still be the same person if she gave up these persistent dreams of showing, cut back on her equestrian expenses, and lived through a few months of job-hunting with Brandon's help? Of course she would. James would still be out there, grazing in the dark, doing the only thing horses really cared about.

Eating grass.

Chapter Twenty-Four

CASEY FLOPPED OVER in bed and looked at the ceiling. Next to her, Brandon stirred and sat up. "Why are you still up?" he asked, voice gravelly with sleep.

"I'm thinking." She'd been pondering her problems for hours. Part of her was really, really glad the Sheridan show had been on a Saturday. She had all day tomorrow to catch up on sleep. If there was one thing Casey was not planning on doing the day before she faced the firing squad, it was doing any additional work on the weekend.

"Do you want anything to help you sleep?"

She laughed and gave him a cuddle. "Like what? Warm milk? You know I don't like sleeping pills."

"Benadryl could help," he suggested.

"Go back to sleep, love. I don't need you up, too."

"Well, now I am." Brandon kissed her hair and Casey sidled up against him, feeling very warm and fuzzy despite all her fears. An idea came into her head and she voiced it without pausing to filter it for potential mistakes.

"Should we plan on going on a trail ride sometime soon?"

"A trail ride!" Brandon stared at her as if she'd suggested going on a last-minute drive to the county dump. "You're up at two a.m. thinking about going on trail rides with me?"

"What else would keep me up at night?" She'd been running through a hundred and one subjects that weren't trail riding before he'd woken up, but none of them seemed to matter now. She wanted to go riding with her boyfriend. That was the answer. She wasn't quite sure of what the question was, but *that* was the answer. "I've been way over the top with this whole horse show thing," she admitted. "And I'm trying to start over again on the right foot. With you."

"I have to talk to Maria about riding Chico," Brandon said, "but I'd like that. I'd like that a lot."

"Me, too," Casey told him. And she meant it. She wasn't sure who she was supposed to ride, because James would be bonkers on the trail, but at least she'd made a start.

A few minutes passed. Brandon slid back down onto his pillow, but Casey remained upright, her back against the headboard. He looked up at her, eyes heavy. "Was that really the only thing you were thinking about?"

She sighed. "No. I was also thinking about quitting my job."

Brandon didn't bother getting up this time. He just wrapped an arm around her and tugged her back down to the bed. "You're the most troublesome woman," he murmured. "It's Saturday night. Worry about this tomorrow."

It was tomorrow, she wanted to tell him. But he was sinking back into sleep. Somehow, Casey found that comforting. Brandon wouldn't lose sleep if she did quit, or got fired, on Monday. She ought to take a leaf out of his book. Casey closed her eyes and tried to match her breathing to his. Sure, she couldn't sleep, but she could definitely try to relax.

Sunday brunch by the ocean: it wasn't quite the regular thing it had once been, but now and then, Casey gave up a ride and Brandon gave up a quiet Sunday doing whatever he did—now she knew he'd *been* riding, too, which was wild—and they went out. Casey had pulled on one of her sundresses this morning with a smile on her face. For one thing, this was a perfect day to skip riding. She could leave cleaning up Liz's trailer until Monday afternoon, and give James a few days to recover from their calamitous horse show. For another, she was looking forward to just spending a little time with Brandon, out of their normal surroundings. In her experience, that was the best time to talk. And in the wee hours, he'd given her the impression he would be much more supportive of a brief jobless period than she'd previously suspected. She was eager to talk it out.

So when they were spotted by one of Brandon's work buddies as they stood at the hostess stand, Casey had to suppress a sigh of frustration.

"Nolan!" Brandon exclaimed. "What's a guy like you doing at a fish shack like this?"

The hostess pursed her lips. They were standing in front of a very fancy glass and wood structure with a sensational view of the Atlantic. Casey could tell she didn't appreciate having her place of business called a fish shack.

Nolan bowled over several well-heeled seniors standing just inside the front door. Cold air blew out around him. He was a bulky guy in a Hawaiian shirt and board shorts, and a skeletal woman with red lipstick and a frosty smile trailed behind him. "This is our favorite brunch spot," he informed Brandon. "Isn't it, Corinne? Our *favorite.*

You have to sit with us." He rounded on the hostess. "We need to change our table. There are four of us now."

Her chin jutted slightly. "There's a wait for a four-top."

"That's fine!" Nolan gave Brandon a jovial squeeze. "I know this guy doesn't mind."

Casey glanced at Corinne. She flicked her gaze back, ice-blue eyes showing how much *she* minded. But Nolan didn't ask her, and Brandon was completely overpowered. Casey smiled at Corinne. "I guess we're waiting," she said, stepping away as Brandon and Nolan launched into conversation, something about work and dolphins. "I haven't eaten here before. It's good?"

Corinne shrugged her thin shoulders. "We like it." Her tone implied an unspoken 'obviously'.

"Super." Casey never said 'super', but it seemed appropriate here. As in, *you're super-awful.*

They looked at each other for a long moment, then Corinne turned her gaze towards the ocean visible through the restaurant windows, and Casey glanced back at Brandon, hoping for rescue.

Luckily, the hostess provided it, as a group of four walked out, laughing and clearly enjoying one another's company. Casey watched them enviously as the hostess gathered menus and silverware. "Right this way," she announced.

"So, my sister rides horses," Nolan said, once he'd ordered the bottomless mimosas. "Maybe you know her. Violet Harrell? Her horses have the funniest names. Let me see, they're called Dune Buggy, Mystic Mike, and then there's something I can't remember that starts with a V. *He* came from Europe," Nolan added, turning his gaze on Brandon. "Popped that horse on an airplane and flew him over. I had no idea stuff like that went on until her trainer insisted he was the perfect horse for her. Her husband didn't know what hit him when the bill came."

"People do a lot of crazy things with horses," Brandon agreed cheerfully. "But Casey's horse is a retired racehorse. American-grown."

Casey forced a smile as Corinne and Nolan both pivoted, their faces astonished.

"A *racehorse*," Corinne repeated, looking as if she hadn't known Casey had it in her.

"He's a really nice, quiet horse," Casey told them, pulling out her phone to show off some pictures. "He wasn't a very good racehorse, but he's a great horse to hang out with."

"Oh, look at those little white and black spots on his back feet!" Corinne was gazing at James's picture with an intensity that reminded Casey of Cruella De Vil. She took the phone back quickly.

"The black spots are called ermine," she said, but Nolan was already talking about his sister's horses again, drowning her out as he described how much money they cost to feed and shoe and board every month.

"You have to be rich to have horses," Nolan declared. He looked at her, waggling his eyebrows. "You're the rich one, right? Because we know Brandon isn't!"

A chorus of tinny laughter rang out as the conversation turned to non-profit salaries and horses were forgotten. Casey gazed out to sea, watching for the occasional dolphin fin as the turquoise waves curled in on the shore. After a while, she noticed Corinne was doing the same. She decided to try one more time with the other woman. She had no one else to talk to; Nolan was completely monopolizing Brandon. "So, I'm not rich," she said, laughing as if there was a private joke between them.

Corinne cast Nolan a baleful glance before she looked back at Casey. "Oh, just ignore Nolan. Everyone else does. I've been ignoring him for years."

"Have you been together a long time?"

"An eternity," Corinne said.

Ouch. "It can't be that long," Casey replied, going for the flattery angle. "You're not old enough!"

Corinne did something with her face which might have been her muscles preventing a truly nuclear eye-roll. But her voice was light when she replied, "I pay a lot of money for this skin. Thanks for noticing."

"I'm jealous. I spend too much time in the sun."

Corinne leaned forward and gave Casey's face a speculative look. "You're doing all right," she pronounced. "Don't let up on the moisturizer, though."

"Okay. Thanks." Casey resisted the urge to rub at the skin around her eyes, as if Corinne had seen the beginnings of a thousand crows-feet there.

"You're welcome. I see a lot of women let their skin go down here. It's sad. The sun in Florida is no joke."

Casey absorbed this and cast about for something else to talk about. "Do you have hobbies?" she asked eventually.

Corinne shrugged. "I guess, I knit? I suppose that's a hobby, even though I only do it because my therapist said to. It's fine. It keeps me from obsessing over work while I'm watching TV, anyway." She suddenly grinned at Casey. The open expression didn't match her face at all. "Is this about your horse thing?"

"My...horse thing?"

"Yes, the horse thing. Riding all the time. It takes a lot. Nolan's sister does nothing else. Their nanny practically raises their children." Corinne actually rolled her eyes this time, but in a conspiratorial way. Like Casey was in on the joke. "Although between you and me, I wouldn't raise that woman's children, either. Little nightmares."

Casey had no idea what to say, so she just nodded along.

"Anyway, Nolan doesn't make as much as the brother-in-law, so even if I wanted a horse, which I don't, not particularly anyway, I wouldn't be able to have one." She fluttered her lashes at Nolan, who had heard his name and was looking at them with a bemused expression.

"What's that, dear?"

"I was just saying we can't afford horses."

"Not for a thousand dollars a month just to feed them, we can't!" Nolan exclaimed.

Brandon's mouth fell open. *"How* much?"

"My sister's horses live at the Ritz," Nolan said, tipping back his mimosa.

Casey met Brandon's shocked gaze. She shrugged. She'd told him how expensive West Palm could be.

"And," Nolan added, setting down his empty glass, "Brandon here has a horse. But we don't, Corinne. If I can't afford a horse, what am I even doing in programming?"

"Saving the oceans?" Brandon suggested.

"That's entirely on your shoulders," Nolan informed him. "You know I only run back-up on your division."

"That's right." Brandon agreed. "You're on the side of the company making money, not giving it away."

"That's hardly a distinguishing attribute." They all swiveled to stare at Corinne, whose ivory cheeks had flushed slightly. "Making money isn't exactly unique, is all I'm saying. Brandon over there is saving the ocean. That's pretty admirable, *I* think."

Casey wondered if Corinne had pregamed before brunch.

"You're just saying that because I won't buy you a horse," Nolan said finally. "If I was making horse money, you'd be telling a different story."

"I don't *want* a horse," Corinne insisted. The tips of her ears were pink now.

"Horses are a lot of trouble," Casey said quickly, wishing the conversation would turn to anything else.

"Better off with a dog," Nolan suggested.

Not that, though.

"Dogs are dirty," Corinne said. "Dirty, dirty dogs."

Good heavens, Casey thought. *She's really drunk.* No wonder she'd been so quiet and stared at Casey so hard before. She was just trying to hold it together. Casey put her hand over Corinne's. "I'm going to go to the bar and ask for a cappuccino," she said. "Do you want one?"

Corinne nodded. "That would be nice."

Brandon's eyes followed her as she got up, but she shook her head slightly, imploring him not to say anything. This was just one of those times women had to stick together, she thought ruefully, leaning on the bar while the woman behind it steamed milk for their drinks.

Her gaze drifted back to the ocean; it was impossible to ignore here, in a dining room made almost entirely of windows. She remembered their casual, outdoor brunches back home; hanging out almost all day with Heather, Alison, and Brandon's old work buddies. Easier times, she thought. Then she wondered if Raina liked brunch. Or Sharmayne. Maybe she could find a more easygoing kind of place where they could all meet once or twice a month, to sit around and talk about their horses and their jobs and the crazy people they'd met out there, under the hot Florida sun.

Maybe the best was yet to come, and she was just getting started at crafting her new life here.

"Two cappuccinos, extra shots," the barista droned, plunking the china cups down on the bar beside her. Casey slid a few dollars her way and picked them up, taking a moment to prepare mentally for the people waiting back at the table. These weren't her people, but they weren't Brandon's, either. She had to believe that this wasn't as good as it could get. Better things were waiting.

"Well, that was certainly a thing that happened."

Casey slid into the car, smiling at Brandon's assessment. "Now I know why you work from home so much."

"Nolan's not the kind of guy I'd choose to be my closest colleague," Brandon admitted. "Or a regular brunch guy. You do realize we can never go back to that restaurant again. They might be there."

"I don't know. The dinner menu looked intriguing." Casey took out her phone, checking her messages. She was still on edge about the Sheridan Farm situation, although since her conversation with Brandon in the wee hours of the morning, she had been considerably less fixated on what might happen with her job. "It's possible they have another regular spot for dinner—oh."

He looked over at her. "What? Is it work?"

She read the email over a second time, her heart sinking. "I have to go up to the office for a meeting tomorrow morning. Early."

Brandon put the car back in park and placed his hand over Casey's. "Hey. Don't sweat this. If this is the end, it wasn't meant to be. We'll figure it out, okay?"

"Yeah." Casey nodded, blinking back tears. She didn't want it to end this way. She wanted to end things on her terms—or better yet, she wanted things to work out, to improve to the point where she didn't have to worry about quitting or getting fired. "Thanks, babe."

He squeezed her hand. "Now let's go home and have a drink. I need to recover from all that madness."

Casey laughed despite herself. In all their years of brunches at the beach, they'd never abandoned bottomless mimosas so quickly before.

Chapter Twenty-Five

MONDAY MORNING CAME a little earlier than usual. Casey sat up in the darkness and looked around, confused by the sound of her alarm. Then she realized all that racket was her own doing. She put out her hand and found her phone, but she didn't get it turned off before Brandon stirred and sat up as well.

"Five o'clock?" he murmured. "On purpose?"

Casey gave him a kiss. "Go back to sleep," she said. "I have to go to Merritt Island this morning and it's a long drive."

He made a grumbling sort of noise, put his head back on the pillow, and was instantly asleep. Casey doubted he'd even remember this conversation when he woke up in a few hours, so she left a note on the coffeemaker. *Working in office today, back by six!*

The morning rides on James had her primed to wake up before sunrise anyway, so getting into the car for the long drive so early in the day wasn't quite as awful as it would have been only a few weeks before. The drive up to her old haunts was almost relaxing. By the time she got to Merritt Island, though, the long stream of commuters heading for Kennedy Space Center had taken over the roads. She was grateful to pull into the parking lot of the strip mall where Atlantic Horse Show Productions was headquartered. For a moment, anyway.

Then she remembered what was coming next. Or rather, what she *thought* was coming. It would be so much easier if she knew what they wanted from this meeting. Was it a firing? Or a slap on the wrist? Something in between? The anticipation was murder.

Casey let herself into the office, turned off the alarm, and made coffee in the tiny kitchen. When no one else turned up early, she sat down at her desk and started going through her emails as if it was a normal day.

Sharon came at last, dropping her purse on her desk with a thud. "Casey, it's good to see you."

Casey turned in her chair. Sharon didn't look mad. A strange sensation fluttered in her stomach, her brain halfway between elation and disappointment. Did she *want* to get fired?

"I made coffee," Casey offered. "And I brought bagels."

"That's my girl," Sharon said, and headed for the kitchen.

Phillip came in a few minutes later, and their exchange was similar. Casey was conflicted now. Maybe she hadn't walked into her own termination meeting. Maybe they wanted her to do more horse shows.

In which case, she'd be forced to quit.

She didn't want to get fired, but she kind of wanted to quit. Or was it the other way around? If they fired her, she wouldn't go home feeling guilty about quitting her job.

It was all very confusing.

Once everyone was settled in with coffee and bagels, Casey waited for their meeting to begin. She'd been summoned here early, after all.

But when the silence of Monday morning emails took over, she realized *th*ings weren't that simple. Neither Sharon nor Phillip enjoyed confrontation. So even though they'd called the meeting, both were probably hoping they wouldn't actually hold it. Casey supposed if she simply sat at her desk all day and refused to bring it up, it was possible the entire thing could be swept under the rug. By phone, they could easily tell her off. In person, neither would be the first one to address it.

But Casey knew if she didn't handle this, things would just get worse. Until she quit, or really did get herself fired. And it was probably fifty-fifty which one would happen.

You have to do fix this now, she told herself. *And if they don't agree, you have to quit.* It was the deal she'd made with herself last night, and she had to stick to it. She steeled herself, tensing all her muscles, forcing them to relax again, shaking out her shoulders.

Go time.

"Guys," Casey said, turning in her chair. "I think we need to talk."

They looked at her. Sharon was the first to square her shoulders and stand up. "I'll get us more coffee," she said.

Casey nearly laughed. The stalling techniques were unreal! But she just held out her mug. "Yeah, good idea."

Phillip twisted his fingers together anxiously as Sharon went into the kitchen. "It was a rough weekend," he ventured. "We didn't get all that rain up in Jax, but that just meant it was a million degrees, instead. We had three paramedic runs for heat stroke."

Casey gazed at him sympathetically. "It was hot up there," she agreed finally. "Summer horse shows are really rough."

"When I was young, we didn't even hold horse shows in June." Phillip shook his head. "No sir, summer was for turning horses out and taking a break."

"No breaks allowed these days," Sharon trilled, bringing in the mugs on a tray. "Here you are, and here you are," she added theatrically, passing Casey and Phillip their coffees. "And here *I* am." She laughed at herself and sat down, swiveling her chair to face them.

"Who's going first?" Phillip asked, his face uncertain.

"You are," Casey announced. "Go on. I'm listening."

Casey listened attentively while Phillip listed the complaints from the Sheridan show. He didn't have the figures yet, he said, but chances were high they'd taken a bath financially, losing out tremendously with all those refunds. "And Mrs. Sheridan says she won't be using us next summer for her show, which is a real shame," he added. "She was one of our first clients."

"It's entirely my fault," Casey said. "And I—"

"It's only Sheridan Farm, though," Sharon interrupted. "It's one show a year, and a basic package at that. It's not a huge loss, on an annual basis. Phillip, I'm inclined to just let this go. Natural order of things, and all that. It's high time we let Sheridan go."

Casey stared at her. "I don't understand. This is going to be terrible word-of-mouth. You can't play that down."

"But think about this before you martyr yourself," Sharon said briskly. "If there are any PR problems from this, who's going to fix them? You are. That's *your job.*"

"Sharon's got a great point," Phillip agreed, visibly relieved. "We need you. If we lose you *and* Mrs. Sheridan, then that's a real problem. But just Mrs. Sheridan? You can handle that for us."

"We've had a good chat," Sharon continued, "but I think we can all agree it's time to move on. Casey, you're good at your job and we need you."

"Well, then stop making me do your job!" Casey shouted, jumping to her feet.

They stared at her in stunned silence.

Casey put her hand to her head, suddenly dizzy. "I'm sorry," she said. "I shouldn't have—I think I might be getting sick."

Sharon jumped up and took her by the elbow. "Sit back down and drink your coffee."

Casey was pretty sure coffee was the worst thing for her, but she sat down and sipped it, anyway. Sharon and Phillip watched her anxiously, as if they had no idea what had set her off, as if they hadn't been the ones to call her up here to give an account of herself and her sins. Casey felt like she was taking crazy pills. That had to be it, right? There was no other explanation for their behavior.

Or they really had realized, right before they fired her, that they couldn't run this business without her—or someone like her. Someone who did everything asked of her without complaint, no matter how inappropriate the request.

And suddenly Casey remembered Sharmayne, a working student for a woman who wouldn't let her go, and wouldn't let her move up— doing everything and anything for her boss, because no one else had given her a chance.

But if Sharmayne could say enough and make a plan to get out, so could she.

Casey put down her coffee cup. "Okay, guys. Listen to me for a minute. Because we need to take a really honest look at what has happened here over the past few months."

There were nods. She took a breath and went on. "I'm here to do marketing and PR. But in the past three months, I've taken on three horse shows that are not in my scope of work because you asked me to. My first client completely ghosted me and then said that I'd planned the entire show without her and against her wishes. Then, on my first on-site, I dropped the ball on the engineering issue and I've cost the farm thousands of dollars in refunds. I now have to work overtime on PR issues that I created. I am not good at planning and organizing horse shows, guys, but that's because it's *not my job.* And I can't do it anymore."

Sharon and Philip exchanged nervous glances. "Well, Tildy likes you a lot," Phillip finally ventured. "Everything seems to be going well over at her place." Sharon nodded in agreement.

Casey's vision actually blurred for a moment. Were they for real? "Guys! Come on! You can't be this afraid of confrontation. Tell me that I absolutely bungled two out of three shows I've worked on!" Casey couldn't believe she was begging to have her mistakes acknowledged. The world was upside down with these two. She needed them to admit she was failing, or her next argument wouldn't even make sense. "Here's the truth: I've been giving you two hundred percent on the horse show organizing, which is obviously way more than I have to give, and they're still going wrong. And I need you to tell me you will not ask me to touch another show, except for marketing and PR purposes."

Slowly, realization dawned over their faces. Phillip shook his head. "Casey, I know that's not what we hired you for, but this is a start-up, and in start-ups, everyone wears a lot of hats—"

"No," Casey interrupted, holding up a finger. "Nuh-uh. This *was* a start-up. Now it's a business which acquires other businesses and expands. And that's where it stops being a start-up and you have to stop using that excuse. I am very sorry the other company's employees all quit, but you can't use that excuse anymore. And, even if it were still the case, if I'm wrecking your business because I'm working outside of my title, how does that help anyone?"

"I wouldn't say *wrecking*—" Sharon stopped speaking. Casey knew she was making an absolutely ferocious face, but it was working, so she didn't stop.

"It's *wrecking*. Maybe what happened with Goldie was fixable, but yesterday? That's going to be a problem for a long time. It's going to come up over and over again. I have *dozens* of local trainers all furious with the company, and they all have social media and they're very unafraid to use it."

Casey leaned back in her chair and stared at the ceiling, suddenly exhausted. She didn't even know what case she was making anymore. She'd come in this morning expecting to get reamed out, with her planned defense ultimately that she wasn't doing the job she was trained and ready to do, and they needed to hire someone else to handle organization. Instead, she was using her defense to explain to them what an awful employee she was.

Make it make sense, she thought miserably.

"Casey, I didn't realize you felt like this," Phillip ventured. "And I guess that means we were approaching what happened over the weekend all wrong. We thought you were learning, and it was just growing pains."

"I am, and it was," Casey sighed. "But it's not my job, and I'm not going to grow into it. I'm a marketer. I can bring in business. I can sell what we're doing. But I can't spend my days and nights traveling and setting up shows." *I have other things in my life,* she added silently. *I have to find balance. Away from you guys.*

"I think we can find room in the budget for someone else," Sharon said. "An assistant planner, something like that." She looked at Phillip. "Want to drop up a position, responsibilities?"

"Sure." Phillip turned his attention back to Casey. "Any ideas on who could fit the bill?"

And a whole new solution appeared to Casey. She leaned forward, feeling a weight lift from her shoulders. "You know what? I do, actually."

Chapter Twenty-Six

CASEY HAD BEEN standing in the barn aisle for a while, just watching Maria. She'd timed her visit to the farm strategically, knowing Maria's schedule well enough to be certain she would be there on an early Monday afternoon. The drive back from the office had flown by as she'd gone over her plans, sorting out everything she wanted to accomplish in the next month. One of the most important items on her list? She needed to sort out the situation with Brandon.

They needed to go riding together. And Casey thought Maria might help her make it happen.

The older woman was brushing out Chico's mane, slowly teasing a comb through his mottled brown and white strands. Unlike James and Caruso, Chico's mane had been allowed to grow long and luxurious, its tips falling below the curve of his neck. Since he never had to be braided for horse shows, his tresses could grow as long as they cared to. Privately, Casey found the look a tad messy.

But she and Maria had different motivations in the saddle, and those differences showed in their taste as well. Maria was a casual rider, a woman who enjoyed trail riding but not hard work. Casey didn't know how to be anything but a worker, a woman who got in the saddle and chose the hard way every single time. She used to be certain her way was the right way; now she wasn't so sure.

And now that she needed to ask Maria a favor, Casey's old prejudices were making it hard for her to begin.

So here she was. Just standing in the aisle. Like an idiot.

Finally, Maria tossed the comb into her grooming bucket and turned. A smile played on her lips. "You've got something on your mind, Miss Casey."

"I do," Casey admitted. "But it's going to be hard for me to put into words."

"Just spit out." Maria shrugged. "I'm getting ready to take this guy out for a ride."

"Okay, well...Brandon's birthday is in three weeks. He wants to go on a trail ride with me and I've been putting it off, but I thought for a birthday surprise...Anyway, he said he'd talk to you about borrowing Chico?"

Maria nodded. "Brandon's always welcome to take Chico out for a stroll."

"That's good." Casey took a breath. "The problem is...I don't have a horse to take."

"James can't do it?"

"I've never taken him out on the trails here. And I barely took him out at my old farm. We didn't have access to a lot, honestly." They'd ridden down the farm driveway and out on the road a few times. Riding with the teens had made it fun—especially when Gwen gave her tips on relaxing with James out there. But she couldn't imagine taking him out on the trails here. The spaces were too big and open.

Maria regularly disappeared for hours on end. "I was wondering if... you'd take us out."

"I'd be happy to! You know I think every horse needs some time on the trails."

Oh, Casey knew. Maria reminded her of that every chance she got. "That's right," she said, as if she'd just made the connection. "You do say that."

"I believe it, too." Maria picked up a saddle blanket and settled it over Chico's broad back. "Do you want to go out right now?"

Casey would rather never actually go on the trail ride, but she figured that would be a weird response. "I would. There's just one thing...James can be really spooky in new places."

"We'll put you in one of Liz's old saddles," Maria assured her. "When you take a horse out on the trails for the first time, it's nice to have a deep seat and something to grab hold of. And if things get really bad, just shove his nose right into Chico's butt. Chico won't mind none."

"Oh my goodness, look at that gator." Casey pointed to a massive alligator stretched on the bank opposite the trail.

Maria turned her head and Casey saw a smile on her face. "That's just George," she called over her shoulder. "He won't hurt you any."

"I guess I have to trust you, or I'd be too scared to keep riding." Casey kept an eye on the alligator as they rode past. Maybe George could have eaten them in one bite, but he wasn't in any hurry to move. The gator looked as if he'd melted into the mud. He might have been camouflaged on a cloudy day, but his glossy hide was glistening in the bright sunlight.

James never even saw him. Her goofball horse was too busy snorting at fluttering butterflies to notice the potential man-eaters snoozing on either side of them.

They'd been riding for twenty minutes, as the steamy Florida morning gave way to a sultry midday. Just a few fluffy clouds floated through the cheerful blue sky, their gray underbellies offering occasional, appreciated shade. The countryside beyond Twin Palms was flat and swampy, with few trees outside of small hammocks of high ground where palms grew in tight clusters. They mostly rode on high swales above wide, deep drainage ditches, which gave them an excellent view of the creatures living around and in those still, dark waters. Alligators snoozed on banks or swam through the canals, their tails flicking back and forth while their snouts cut through the water like ship prows. White egrets, multi-hued herons, and plain brown limpets stalked through the water's edge, their long legs bending backwards as they searched the water for prey. Fish jumped for bugs, creating sudden splashes which made James flutter his nostrils and dive for the safety of Chico's hindquarters. Casey frequently found herself thankful that Chico was a reliable trail partner—no kicking, no fussing.

Despite Maria's assurances, Casey felt herself tensing as they passed the alligator, even though George was a good fifteen feet away and on the other side of a canal, to boot. What was to stop a dinosaur like that from diving into the water, swimming across like a flash, and racing up the bank to devour them? Then she considered how fast James would take off if that alligator so much as twitched a toe, and her taut shoulders relaxed. There was no chance her spooky horse would allow a snoozing gator to wake up and catch him. The two of them would be halfway to Lake Okeechobee before old George so much as slid into the water.

The trail eventually led them into a dark hammock of live oaks hung with vines, and they had enough space to ride alongside one another. The air was cool and damp, and the horses slowed, hoping to prolong their time out of the sun. James's shoulders and neck quivered against mosquitoes, which hung around in the damp, shady forest.

"Have some more Off," Maria suggested, tugging an aerosol can from her saddle bag. "It works real good on horses, too. Better than fly spray."

James danced sideways at the hissing sound, but Casey got both of them doused. The mosquitoes disappeared immediately. "Why don't we just use this every day on horses?" she asked, handing the can back over.

"This stuff is pricy," Maria laughed. She sprayed Chico's neck and her own legs and shoulders. "And not waterproof. I keep it around just for emergencies like this."

"Emergencies?"

"When the sun's so strong you don't want to leave the shade right away."

"That definitely qualifies as an emergency use," Casey laughed. "So, um, is this a good time to talk about Brandon's birthday trail ride? It might be fun to make it a group thing—do you know if anyone else would want to come with us?"

Maria gave her a sideways grin. "Well, we could invite any number of folks from his ranch."

Casey blinked. "His ranch?"

"Sure. The folks he rides with already."

"I'm sorry...do you know something I don't?"

Maria peered at her. "You don't know where Brandon rides?"

"He's been kind of hush-hush about it," Casey said, feeling miserably embarrassed. "I think there was supposed to be an element of surprise at first."

"Oh, right. Well, he came to me for advice." Maria smirked at

Casey's astonished expression. "Honestly, it coulda been anybody. I just happened to be the one hanging out in the barn aisle when he showed up askin' questions. So now he rides with Park Chance at Good Chance Ranch over on Rattlesnake Trail. Park's a good friend of mine. I sent Brandon there because Park's got a good way of teaching men to ride. He's got a whole riding club over there. I bet a few of them would like to come."

"We could have a party," Casey suggested, trying not to feel too dazed by Maria's succession of bombshells. "Would he like that?"

"He's *your* boyfriend. Would he like a party?"

"I mean, yes. He would. But with those guys? From the ranch? I don't even know if they're friends. We don't talk about it all. We kind of...I might have made Brandon think I didn't want to share horses with him."

Maria shook her head. "I've never seen one girl make her own life so difficult. What do you do, stay up at night figuring out new problems for yourself?"

"It really seems that way," Casey admitted. "But now I'm trying to fix them all."

"How many do you have under control now?"

Casey ran her hand along James's hot neck. They were coming out of the trees now, and the sun was dazzling, shining down on a vast lake she hadn't even known existed out here. James pricked his ears and quickened his pace, tugging her towards the water. She pushed him towards Chico with her seat and leg, hoping he'd settle alongside the other horse, while answering, "If I get Brandon's birthday handled, two. I think I have work under control now."

"Good for you!" Maria gave her a sideways grin. "Can I ask you a favor for your next project?"

"Well, I can only try." James shoved against Chico. "Oh, sorry."

"Do something about that Hannah," Maria said, ignoring James. "The girl's a handful without you keeping her in check."

"I'll add that to my list," Casey promised. "But I don't know if I can fix things. She's headstrong. She barely ever listens to me. Hell, sometimes she convinces *me* to do things I didn't want to do."

"Oh well," Maria sighed. "I tried."

Casey called Sharmayne on her way home, putting her on speakerphone while she drove carefully over the wet roads. A postage stamp-sized storm had blown over the ranch while they were riding, missing their trail, but leaving puddles back at the barn. Florida was funny that way.

"Casey! What's going on?" Sharmayne sounded delighted to hear from her.

"Just checking in," Casey replied. "I've been thinking about you. Everything going okay with Goldie?"

"It's okay, I guess." Her voice darkened. "I think she's decided it's time for me to go."

"She's going to fire you?"

"No, she's just making me feel unwanted. She won't actually fire me. She'll just make me quit. Passive-aggressive, you know. Like most horsepeople. Why is that a thing? Am I making that up?"

"I have no idea, but it is *definitely* a horse people thing." Casey could think of several trainers in her past who had behaved in similar ways. "So are you on the job hunt, officially?"

"I am, but I don't know that I'll get a reference. That might make things hard."

"Well," Casey said, "I actually have an idea about that. Is Goldie in the office right now?"

"Yeah, she is. You want to talk to her?"

"I'll call her. Don't say anything, okay?"

"Got it." Sharmayne lowered her voice, ready to conspire. "Want me to do anything on this end?"

"How's your luggage looking these days? Got a good carry-on?"

Sharmayne barely managed to bite back a squeal of excitement.

She called Goldie while she was still sitting in the car, parked in their condo's parking lot. The sky was clouding over again, and she could see the living room lights turned on. Brandon, tired of working in darkness. *We need a place with more windows,* she thought, listening to the phone ring. A bigger place. An extra bedroom for a second office. A yard. So many needs.

She half-expected Goldie to ignore her call, so she was a little surprised when the woman answered, her voice cheerful, as if nothing bad had severed their relationship. "Well, if it isn't Miss Casey! How are things in sunny Florida?"

"Cloudy," Casey laughed. "The usual summer storms. I called to check in and see how the show run-up is going. You getting your entries?"

"Plenty of 'em," Goldie said with satisfaction. "No complaints here. You're doing a good job with your ads. You really know your stuff."

"Well, good. And thanks." Casey marveled at how Goldie could shift gears. From accusations to accolades, without a single apology in the middle. Sharmayne would be better off without her. But she would not let her friend burn bridges. She'd help Sharmayne find her next job without pointing a single finger at Goldie. "I was wondering—I have a big series down here that I've been working on. I could use some help, and the bosses okayed a temp hire. Do you think I could borrow Sharmayne from you for a couple of weeks? We'd pay her airfare and lodging."

There was a moment of silence. Casey imagined Goldie leaning back in her desk chair, trying to wrap her head around this out-of-the-blue request. When she finally spoke again, her voice was suspicious. "Did Sharmayne put you up to this?"

"Sharmayne doesn't even know I'm asking," Casey said truthfully. "This is strictly because I need a temporary assistant while we're looking to hire a full-time one."

"Well, I'll see what I can do," Goldie said. "It's hard to manage around here without an assistant, though."

"I know it," Casey said with sympathy. "I bet one of your grooms is just waiting for a chance to prove themself, though. Or one of your students. I bet you have a long line waiting to be your next full-time working student." She almost felt bad for whatever kid was next up. But that was the horse business. Casey couldn't change it for everyone, but she might manage to change it for one person. "Maybe you could take someone on trial, see how they do."

"You might be right. In fact..." Goldie put down the phone. Casey heard her actions almost second-hand, muffled, as Goldie went to the door and shouted for someone. There were a few minutes of brief discussion, which made Casey tense in her seat, and then Goldie returned. "I think we have a solution that works for everyone."

"That's great! I'll touch base with Sharmayne and see what she thinks," Casey lied. It was the only lie of the call—she knew exactly what Sharmayne thought of a trip to Florida—and Casey congratulated herself on getting through it without resorting to any crazy stories. She did a little dance as she ended the call. Sharmayne was coming to Florida! It was as good as done.

Chapter Twenty-Seven

SHARMAYNE AND RAINA worked together like they'd been partners their entire life. Casey watched them walk around Tildy's farm, their heads close as they plotted courses and show set-up, and felt a little glow of pride—coupled with some jealousy. *Three's a crowd,* she reminded herself, every time she thought about butting in to their conversations.

Luckily, Sharmayne waved her over. "Casey! You have to see this. Raina is a course design *genius.*" She started pointing out the combinations Raina was suggesting for the late jumper classes. They were complex and interesting. "This is going to throw even the experienced kids through a loop," Sharmayne laughed.

"I didn't know you were a closet course designer," Casey said to Raina, impressed.

Raina shook her head. "I pick up things from my dad. He walked out here with me yesterday and showed me some new ways of looking at the fences, the way we use space, that kind of thing. Just some inspiration."

"We should put him on the payroll."

"Don't even joke about it." Raina made a show of looking around. "Tildy would take out on a hit on you. She relies on him for everything. And now? With the show just a couple weeks away? She's barely letting him out of her sight."

"Casey and Tildy are going to have to fight it out for your dad," Sharmayne giggled. "Come on, Casey, offer him the big bucks!"

Casey rolled her eyes. "Yeah, because we have big bucks to offer."

"Oh yeah, that reminds me—about that paycheck..." Sharmayne's eyes twinkled with mischief.

"Nice try. We agreed on no payment." Casey noticed Raina's wide-eyed look. "I'm *kidding*. We don't have unpaid interns...yet."

"Hopefully not ever," Sharmayne added. "Everyone deserves to get paid. Ask me, the career working student."

"We won't," Casey said absently. It was an easy promise to make. They barely had *paid* interns—or a paid temp, to be completely accurate. Most of the budget she'd gotten allocated for Sharmayne was going towards paying for her travel and living expenses. But Sharmayne was resourceful. Casey had heard her talking about looking at rentals with Raina, and she'd mentioned picking up some work teaching riding lessons at Tildy's barn as well. She was making the most of her time in Florida, using every moment to turn it into an opportunity that would catapult her career forward. "I'm so glad you guys are handling this," Casey told them. "You know it's the same day as Brandon's birthday? I'd be in so much trouble if I had to man the show."

"You'll be around a little, won't you?" Raina looked disappointed. "I want you to see how amazing we are in action."

"In the morning," Casey promised. "But only to watch and be

wowed. You won't need my help."

"Not a chance," Sharmayne laughed. "Don't even bring your work phone."

Casey walked back to her car alone, satisfied the two of them had the show plans in hand. She had to get home and work on advertising. It was so nice to hand all this show prep over to someone else, she thought happily. So freaking wonderful. She was in such a good mood, she didn't have a minor freak-out when her phone buzzed and she saw Sharon's name on the screen. She ducked into the shade of the barn atrium and answered. "Sharon, hey, what's up?"

"Surprise news," Sharon declared, her voice flat.

Casey went very still. She knew Sharon didn't care for surprises. And when it came to work, neither did she. This was something bad. "What's happening?"

"The new girl, the one you had us bring out on spec?"

"Sharmayne? She's doing awesome, by the way."

"Well, her boss is coming out."

"Her *boss*—"

"Goldie. The one who loves you, hates you, loves you again. She called us to get details on the show Sharmayne's working. I let it slip that it's at Tildy's place before I realized what was going on. So she knows where Sharmayne is."

"She isn't like, stalking her or something, is she?" Casey crept into a tack room and sat down on a bench. Her legs had gone a little wobbly. Goldie out here was the last thing any of them needed. The woman was too unpredictable. "Should I take her back to my house and hide her?"

"No, I don't think it's anything like that. She just said she wanted to see how Sharmayne was doing with this other show. She's going to come be a few days beforehand and go as a spectator, she says."

Casey ran her fingers through her hair. "Well, the show is coming together, and between Raina and Sharmayne, it should be a hit. I told them I'd make sure to be around in the first half of the day, then they'll take over. Sharmayne will be our company rep."

"I might need you to stay all day," Sharon warned her.

"I can't," Casey said, panicked. "I have my boyfriend's surprise party in the evening. It's at my barn, and there are a million details to handle. I absolutely cannot stay at the show all day."

Sharon's sigh was hardly reassuring.

But Casey would not be deterred. Not this time. She'd made plans for every eventuality, dammit.

Except, she had to admit, for Goldie.

Casey woke up on the Friday before the horse show weekend and checked every weather app on her phone, clicking through the stats obsessively. As the weekend crept closer, she'd been seized with a terrible certainty a hurricane would emerge from the Atlantic and sweep over West Palm, canceling the show and wrecking the triumph she'd planned for Sharmayne and Raina. It was a terrible time for a horse show, in weather terms—the end of August was the height of hurricane season, and the days were still hot and sticky with a chance of severe storms nearly every day.

But in terms of guaranteed attendance, Tildy's decision to hold a show before Labor Day weekend was a stroke of genius. A Saturday show at the end of August was always well attended—kids had just gone back to school, and they were big mad about it, raring to show off all the skills they'd acquired during a summer of riding camps and nonstop barn time, and dying to blow off steam after two weeks of confining desks and classrooms.

The only issue they'd run into had been a slowdown in entries after the Sheridan Farms fiasco. True to Casey's prediction, the trainers who had gotten refunds had taken to their keyboards and phones to complain about the show's lackluster response to the severe weather. Casey had to work serious damage control on her social media ads, deleting the negative-for-negativity's-sake posts and replying with concise answers on the posts which simply wanted more information on what had happened and how it would be prevented the next time around.

The negative attention definitely had a chilling effect on the show's early momentum. When classes didn't fill up by the initial closing date, Casey had Sharmayne extend the closing date, and even allowed last-minute entries without an extra fee tacked on top.

Now, she checked her social posts with a trepidation. Things were slightly worse than usual this morning, which she expected. Every time she increased ad spend to try to boost entries, the trolls amped up their comments by a factor of ten.

But she couldn't get too focused on the negativity. They'd gotten a lot of entries, anyway, and Tildy's show was going to be fantastic no matter what. There was no hurricane coming, the show would go off without a hitch, and that would put all these moaning and groaning Facebookers to bed. Speaking of which, time to get out of her bed. She slipped from beneath the sheet without waking Brandon and grabbed her riding clothes, heading into the living room to change.

She wasn't about to take James out on a group trail ride this evening without tiring him out a little first.

"Goldie!" Casey staggered backwards. Yes, it was overkill. But if there was one person on this planet she hadn't expected to see at Twin Palms this morning, it was Goldie.

Worse, Goldie in full riding attire and wearing such a satisfied grin on her face. Casey was well aware there were two sides to Goldie. She was pretty sure this was the manic side.

The side she'd been hoping against hope wouldn't come to Florida.

"Good morning, Casey! I came out to see that Thoroughbred of yours! Is that him?"

She pointed in the direction of the pasture, where the horses were milling around near the gate, already thinking about breakfast. There was no way to discern which horse she meant.

"The dark bay," Casey murmured. "I was just going to take him for a little hack this morning, though. We have a big group trail ride this afternoon, for my boyfriend's birthday, and I'm not sure how he's going to behave."

"A trail ride! Looks like maybe you learned a thing or two from me, right?"

And while Casey hated to admit it, she *had*. Goldie definitely spent more time out of the arena than in it, and her horses were laid back, happy, and easy to ride. Three things she couldn't always say about James. "Maybe you could give me a few pointers on relaxing him?" Casey asked, hoping she wasn't making a mistake. This could go either way. Goldie might be unpredictable. She might even be dangerous. But she was a very good trainer. And Casey hadn't had a riding lesson in a long time.

Goldie's smile was ear to ear. "What a fun idea! I'd love to!"

"Great. I'll go get him. You can...uh..."

"I'll wait right here." Goldie threw herself into one of the camp chairs which lived in the aisle. "Go tack up your pony and we'll see what we've got."

An hour later, Casey dismounted from James. She leaned against him for a moment, her hands gripping the stirrup leather. "Wow," she muttered. "Wow."

"You okay, Casey?" Goldie called. "That was a real good ride. You both did great."

It was an *incredible* ride. Casey's thighs were burning, her arms were trembling, and her ankles were so loose they felt like only her boots were holding her joints together, but the ride had been amazing. She slowly let go of the stirrup leather and straightened, walking to James's head to lead him back to the barn.

Goldie was grinning at her, one hand on the arena gate. She pushed it open theatrically. "I thought you said that horse was giving you trouble," she said with a wink.

Casey was too exhausted to speak. She just gave Goldie a grateful nod as she led James past. They'd worked on transitions, leg-yielding, and lateral movements—all movements which would help bring James back to her if he was starting to lose his head, all movements which required tremendous leg and core strength—and all movements which were hard to work on alone, without feedback or help, for months on end.

In the barn, Goldie gave a little speech about how Casey could use the principles they'd worked on while she was out on the trail with the group later that day. Then she looked at her watch and started edging towards her rental car. "I better get over to Ivy Place," she said. "I want to see how Sharmayne's doing."

Casey watched her go, hoping the lesson had snapped Goldie back to her sane, teaching brain. The manic glitter had left her eyes, and her voice had calmed as she'd called out instruction in the arena. It was possible, Casey thought, that Goldie wouldn't do anything to upset Sharmayne today.

Perhaps everything really would work out.

Chapter Twenty-Eight

EVERYTHING WAS WORKING out. Could it be? James, Brandon, Sharmayne, Raina, Sharon, Phillip—she'd managed everyone's expectations, horse included. Okay, Hannah was still a wild card. But she'd talk to Hannah tonight, at Brandon's party. Explain they needed to cool it with the constant horse show drama. It was taking up too much of their lives. They should concentrate on getting a regular coach, taking riding lessons, growing as equestrians. The high from her lesson this morning hadn't yet worn off. She wanted more of it.

Casey turned into the drive at Ivy Place, noting the balloons tied to the front fence and the fresh paint on the open gate. There was a gleam of metal shining in the distance as rows of horse trailers caught the morning sunlight. People were here—they'd brought their horses —this was happening! The rush of euphoria she felt was as stimulating as a shot of espresso. Things were shaking out. At last. After almost a year here. Casey felt her face slowly stretching into a smile as she parked the car in the spot they'd coned off for her.

She walked through the barn, craning her neck to get a glimpse of the warm-up arena beyond. Her smile slipped.

"Where is everyone?" she cried, running into the office. "That arena should be *packed!*"

Raina looked up at her with haunted eyes. "No one's coming."

"No one?" Casey felt dizzy. "I saw trailers when I was driving in—"

"Some people came," Sharmayne said. "Raina's being dramatic. Here's the deal: we have enough people to run the morning divisions. The little kids are here, all the hunter people are here. For entries, it's the afternoon jumper stuff we're worried about. Those classes never filled, even when we posted that we'd killed the same-day entry fee."

"Ugh." Casey sat down with a thud. "This is all because of the Sheridan mess." *My fault,* she added internally. If she'd only handled that better...

"And there's one more thing." Sharmayne shrugged her shoulders elaborately. "We lost our second judge. So we can't actually run all the hunter classes as scheduled. We only have a judge for one arena."

Raina put her head down on the desk and moaned.

"We're down a *judge?*" Casey stared at Sharmayne, who was acting way too cool about this. "The only classes we got entries for are hunters, and we don't have enough judges for them? How did this happen? When did you find out? Why didn't you call me?"

"It literally just happened," Sharmayne assured her. "We had Judy Friesling booked, as you know, but she called like three minutes before you walked in. Said she had food poisoning. We have one hunter ring judge until two p.m., but after that she's going to another engagement. Something down at White Fences. We can move the second arena classes to the afternoon, and we have a valid excuse because of the food poisoning, but we need someone to do the judging—"

"We can't tell anyone she has food poisoning," Raina interjected. She had folded her arms on the desk and had her head resting on them, like a toddler falling asleep at the dinner table. "That's her private business."

"Well, then she shouldn't have told me," Sharmayne declared. "Because I am using that information. And I am making up gory details to make the story worse. I'm using everything I can to gain sympathy from those hard-ass trainers out there."

Casey looked at the two women, feeling helpless. Raina lifted her eyebrows in a sympathetic grimace. Sharmayne shrugged again. *What can you do?*

What could they do? They'd never find another judge before two o'clock. Horse-people didn't sit around on sunny Saturdays. They went out and worked horses, or taught lessons...

Casey had an idea. Not a very good idea, probably. She didn't even know if...but maybe...? Casey pressed her lips together, mulling it over.

Sharmayne and Raina turned back to each other, digging into the problem as best they could. Raina was flicking through an address book. "I can start calling contacts from my dad's book," she offered. "Although a lot of these people aren't in Florida right now. They go to New England for the summer."

"Lucky them," Sharmayne snorted. "We need the real OGs who aren't afraid to sweat it out in Florida all summer."

"You sure acclimated fast, I'll give you that—wait a minute." Raina held up the address book, tapping a page. "Sharmayne, this isn't *your* Goldie, is it?"

Casey looked up, eyes wide. It couldn't be. Just *couldn't* be—

Sharmayne leaned over to look at the page. "That *is* her. How weird! Although the horse world is really small. I wonder how he knows her."

"This book goes back a couple decades," Raina said. "It might have everyone in the business listed."

Casey decided it was a sign. "Sharmayne, is Goldie a judge?"

"I don't know!" Sharmayne stared at her. "It's never come up before but...I guess she might be?"

Raina looked between them, her face lighting up. "You guys, this is the answer."

"She might not be a judge," Sharmayne said doubtfully. "Then again, I didn't know she was a realtor, either. That just came up one day when a boarder asked her for a recommendation. Goldie's the kind of person who just does a little bit of everything on the side, you know? And she doesn't always tell me where she's going when she leaves for a few days. She can be very secretive, for no reason at all."

"Oh my God," Casey muttered. She tugged out her phone. "Girls, this is going to work out. I am manifesting it."

"Manifest me a venti latte while you're at it," Raina said, rubbing at her dark hair. "With a shot of bourbon."

Casey tossed her credit card on the desk. The phone was ringing, ringing, ringing. "Send someone on a caffeine run," she said. "Quad for me, thanks."

Four shots of espresso would be good for a start, she figured.

"Goldie's on her way," she told them a few minutes later. "We can start the second ring a half-hour late, and it will just feel like a regular show for the veterans. Now, we need to figure out the jumper classes. We can't run classes with two or three horses in them. It's an embarrassment." Any photos from a sparsely attended jumper ring would bolster the positions of the trainers who had talked trash about the company. It would be a failure on top of a failure. Casey wasn't so worried about her job anymore, but she needed to preserve Sharmayne's position. She knew Sharmayne had no interest in going back to California with Goldie, and she was a natural at running horse shows.

Raina picked up her phone. "I know some trainers who aren't here today. I'll call around and see who I can convince to come out here. We can push back the classes by an hour or two, give them a chance to get here. Folks won't freak about a delay if they're aware it's coming."

"Not as if it's a major power outage or anything," Casey said with a wry smile. She looked back at her own phone, wishing she had contacts she could reach out to. But the only horse-people she knew anymore were the riders at St. Johns. And St. Johns was two hours away...

"Worth a try," she muttered, and left the office.

She'd make this call in private.

"Hey, Sky?"

"Casey!" Sky's ebullient voice nearly blew out her speaker. It seemed that way, anyway. Casey leaned her head back against the car seat headrest and closed her eyes, wishing she could be with her old friend right now. But that's what this call was about, right? She opened them again.

"Sky, I'm so sorry I haven't kept in touch."

"I see your pictures online. You like mine. It's all good." Sky's voice was light. "We're both at busy phases in our careers, right?"

"Sometimes I think my career is eating my entire life," Casey admitted. "And yet, somehow, I'm not even sure what my career is. Does that make sense?" She was getting off-track, but it had been *so* long since she'd enjoyed a good conversation with Sky. The younger woman always gave her new energy and positive advice. She'd forgotten about that—how?

"Perfect sense," Sky laughed. "I'm doing what I wanted to do when I grew up, but now I'm less and less sure of what I want to do when I grow up. How's that for a conundrum?"

"Oh God. We're hopeless."

"Admitting that is the first step on the road to hope. So, what's up? You didn't just call because you were thinking of me," Sky teased. "And I don't expect you to, by the way."

Easy-going, undemanding: these were a few of Casey's favorite things in a friend. The only way she could manage a friendship, actually, was if the other person had absolutely no expectations of her. A lesson to unpack on another day, though. "I'm in a tight spot, and I had a crazy idea that might work out for everyone, if you're free and able."

"Oh? Color me intrigued. Whatcha got, Case?"

"I'm running a show at Ivy Place today—"

"Fancy! I've been there once or twice, looking at horses. That place is like a luxury resort for equestrians."

"Everything but the hotel," Casey agreed, encouraged by Sky's interest. "And I hear that might be coming. Well, here's the thing. You might have heard about the Sheridan show a few weeks ago..."

"Totally not your fault, by the way."

"It was, and it wasn't. I can admit that. But it's cost us our jumper ring this afternoon. As in, almost no one has entered the jumper classes."

"Oh. That's a shame."

Casey wished Sky would just guess what she was asking already, but that was probably asking too much of the universe. The universe had already given her Goldie as a judge. She had to meet it halfway here. "Are you busy this afternoon? Because I can offer you free everything.

I'll even cover the insurance and medical fee."

"Wait. Are you asking me to come down there and show?"

She didn't sound skeptical or annoyed. She sounded interested. Casey had suspected Sky's spontaneous personality could work in her favor here. Looks like she might have guessed right. "I know it's crazy last-minute, but if you load up a trailer and bring some kids down, that gives us six more competitors in our classes. Raina's adding in a few more. If I can just get it to a dozen or so per class, we won't look like a total failure on social media tomorrow."

"And that's what it all comes down to? This is about reputation?"

"You got it. You know me, reputation management is in my wheelhouse." Casey leaned forward, tipping her forehead against the steering wheel. She was so close. "Sky, a lot of people's futures are riding on this show today. It's hard to explain. But there are some really cool women here today that I'd like to introduce to you. And then I think you'll understand why I decided to ask you this crazy favor. Plus," she added, humor finally entering her tone, "I think everyone will have fun and your kids will clean up."

"Fine," Sky said.

"Fine?" Just like that? She didn't have to do any more negotiating, any more wheedling?

"Yeah, fine. It sounds great. I've got a crowd here today—Arden is here, Gwen, a couple others—so I'll just send one of them to get signatures on some release forms while the others load the trailer. I'm guessing we can get there by four at the latest. Will that work?"

Casey let out a gusty breath. Four was late, but if Raina pulled in any local trainers, they'd still have some competitors for the lower divisions. All of Sky's students could jump in the higher classes, anyway. "That will more than work. I'm so grateful, I can't even tell you."

"Come on, Casey," Sky said warmly. "That's what friends are for. I got your back, sister. See you in a few."

Casey hung up the call. For a moment, she sat in the car, letting the cold air conditioning wash over her. Then she picked up her phone and dialed one more number. There was someone else who deserved to be at this show today. She just needed a little help to get her here.

"Hi, Liz? It's Casey. I have a favor to ask you."

Chapter Twenty-Nine

Liz arrived first, with Hannah hanging out of the passenger window of her truck, waving excitedly at Casey. "I made it!" she shrieked. "I made it!"

Casey shook her head and depressed the accelerator on the golf cart she'd borrowed from Tildy's small fleet, directing Liz back to the trailer parking and into an open spot. Liz put the truck into park and slowly walked over to Casey's golf cart, leaving Hannah to unload Caruso alone.

"Casey, girl, I don't see how this is going to solve that girl's horse-show crazy brain." She slid onto the vinyl seat next to her. "Pretty sure Maria asked you to calm her down, not amp her up."

"I know. But Hannah's problem isn't that she loves horse shows," Casey explained. "It's that she wants to be included. She has a huge fear of missing out. The kids call it FOMO."

"Made-up words," Liz grunted. "The English language doesn't have enough words?"

"Anyway," Casey laughed, "my friend Sky is going to take her under her wing today. Because apparently she can never do me enough favors. It will be good for her to get some help walking courses and getting around the warm-up fences. Maybe it'll be what she needs to focus on finding a working student position and really put her riding first."

Liz nodded. "Well, you might be right."

They watched Hannah back Caruso off the trailer. The horse looked around, eyes wide, and whinnied, hoping to find some friends. From the barns and arenas, several neighs came floating back, carried on the light summer breeze. Hannah laughed and patted him on the neck. She led him towards the barn, unbothered by his dancing jig-jog and high head.

"They're not a bad pair," Liz allowed. "Just need polished up."

"I think today's the day Hannah realizes that."

Liz patted her on the knee. "Here's hoping, Miss Casey. Well, I told her everything was on her today, but I'm feeling generous. You want to hang on a minute and let me pull her tack outta the trailer? And then we can drive it up to the barn."

"No problem," Casey said. "Here, I'll even help."

Liz opened the tack compartment, and they tugged Hannah's saddle and grooming gear out, piling it on the golf cart's backseat. Nothing was particularly clean—Hannah wasn't big on cleaning her tack every day, and she'd probably just thrown everything into Liz's trailer the moment it had come to a halt outside the barn—but it was all good, serviceable leather. Hannah had a good foundation, Casey thought. She had the tools. All she needed was to learn how to use them, and how to be patient with the process.

Could Sky impress a lesson like that on her in a few hours this afternoon? If she could, Hannah might really have the future of her dreams.

By one o'clock, Goldie was sitting underneath an umbrella judging the under-14 equitation, Hannah had ridden Caruso in a long stirrup division and no one had been injured in the process, and Casey had ordered sandwiches and a second caffeine infusion for her tired show office. She was already dreading the evening. How had she ever thought she could run a horse show *and* put on a birthday party in one day? The answer, of course, was that she'd underestimated how wrong things could go, and how quickly it could happen. But she was learning that horse shows, like a lot of equestrian matters, only existed to test how many ways one fool-proof system could fail.

Raina looked exhausted, dark circles under her eyes as she bent her head over her lunch. Sharmayne, on the other hand, looked exhilarated. She'd even squared her shoulders and handled Goldie, taking on fitting her boss—her former boss? Casey could only hope so—with her radio and name badge, escorting her out to the judge's stand to oversee her arena, and taking her coffee order.

Now she tore into her sandwich with one hand while she flicked through her phone with the other, checking social for any mentions of the show. "Look at this!" She held up an Instagram photo for Casey and Raina to admire. "Caption says, '*Having a great day at Ivy Place. This farm is gorgeous and the show is great.*'" Sharmayne nodded her head at the phone. "Can't ask for better publicity than that."

"I'll go through the posts in a little while and repost some of them," Casey said. "Right now I don't have the energy."

"I'll do it right now," Sharmayne said, throwing the rest of her sandwich into her mouth. "You just have to ask for permissions, right? Here, let me do that." And she started typing, fingers flying over her phone. Casey watched, dazed by her energy. Whoever said youth was wasted on the young had never met anyone like Sharmayne.

Luckily, her high spirits spread around the room. Raina picked up her phone and started skimming, too. "Oh, hey! The crew from Waverly Farm is coming, too. They posted that they're coming to do jumpers this afternoon." Raina smiled with satisfaction. "I called them first. Glad I trusted my instincts."

In all, Raina had convinced four trainers to hitch up and bring their students and horses to the show for the afternoon. It would add up to nearly thirty horses, with more riders. And with Sky coming as well, plus anyone who might be enticed by her frequent Facebook posts about waived same-day fees, Casey thought the afternoon might not just be saved...it might be a roaring success.

And the sooner the better, because she still had to get out of here at a decent time. Brandon's party at Twin Palms was due to begin at six o'clock.

Sky arrived at three-thirty, hauling her six-horse trailer and with kids crammed into every available seat in her truck. A weary-looking horse show mom followed in an SUV, also crammed with kids. Casey had never been so happy to see anyone in her life. It wasn't about the horse show now; she was thankful to see her friend after so many months.

"And I phoned up some friends to come as well," she said over Casey's shoulder as Casey squeezed her in a tight hug. "Some local girls I know here, a few in south Brevard. They'll make it for some classes later. It's not a sell-out crowd, but it's something."

"It really is. Thank you so much for coming! I can't believe it. Thank God for casual dress codes, right?"

Sky laughed. "No doubt. It's a lot easier to hit the road last minute when you can wear polo shirts and breeches. Gives everyone a chance to show off the St. Johns polos I gave them at Christmas." Sky turned, watching as Gwen and Arden started to unload the horses. "Take them into that barn and look for a girl named Hannah," she called. "She should be jumping up and down waving at you, if I got the right idea of her personality."

"You nailed it," Casey said. "Thank you for taking her under your wing this afternoon. She needs it so badly."

"It's no problem. Training eleven kids is the same as training ten. Everything else all set? You got this whole circus under control, didn't you?"

Casey nodded. "I think we did! I've got Goldie, the woman from California, judging. We delayed the afternoon classes just a little to give folks some time to get here, and a few more barns have showed up. Like you said, it won't be full, but it's not empty. And I don't think there's going to be a tropical deluge, either." She glanced up at the sky, noting the wooly cumulus clouds weren't threatening to turn into thunderstorms. At least, not yet. You could never be sure in August.

"And hey, no power outages, no problems, right?" Sky grinned at Casey's grimace. "It'll get forgotten."

"It was just such a nightmare. I thought for sure I'd get fired, and then everything would have been for nothing."

"Everything?"

"You know...moving here, having to leave you and your barn, all of that."

"It's not for nothing," Sky told her. "You came because Brandon's your person. He still is, isn't he?"

"Oh, definitely. He is my person—that's such a nice way of putting it. And I was trying to throw him a party tonight, but with the show going haywire, I'm not sure how our final set-up is going to happen."

"If you're stuck here for a while, can't you call anyone else to take it on? I know it sucks asking for favors, but people really do want to help you out." Sky put a hand on her arm. "People *like* helping you, Casey. Because we always know you'll be there to help us out. You've got that kind of personality."

"A pushover?" Casey grinned.

"A good and giving person," Sky said seriously. "The sort of person who never asks for favors, but always should."

Casey nodded. "Right. Well, I've already called in every horse show favor I have today...I guess I might as well call in a party favor."

"Hah! I see what you did there."

Casey rolled her eyes. "Totally inadvertent."

"Admit it. You're punny."

It took her a minute—and a little distance from the crowds—to get up the courage to call Maria. She'd already asked Maria for so much, and given her nothing in return. But she didn't have a choice. The day was slipping away. And there was no way she could leave Sharmayne and Raina here to take the heat if anything else went wrong with the show. She looked at the phone number on her screen for a long moment, and then she hit *call*.

"Maria? Hi, it's Casey."

Casey stood near Goldie, watching as Gwen galloped her bay warmblood, Juniper, over the course. The girl had only gotten better in the saddle since Casey had left St. Johns, and she'd already pulled two blue ribbons for the afternoon. It was looking like another one was in her future. Casey had brought Goldie a fresh coffee and the entries for the next class, but she found she couldn't pull herself away from Gwen's ride.

The duo was leaving the arena to scattered applause when Goldie leaned over. Her eyebrows lifted as she asked Casey, "Do you know that girl?"

"Yeah, that's Gwen, from my old barn up in Brevard."

"How old is she?"

"Fifteen?" Casey guessed. She'd never been good at remembering anyone's ages. "That might be too high. She's something, isn't she?"

Goldie was wearing sunglasses, but Casey could tell her eyes were following Gwen as she rode away. "She's damn good," Goldie said finally. "I'd like to poach that girl for myself when she's eighteen."

Casey thought about Gwen in Southern California, riding horse after horse at Sungold Ranch. Her cool, no-nonsense demeanor would mesh perfectly with Goldie's particular brand of crazy. But Goldie was unpredictable—look at the way she'd turned on Sharmayne and Casey, and the way she was treating both of them right now, like they were her most precious friends. Casey was certain that Goldie had flown all the way out here to make sure no one poached Sharmayne from her, *after* she'd gone out of her way to make Sharmayne feel like trash for stepping up and taking charge of the show series. Then she'd flipped the script and made nice, giving Casey that lesson this morning—so long ago, now—and stepping up to judge.

People like Goldie were a dime a dozen in the horse business—all ego and no sense—and Casey didn't want to see Gwen end up as her pawn. "She's going to FSU like her sister," Casey lied. "She's a Florida girl through and through."

"Too bad. I'd offer her a job the second she graduated high school."

The next rider was trotting into the ring, taking Goldie's attention back to her job. Casey turned and headed down the steps. She didn't feel bad at all about denying the precocious Gwen a job offer before she'd even turned eighteen. Goldie would go back to California and continue her reign of terror there, but it would not be at the cost of Casey's friend's careers.

And that included Sharmayne.

Casey found her in the office, rummaging through a stack of entries, while Raina looked on.

"Everything okay, ladies?"

They both nodded. "Just doing a final count," Raina murmured, not wanting to disturb Sharmayne. "Wanted to make sure it matched what we've got in the spreadsheet."

"Two-hundred and thirteen," Sharmayne said. "Is that it?"

Raina glanced at her laptop screen. "That's it!"

"Well, not too bad," Casey said, "considering what we went through to get folks here this afternoon."

"We won't make money," Raina said, "but Tildy wasn't doing this to make money. She just wanted to say she had a horse show circuit of her own."

Casey shook her head. "I rarely say this, but thank God for eccentric rich ladies."

"Emphasis on the rich part," Sharmayne said. "The eccentric part gets a lot more leeway when they're willing to spend money."

Casey knew she was talking about Goldie—not rich, just eccentric. And controlling. "Sharmayne, can I talk to you when you have a minute?"

Sharmayne and Raina exchanged meaningful glances. Casey immediately knew they had left her out of a conversation. "Sure," Sharmayne agreed. "Let's go get a Coke."

They sat down at one of the patio tables set up beneath a cluster of oak trees near the concessions. "You did an amazing job prepping this show," Casey began.

"Let me stop you real quick," Sharmayne said. "I helped you and

Raina, but *I* didn't prep this show. The three of us did. It's a big job, and I kind of can't believe your bosses ever expect one person to do it. *They* don't do it alone—those two are always connected at the hip, from what I can tell. This was a team effort, and I'm proud of the three of us."

"Okay," Casey said, momentarily distracted. "That's very kind—"

"It's the truth. And I'd do it with the two of you again. But this isn't the job for me."

Casey stared at Sharmayne. "You knew I was going to offer you a permanent job?"

"I figured. And I appreciate it, really. But I've had another offer."

"You have? From who?"

Sharmayne smiled. "From Raina."

"From *Raina?* But—I don't understand—" Raina couldn't hire anyone...she worked for Tildy. Did she mean that Tildy hiring Sharmayne for—something?

"Raina's dad put down a deposit on a place. It's up north a little ways. Near Indiantown, Raina says," Sharmayne explained. "Whatever that means. Anyway, he's been living here and working for Tildy all these years, because he was saving every penny to buy his own farm. And he wants Raina to run it. And Raina wants *me* to run it with her. We're going into business together."

Casey didn't know what to say. She felt her mouth falling open. They were both leaving? At least Indiantown wasn't that far away. But still, she'd thought they were building a team and now...it would be just her again. She squeezed her fingers together tightly, waiting for Sharmayne to finish. And then what? She'd just fall apart, that was all.

Sharmayne hadn't seen her discomfort. Her face was lit up with excitement. "We have a lot of work to do, obviously, doing the business plan and all of that boring bank stuff, but the important fact is, we work great together and we owe that to you! We lived on opposite ends of the country, and we never would have even *met* if you hadn't put us together. So thanks, Casey." Sharmayne leaned forward and took her hands. "I mean it. This is the chance I needed. Not to go work for another snooty northeast trainer and have people look at me funny because my big hair doesn't fit in a tiny bun. Now, *I'm* going to be the snooty trainer," she laughed. "And I'm going to make sure everyone feels like they belong."

Casey nodded her head. "I'm really happy for you," she said tightly.

Sharmayne took her hands, prying her taut fingers apart. "Hey," she whispered. "This isn't the end of anything. We're going to be right up the road. This could be good for everyone. Maybe you could even bring James out there to live. We'd cut you a friends and family discount. You're both of those things, as far as I'm concerned."

"That's really kind." Casey tried to swallow her grief. "I just feel like I'm losing the best coworkers I've ever had. It's going to take a minute."

"Nothing really has to change," Sharmayne insisted. "We can all be friends. And you're not going to be working on horse shows anymore, remember? You're just going to be doing the marketing out of your home office like before. Which is what you wanted."

Casey managed a smile and nodded. She hoped Sharmayne was right. But something told her that Sharon wouldn't hire someone right off the street. She'd taken Sharmayne on as a temp, and it had worked out. But who would handle the coming shows? They'd come right back to Casey.

"You're still upset." Sharmayne tipped her head sideways. "I can tell. You don't think this is going to work out?"

"For *me,* not for you. I'm really happy for you guys," Casey insisted. "Don't read anything into my awful behavior. I'm just tired. This job wears you out. You're right to go and do something else, honestly."

"I think you should quit," Sharmayne said.

Casey raised her eyebrows.

"No, I'm serious. You hate doing this. You hate running shows. And it's just going to keep happening. Let's be real. It's never going to be a huge business with tons of employees. The horse business is hands on. You know that."

Casey sighed and looked away, glancing over the piles of paperwork, the detritus of a half-dozen desperately needed coffee breaks. What a full day it had been. And she was leaving now, but Sharmayne and Raina still had hours and hours left. "You're probably right. But I can barely afford to keep James as it is. And I was hoping to get a bigger place. Brandon and I need more room—he wants a dog, and I keep saying no, and then there's the fact that he really needs his own office..."

"Don't give up hope," Sharmayne told her. "I've found that if you want something and need something enough, the universe will provide." She wrapped Casey up in a warm hug. "Like it provided *you.*"

It was a nice thought. *The universe will provide.* Casey walked out of the show office, her unshed tears finally drying, and tried to think back over her recent history to see if the saying was true. In a way, she supposed, it had. Maybe Sharmayne had a point. She had been sad and miserable last spring, and the universe had led her to St. Johns, and to James. She had been desperate for a job that would let her move with Brandon, and the universe had led her to her horse show job. She had been confused and lonely in West Palm, and the universe had led her to Raina and Sharmayne.

What if the universe was trying to lead her to something else, and she just hadn't seen it yet?

She went over everything weird and different in her life, looking for roadsigns. Brandon learning to ride—that was a weird one, for sure. Her sudden feeling of claustrophobia in the condo—well, that might just be more of a complaint than a sign that she should be finding change, right? The realization that she was losing Sharmayne —the girl she'd brought here to be her colleague, the girl she'd been trying to *save* from a life of drudgery—to start her own business with Raina...

Yeah, that could be a sign, for sure.

But of what?

Casey's phone buzzed. She glanced at it, eyes scanning the message from Maria. At least the party was under control. For once in her life, she didn't have to feel panicked about an event she was planning. Maria said everything was ready. Now it was just time to wait for the party's main guest to arrive. And for her. Maria had a way of phrasing her texts; Casey could just see her adding that last line, a sly smile on her lips. *You have to get here, now,* that little side comment was saying.

The panic rose again. Time to get to the barn? Was it that late already? Casey felt simultaneously as if the day had flown by and as if the day had lasted a record number of hours. A hundred, maybe. This morning's five a.m. alarm seemed to belong to another era of her life.

Casey looked around the show-grounds. The small afternoon classes were turning out to be a hit with the exhibitors. No one had to wait around in hours-long crowds by the in-gates, and eager kids were entering more classes than they'd intended to because Raina's courses were so exciting and fun to ride. Tildy might just break even on the show, and with the good will spreading online, the next one would be fully attended—Casey was sure of it. She'd trained two people to run one fantastic horse show, and while that accomplishment might not make a difference in her current job, it would be good for them at their next one, running their own farm.

Heart suddenly full, Casey sent a quick text to Raina and Sharmayne, letting them know she was heading to pick up Brandon, and she was leaving the show in their capable hands.

Chapter Thirty

BRANDON WAS WAITING for her when she got home, wearing his jeans and cowboy boots as she'd requested. She nearly stumbled over him in the entryway.

"How's the horse show going?" he asked, picking her up by the elbows.

"Like a well-oiled machine," she said. "Now, anyway. It was a bumpy morning. I meant to be home *way* before this. Are you ready to go? I just need to change really quick."

Brandon displayed his boots. "I'm wearing my boots, as you requested, although when I read that text, I considered calling the FBI to report a hostage situation. Are you sure I'm allowed to wear my boots in public? You won't die of embarrassment?"

She rolled her eyes at him. "I might cringe a little, but you can help me through it by simply proving they were a good buy." Casey moved into the bedroom and tugged off her sweaty horse show gear. It was almost painful to put on riding tights again; she wanted to take a shower and get into an oversized t-shirt, instead.

Brandon followed her, stepping carefully on the sand-colored carpet, as if there was any damage his boots could possibly inflect on such old, battered pile. "But where are we going? Please tell me it's not line-dancing. I didn't learn that part of being a cowboy." Then he noticed her tights. "Oh."

Casey pulled a riding shirt over her head. "Well, Brandon, I've decided to embrace your new cowboy spirit."

"Well, it's about time." A grin spread across his face. "I know I look a little glitzy next to you in your breeches and boots, but it's okay, hun. People will still think you're pretty. They'll just think I'm prettier."

Casey laughed and dragged him out to the car. They drove west, towards the approaching sunset, and a heavy border of distant thunderstorms hanging along the horizon. While it wouldn't rain this evening, they'd likely get a little shade for the trail ride...and probably a nice sunset of pink and purple, too. Casey smiled. At last, things were going to plan.

Twin Palms Ranch had never looked so festive, she was sure of it. As they drove up to the barn, her breath caught in her throat. She'd done some of the work the day before, but Maria had finished the job, including hanging a dazzling array of Christmas lights along the barn's front porch and in the two palm trees which leaned over the roof. They were weak against the evening sunlight, but the effect was still pretty good—and it would be sensational after sunset. Worth the mosquitoes, and the prodigious amounts of Off spray the party would require, for sure. Casey grinned as she heard Brandon suck in his breath.

"Casey! A ranch party? This is incredible!" Brandon clapped his hands like a little kid. "And everyone's here! You got my IT friends to come to a ranch—Casey, that's like witchcraft, seriously. And isn't that Park's truck and trailer? Wait—how did you know about Park?"

"I asked Maria," she admitted, parking the car. "We had a lot of time for talking while she helped me get James used to the trails here."

He stared at her. "You've been trail-riding?"

"For the past three weeks," Casey said. "And you were right. It's pretty relaxing. I think I needed the vacation. But everything in its place. I had an incredible riding lesson with Goldie this morning, and we had some major break-throughs. I'm never going to stop working hard to be a better rider, you know that, but I think I can balance things a little better."

Brandon leaned over and gave her a kiss. "You know you can do whatever you want with horses, and I'll never try to stop you, right?"

She laughed a little uncertainly, wondering if there was some hidden meaning behind his words. "That's—certainly what I would hope."

"I mean, I wouldn't tell you were wrong if you chose to change things. Like, with James. Or the barn, or whatever...it's coming out wrong. Sorry." Brandon shook his head. "I just want you to be happy. All the time. And when you get stressed, I worry."

"Well, no one's happy all the time," she hedged. "I can't really promise that I won't be stressed quite a lot. Work threw me another curveball today and I just—" She shrugged, trying to dump the hidden weight from her shoulders. "Stress seems like a big part of my life, is all. I'm trying to accept it."

"Casey. Let's not be like that. Let's not just accept things. We want to be happy all the time. That's certainly what I want for you." Brandon took her hands, gripping them tightly. His face was so earnest, Casey was a little taken aback. Was everything okay? He was being kind of weird. But, she reminded herself, Brandon could be over the top emotionally sometimes. It was endearing. Most of the time. "Anyway, what I want to say is, if you're happy riding James on the trails with me, that's great. And if you're happier prepping for big horse shows, that's great, too. I'll be okay with either. That's...that's all I wanted to say."

She peered at him. It didn't really sound like that was all he wanted to say. But there wasn't any time to dig deeper. The party had emerged from the barn, and they were headed for the car in a big, cheering mass.

Casey leaned over and kissed him. "Happy birthday, Brandon," she said, and turned him over to his welcome brigade.

"This is a good place to be," Brandon said, looking around. Then he waved his arms. "Except for the mosquitoes. I hoped the Off would work a little harder."

Maria appeared with a small brass tray, which was emitting a cloud of scented smoke. She dropped it on the table between Casey and Brandon with a *plunk*. "Mosquito coil," she explained, and headed off to her own table.

"Well, that should help a little," Casey laughed, tugging her hoodie over her head. "That and covering up. They'll mostly clear out once it's fully dark."

"The smoke smells pretty good, anyway," Brandon said. "Like a weird incense."

"Yeah, I like it. Hopefully, it isn't killing us. But if not the smoke, the West Nile and the Zika." She shook her head. "Why do we live in Florida?"

"Because we're crazy," Brandon supplied. "And we love it here."

"We really do." Casey thought about her time in San Diego. It was beautiful, but it wasn't home. "Look at the palm trees silhouetted against the sky."

Brandon turned in his chair, following her gaze. The twin palms were black against the luminous purple-blue sky, their Christmas lights twinkling in the soft breeze. Beyond them, far out over the peninsula's interior, lightning flickered on and off, illuminating massive thunderheads. They looked like heavenly paper lanterns. "I appreciate the fireworks show," Brandon said. "That must have really set you back."

"That's just Florida for you."

The party had quieted around them, people were winding down, settling in chairs to enjoy the cold drinks and leftover snacks. The trail ride had been brief, but fun, since Brandon's work friends couldn't come along. They'd ridden across the open prairie as flocks of ibis and lone herons made their way home to roost, their long legs and wings black against the candy-colored sunset. Along the high trails between the drainage canals, their horses had snorted as alligators slipped into the water, splashing noisily as if to complain about the party's intrusion on their late evening sunbathing. And best of all, they'd ridden home to a stereophonic symphony from a pair of owls hidden in twin oak hammocks, listening to the enormous birds calling out, *Who cooks for you?* to each another in their deep, melodic hoots.

While they were out savoring the sounds of wild Florida, the non-riding members of the party hung out at the barn, listening to music and fishing in the pond, watched over by a beady-eyed Liz. Once they'd returned, Liz hopped back into her truck and drove off to pick up Hannah from the horse show. Hannah had been texting her all afternoon, she told Casey grimly. "She says today was the best day of her life. So we've got that going for us."

Casey could only shake her head, in awe at the things

accomplished in one day.

And except for the cloud of mosquitoes which rose at dusk, sending everyone running for the DEET and Maria calmly wandering with her little censers of magic bug-clearing smoke, the party was a roaring success. Casey felt like she'd successfully entertained two different factions: the horse-people and the non, and that, she decided, was the secret to a happy equestrian life.

"Things are okay," she said, just thinking out loud, and Brandon smiled at her.

"You better believe they are."

There were so many things she wanted to fix, so many things which still stymied her. But at least she had this moment. She leaned across the table, taking Brandon's hands in hers, and—

"Casey! We did it!"

She spun around, shocked to see Sharmayne and Raina. They were getting out of Raina's truck, both women looking tired, but happy. Casey jumped up to meet them. "You guys! Congratulations on—on everything!"

Her friends wound their way through the tables to her, wrapping her up in one big group hug. "What a day," Raina said, her voice husky with overuse. "I can't believe we got through it in one piece. And it was a success! I'm proud of us."

"I'm proud of *you*," Casey assured her. "Both of you. An amazing team. I'm so happy you're sticking together. Sad for me, of course."

"We were talking about that this evening," Sharmayne said. "While we were cleaning up, and sending folks on their way, we had time for a really good talk. And there's something we want to discuss with you."

"Can we go somewhere quiet?" Raina asked. "Just for a minute."

Casey glanced over her shoulder; Brandon waved her away. "I'm fine."

"Come over here," Sharmayne said, dragging her away from the party and into the dark night.

"I'm nervous," Casey joked as they left the circle of light. "And not just because there are probably gators out here."

"Casey," Raina began, "You know my dad is setting us up with a farm."

"Of course, and I'm really happy for you."

"Casey, please hang on a second. Listen to me."

Casey looked at Raina. Her friend's face was hard to read in the dim light from the barn, but she could tell something was up. Something major. Casey felt her hands clenching at her sides.

Raina took a breath. "Here's the deal. There are three houses on this property. The place is huge—it used to be a cattle ranch. My dad is taking the small cottage in the back of the property; he's retiring and he just wants to sit around and fish, or something. Sharmayne and I, we're taking the main house, by the barns."

"We want the opposite of her dad," Sharmayne interjected. "We went to be in the thick of everything, all the time."

"Right," Raina agreed. "But there's a little parcel by itself, off to one side. It's like its own little mini farm, honestly...So here's the thing, Casey. We want you to come work with us, and we want to offer you the house and board for James as part of your salary."

"Most of your salary," Sharmayne amended. "We can't pay much, and we were going to rent this place out but...we'd rather have you, if we can have you."

"We need your business know-how," Raina said. "You know how to run a marketing campaign, you can run an office, you can get sponsors and partnerships. You have all that corporate stuff we don't have. Yeah, we got this show off the ground, but we did everything with the supplies you gave us. We didn't do a thing on our own."

"So we need you," Sharmayne went on. "This is as much you doing us a favor as anything else. We have no guarantee this business will work out. But we are going to give it everything we've got, and we're going to have a lot of fun doing it. It just—it would be perfect if you were part of it."

Raina nodded. She tugged Sharmayne close, wrapping one arm around her shoulders. Casey noticed the easy intimacy, and for a moment she forgot the opportunity they were offering her. She just felt proud and happy, once more, that she'd brought these two together. "Casey?" Raina asked. "What do you think? Do you need time?"

"Come on," Sharmayne said cajolingly. "What's there to think about? It's *us*. It's a horse farm. It's going to be great."

Casey couldn't speak. She looked from Raina to Sharmayne, then back over her shoulder, where Brandon had gotten up and was talking with Park and his friends. Brandon, in cowboy boots. Brandon, who had ridden Chico with such easy balance and comfort on the trails tonight. Casey had always thought of him as her city boy, but...could he be a farm boy, after all? Could *they* move to a farm? It would certainly solve the space problem.

She turned back to the women, who were watching her avidly.

"Well?" Raina asked again.

Casey smiled. "Would we be allowed to have a dog?"

Chapter Thirty-One

"I HAVE TO admit, it's wilder out here than I'd expected." Brandon leaned on the porch railing. He cocked his head, listening to the wood creak. "And a little more rickety. This is going to take some work to make it livable." He pushed on the railing again. "Or even to make it *insurable*."

"I know." Casey looked around the porch, taking in the half-rotted floor boards and the sagging rails. The house behind them was showing its age as well. It was an old wood-frame house, and while it had been kept up to some degree, decades of exposure to the harsh Floridian elements showed. Also, there was definitely a mouse skeleton in the kitchen. Casey wasn't sure if a skeleton was better or worse than a living rodent.

The house nestled into the pine forest like a rabbit tucking into the underbrush. On three sides, the woods were taking over, tall longleaf pines rising over palmetto, bayberry, and ferns. In front of them, though, the property was still wide open. A blue pond, so round it might have been drawn with a compass, sat between a scrap of front yard and the pastures surrounding the farm buildings in the middle distance. They were about half a mile away from the steel buildings and wooden barns, which would someday house bright, airy stables and sturdy outbuildings. Beyond the structures, some large earthmover was growling away at its work, prepping the site where the arenas would be laid.

There was so much work to be done, Casey wondered how Raina and Sharmayne had managed to get a grasp of it all. But their business plan, housed in a binder an inch thick, was a thing of beauty. They had a timeline for everything, from replacing the barbed wire in the outermost pastures with diamond-mesh wire and boards, to adding lights over the arenas in time for the short winter evenings. There was already a waiting list for boarders, and the stalls hadn't even been erected inside the first barn yet. They were selling on the name power of Ivy Place, and big promises, but Casey had no doubt they'd deliver. And then some.

And she was part of all those names on the waiting list. She'd dropped to part-time at Atlantic Horse Show Productions, and kept a strict tally of her hours and tasks, refusing to budge even when Sharon and Phillip begged her for more. In response, they'd hired back two of the staffers who had left Perfecto, proving that they'd been capable of more effort to staff up along. That fact alone eased Casey's conscience when she insisted on a drop in hours and responsibility.

With her mornings, she still booked horse show promotions and worked on her advertising portfolio. But in the afternoons, she'd built Raina and Sharmayne a website, all their social media channels, and sign-up forms for future interest in lessons, training, and sales. She'd figured out how to create an online payment portal and taken deposits on stalls. Through it all, she'd learned she was capable of so much more than she'd ever realized—and the work was so fascinating, some days she worked late, staying holed up in her office past nine o'clock, until Brandon intervened and forced her out to eat the supper he'd made.

And she still rode first thing in the morning, although she made time one or twice a week to join Hannah for a ride. Hannah had started working on weekends for a trainer Sky found for her, a small barn where the trainer was still willing to take on the liability of letting a teenager work off riding lessons. She was focused, bringing back everything she learned on the school horses she rode there to begin teaching Caruso the foundations he'd needed all along. The horse was still hot-headed and wired most of the time, but Casey was beginning to see glimmers of hope for him—and for Hannah's future as a rider. She was talking about moving to the other barn full-time, and Casey hoped she could make it happen. Every teenager deserved the perfect barn, full of friends and a big-hearted trainer. Sure, perhaps Hannah would have to work harder for it than some other girls, but teenage horse girls proved year in and year out that when there was a will, there was a way.

Now, she stood on the porch of her future home for the first time, the warm September breeze brushing her skin, and wondered what Brandon really thought of this place. Maybe it would all be too much for him. Maybe he'd say they should stick with their condo, and try to save up for something larger. He'd say they could last another year in their current place, if they really needed to. He'd say he could always spend more time working at the office, and get out of her hair around the house during the day. He'd say—

"I didn't realize it would need so much work," Brandon said. "But I love the idea. I think we should do it. I'm up for it."

Casey spun around, unable to conceal her relief. "Really? You mean it? You want to live here?"

"I mean, yes." He looked around again, shaking his head, as if he couldn't take in all the space, all the potential. "It's crazy. Like, I never would have thought this a year ago, but now the idea of all this space, and riding, it just sounds amazing. I mean, I can just see it: you and me, sitting out here in the evening, watching the sunset, our horses grazing just over there—"

"Our horses?"

He grinned. "Maybe they'll have room for a horse for me. Who knows?"

Casey felt like her entire life had been leading up to this moment. She hadn't known it before, but this was it. This was what she wanted. A home in the woods, with Brandon, and their two horses. And a dog, she reminded herself. They were still in negotiations about breeds, but there would be a dog.

Possibly two dogs? she thought wonderingly.

"And...it's not too far from work?" Casey felt like she was bringing up problems that Brandon might be too star-struck to consider.

"It's only forty-five minutes, and since I only go in twice a week, it's no problem," Brandon reminded her. "Plus, the beach is an hour. I can handle an hour."

"So, we're doing this." Her voice was full of wonder. "We're going to move out here to this farm, and I'm going to be the business manager of an equestrian center."

"If you're up for it."

"I'm up for it," Casey assured him. "I just can't believe it's really happening. How did this happen?"

"The way most good things happen," Brandon said idly, shrugging. "You work with good people, and good things happen."

"Maybe that happens every day for *you,* but it's a new experience for me. And just think, if I had kept on working alone, and if I hadn't brought Sharmayne out here, none of this would have happened." Casey shook her head, hardly able to believe her fortune had brought her here. Here! To a *farm!* "You know I've never been good at trusting people to do a job I thought I could do better, but this time, I did it, and..."

Brandon tugged her close, his arm wrapping around her shoulders. "And here we are."

"Here we are," she echoed. "The start of something new."

"Something *amazing*," Brandon corrected her. "Nice work, Casey. You really turned this West Palm move around."

Casey laughed at that. "All in the plan, Brandon. All in the plan."

There hadn't really been a plan. At least, not one Casey was aware of. But maybe, behind the scenes, the universe had been working away, giving her every sign and tool she needed to get here. Maybe the universe had always known what was best for her, maybe the universe had always planned for her to be standing right here, on this porch, with this man at her side, and her whole bright future in front of her. *Maybe,* Casey thought. She looked up at the sky, tilting her head against Brandon's shoulder, and mouthed, "Thanks, universe."

The End

Acknowledgments

WHAT A RUSH! Finishing *Flying Dismount* feels absolutely wonderful. When I wrote *Grabbing Mane* in 2020, it was with the knowledge I'd write a follow-up, but with no idea what would happen. Dreams were tougher to come by in the summer of 2020, and so all I could do was put a placeholder in the back of the book, promising that if folks waited, something new would come to fill that space.

And boy, did it. I wrote *Flying Dismount*'s first draft in three feverish weeks of writing at a rental house in the mountaintop town of Cripple Creek, Colorado. Sitting at a dining room table with a view of a log which seemed to attract the most interesting birds (I saw my first bluebird!), I managed to pelt out a story which I found inspiring even to myself. The power of friendship, the power of connections, the power of horses to bring people together: I think all of that fuels the story, and I hope it reminds people that the equestrian life is a special one, indeed.

I don't think we're done with Casey's story, but once again I'm going to need a little distance before I start considering where else she could go. Your ideas are welcome—always feel free to send me a message!

I'm deeply thankful to the readers who supported *Grabbing Mane*. The reviews and passion around that book were one of my brightest spots of 2020. I'm so happy to have written something relatable and inspirational to so many people.

For their support in this writing, I must thank my fantastic Patreon supporters. I'm enormously grateful for all of you! It's no secret that I have the best readers in the world, but I also have the best Patrons in the world. As I type this list, I'm amazed at how many times I see your names in the course of a year, and how many books you have helped me write. For your comments, your encouragement, your ideas, your criticisms, and your early reading expertise—and definitely for your financial backing—I am eternally grateful. Whether you're naming horses or telling me where a scene went wrong, or simply sharing how your week is going, you give my lonely job community and shape.

Thanks to Patrons Gretchen Fieser, JoAnn Flejszar, Nancy Neid, Elizabeth Espinosa, Renee Knowles, Libby Henderson, Maureen VanDerStad, Jean Miller, Leslie Yazurlo, Mel Policicchio, Harry Burgh, Alyssa Weihe, Kathleen Angie-Buss, Andrea Parker, Amelia Heath, Katy McFarland, Peggy Dvorsky, Christine Komis, Annika Kostrubala, Karen Carrubba, Emma Gooden, Silvana Ricapito, Risa Ryland, Jennifer, Claus Giloi, Dana Probert, Heather Walker, Kaylee Amons, Mary Vargas, Orpu, Diana Aitch, Liz Greene, Zoe Bills, Cheryl Bavister, Sarah Seavey, Megan Devine, Tricia Jordan, Brinn Dimler, Lindsay Moore, Princess Jenny, Rhonda Lane, C Sperry, and Heather Voltz.

From the bottom of my heart, thanks to all of you who, as readers, give me an outlet for all these stories, and so many amazing days spent writing them.

About the Author

I currently live in Central Florida, where I write fiction and freelance for a variety of publications. I mostly write about theme parks, travel, and horses! I've been writing professionally for more than a decade, and yes...I prefer writing fiction to anything else. In the past I've worked professionally in many aspects of the equestrian world, including grooming for top eventers, training off-track Thoroughbreds, galloping racehorses, working in mounted law enforcement, on breeding farms, and more. Currently I'm a happy amateur rider and enjoy spending time with a very smart chestnut pony, Ben.

Visit my website at nataliekreinert.com to keep up with the latest news and read occasional blog posts and book reviews. For installments of upcoming fiction and exclusive stories, visit my Patreon page at Patreon.com/nataliekreinert to learn how you can become a subscriber!

Made in the USA
Middletown, DE
19 October 2022

12974388R00187